PRAISE FOR
Manda Collins

"When I pick up a Manda Collins book, I know I'm in for a treat."
> —Tessa Dare, *New York Times* bestselling author

"[Manda] Collins is a delight!"
> —Elizabeth Hoyt, *New York Times* bestselling author

"Manda Collins reminds me why I love historical romance so much."
> —Rachel Van Dyken, #1 *New York Times* bestselling author

"A go-to for historical romance."
> —*Heroes and Heartbreakers*

"Manda Collins writes sexy and smart historical romance, with a big dash of fun."
> —Vanessa Kelly, *USA Today* bestselling author

"Sexy, thrilling, romantic…Manda Collins makes her Regency world a place any reader would want to dwell."
> —Kieran Kramer, *USA Today* bestselling author

A Lady's Guide to Mischief and Mayhem

"A delectable mystery that reads like a Victorian *Moonlighting* (with a good heaping of Nancy Drew's gumption)....*A Lady's Guide to Mischief and Mayhem* is wickedly smart, so engrossing it'd be a crime not to read it immediately."

—*Entertainment Weekly*, A–

"This book is proof that a romance novel can only be made better by a murder mystery story."

—*Good Housekeeping*

"Smartly plotted, superbly executed, and splendidly witty."

—*Booklist*, Starred Review

"Both romance and mystery fans will find this a treat."

—*Publishers Weekly*

"Collins blends historical romance and mystery with characters who embody a modern sensibility...the protagonists and setting of this first in a promising new series are thoroughly enjoyable."   —*Library Journal*

"Utterly charming."   —PopSugar

"A fun and flirty historical rom-com with a mystery afoot!"

—SYFY WIRE

"Manda Collins smoothly blends romance and an English country-house whodunit...The twists and turns of the plot will keep readers guessing, but Kate's independent attitude and the interesting friends she gathers around her bring the story to vivid life." —*BookPage*

"With wicked smart dialogue and incredibly strong characters, Manda Collins reminds me why I love historical romance so much. Witty, intelligent, and hard to put down, you'll love *A Lady's Guide to Mischief and Mayhem*."
—Rachel Van Dyken, #1 *New York Times* bestselling author

"When I pick up a Manda Collins book, I know I'm in for a treat. With compelling characters and a rich Victorian setting, *A Lady's Guide to Mischief and Mayhem* weaves mystery and romance into one enthralling tale."
—Tessa Dare, *New York Times* bestselling author

"[Manda] Collins is a delight! I read *A Lady's Guide to Mischief and Mayhem* waaay past my bedtime, absorbed by its spot-on period detail, the well-crafted characters, and of course the intriguing mystery. Brava!"
—Elizabeth Hoyt, *New York Times* bestselling author

"Mystery, romance and an indomitable heroine make for a brisk, compelling read."
—Madeline Hunter, *New York Times* bestselling author

An Heiress's Guide to Deception and Desire

Also by Manda Collins

A Lady's Guide to Mischief and Mayhem

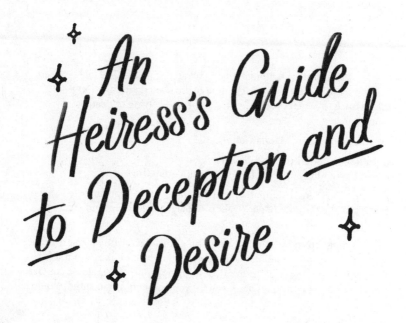

An Heiress's Guide to Deception and Desire

MANDA COLLINS

FOREVER

New York Boston

Forever
Hachette Book Group
1290 Avenue of the Americas, New York, NY 10104
read-forever.com
twitter.com/readforeverpub

First Edition: November 2021

Forever is an imprint of Grand Central Publishing. The Forever name and logo are trademarks of Hachette Book Group, Inc.

The publisher is not responsible for websites (or their content) that are not owned by the publisher.

The Hachette Speakers Bureau provides a wide range of authors for speaking events. To find out more, go to www.hachettespeakersbureau.com or call (866) 376-6591.

LCCN: 2021942529

ISBNs: 978-1-5387-3615-9 (trade paperback), 978-1-5387-0992-4 (hardcover library), 978-1-5387-3616-6 (ebook)

Printed in the United States of America

LSC-C

Printing 1, 2021

To Aunt Dee, who loves a good story.
And to Stephen Catbert and
Charlie P. Underbite. I miss you.

An Heiress's Guide to Deception and Desire

Chapter One

Applegate's Tea Room, London, 1867

They're behaving as if I haven't been on my own, managing my life, for the year they were in Paris."

Miss Caroline Hardcastle set her teacup down with rather more vehemence than she'd intended, and the resulting clink of cup against saucer seemed to echo through the tea room.

"My dear," Lady Katherine Eversham said soothingly, "you knew there would be a period of adjustment once they returned, did you not?"

Caro, who lived with her parents in their opulent Belgrave Square townhouse, had become accustomed to the freedoms afforded to her during their time abroad, and as a result their return had been rather more suffocating than she'd imagined.

"It isn't as if I don't love them." She sighed. "I adore them—of course I do. But Mama has a way of making her negative opinion of my hat or gown known without even uttering a word. And if I don't change after she purses her lips, then I am forced to endure sideways glances until I can stand it no more and must choose another outfit whether I wish to or not."

Kate raised one dark brow. "But you get along well enough with your father, don't you?"

Before the Hardcastles had left for France, Caro had enjoyed a close relationship with her papa. Despite her mother's objections, he had shared with Caro many aspects of his business in which he manufactured tinned food products. She'd even been inspired to write cookbooks featuring recipes using Hardcastle Fine Foods.

But perhaps because she'd become accustomed to going about her business without input or interference from her parents, Caro found even her father's mild questions about where she intended to spend the evening intrusive. To make matters worse, the time away from London had created a distance between them where the operations of the business were concerned.

"Even he is too much for me to bear at the moment," Caro admitted. "It's as if in the time since they've been gone, I've crossed some bridge from child to adult and now they're trying to force me back into the nursery. At least before, Papa treated me as if I were intelligent enough to understand manufacturing. Now he simply follows Mama's lead and relegates me to the role of some delicate creature to be coddled."

Kate took a sip of tea. "I think it could be that you're ready for your own household, my dear."

Caro stared down into the dregs of her cup. Kate wasn't wrong. She was well past the age at which most young ladies of her class were married with children. There had been a time just a few years ago when she'd thought herself on the path to marriage with a man of whom even her exacting mother would have approved. But Lord Valentine Thorn, as he was then, had turned out to be more attached to the opinions of his aristocratic family than he'd been to her. Since the death of his brother, he'd taken up the courtesy title of Viscount Wrackham and was now the direct heir to his father's dukedom. A circumstance she was quite sure had made him even more attached to his family's judgments.

"You are right, of course." Caro leaned back in her chair, suddenly exhausted. "But they will never allow me to set up my own house, no matter how I might wish it. For all that my funds are my own, I cannot quite bring myself to cut all ties to my parents, which would be necessary—emotionally, if not financially—for me to live on my own."

"That's not what I meant and you know it." Kate's eyes were smiling but her mouth was pursed in exasperation. "I do not know what happened between you and Val, but you shouldn't let it keep you from finding happiness with someone else if that is what you wish. I thought before I met Andrew that I would never let another man in my life again, and look at us now."

As if to emphasize her point, the rare sunlight of an April afternoon in London glinted off her friend's sapphire wedding ring.

"Of course, I'm not letting Valentine keep me from happiness with someone else," Caro said with a laugh. Though some hidden part of her wondered if that was the truth. "I've merely been very busy these last years. I've written cookbooks. Collaborated on our column. And now there is the *Lady's Guide* literary salon. How I even have time to chafe about my parents' return to London, I don't know. Really, it's amazing I was able to see you this afternoon."

If Kate heard the hint of desperation in Caro's voice, she didn't let on, merely smiling in commiseration. "You have been quite run off your feet. And I thank you again for taking charge of the salon. I simply couldn't have managed it with the recent changes at the paper." Kate owned *The London Gazette*, in which she published their joint column, *A Lady's Guide to Mischief and Mayhem*.

"I wish you had time to come to more of our meetings," Caro said. After enthusiasts of their column had written to them of their interest in sensation novels, which, like their writing, dealt with crime and murder and secrets, Caro had conceived of their literary salon. It had seemed a natural progression, in Caro's mind, from discussing the real-life dangers to women in the column to talking about the fictional ones they faced in books like *The Woman in White* and *Lady Audley's Secret*. Genteel society liked to pretend that such works were outlandish and bore no resemblance to reality, but Caro, Kate, and their readers knew better. The salon was meant to create a place for their community of readers to confer over their favorite books in an environment where they felt comfortable doing so.

"You needn't read the book if you don't have time. Before we talk about it, we spend at least half an hour chatting about the latest happenings in town. And who would know more about that than the owner of London's most fashionable newspaper?"

"Perhaps I will be able to drop in on a meeting soon," Kate said thoughtfully. "I would like to meet all the new members."

Their conversation was interrupted by the appearance of the shop's owner, Mrs. Jean-Marie Applegate, with a plate of delicate tea cakes in her hand. "Thank you, ladies, for coming today," she said in the lilting accent of her native Jamaica as she placed the dish in the center of the table. Her voice turned teasing. "But it is not like you to drink only the tea with no pastry to complement it. When Annie told me this, I had to come and see your table for myself."

Caro laughed softly. "Have no fear, Jean-Marie. We are as fond of your baking as ever. We are simply waiting for a friend to join us and thought only to have tea while we waited."

The frown lines on the shopkeeper's forehead smoothed. "Ah, thank goodness! I could not hold up my head if the cookery expert should reject my perfectly baked cakes." Her brown eyes twinkled with mischief. She and Caro had struck up a friendship when the shop first opened, and though they shared many of the same opinions on the craft of baking, they liked to tease one another when they disagreed on technique or ingredients.

"I, for one," Kate said, picking up one of the lightly browned cakes, "am grateful you noticed. These look delicious and I must tell you the scents coming from the kitchen have been tempting me the whole time we've been sitting here."

"You enjoy the cakes, Lady Katherine." Jean-Marie smiled. "There will be more when your friend arrives. Just signal Annie when you are ready."

Once Jean-Marie had gone, Caro glanced at the watch pinned to the bodice of her gown and frowned. "It's not like Effie to be late. I wonder what could be keeping her."

Miss Effie Warrington, whom Caro had met through their literary salon and then introduced to Kate, was currently one of the most celebrated actresses of the London stage. Despite their different social backgrounds, the two women had a fondness for the same books, and Effie had been one of the first to write to Caro and Kate about her enthusiasm for the *Lady's Guide* column. The subjects of misogyny and crimes committed were, perhaps because of her profession, of particular interest to Effie. They'd also found they shared some of the same tastes in fashion and haberdashery.

Effie had been particularly enthused about their appointment today, saying she would need the brief respite before playing Ophelia in tonight's premiere of *Hamlet*. So it was odd and out of character for the always punctual actress to be late.

"Perhaps something came up at the theatre?" Kate asked, her eyes troubled. "Or she was unable to get away?"

But Caro knew Effie would have sent word if she couldn't come.

The two women were debating whether to leave when the tiny bells on the door tinkled. Caro looked toward the front of the shop thinking to see her friend but instead saw Effie's maid, Miss Lettie Smith, scanning the dining room before hurrying toward Caro.

"I'm that sorry, Miss Hardcastle," the young woman said as she approached their table. "But I knew my mistress was set to meet you here this afternoon and I thought maybe you or Lady Katherine would know what to do—her husband being a policeman and all. It's Miss Warrington."

Lettie paused to draw breath before sobbing out her next words.

"She's gone missing."

Caro, who had risen upon the maid's entrance, put her arm about Lettie and drew her toward an empty table in a more secluded area of the shop. Behind her, she heard Kate rise as well and whisper to Annie, their waitress, that they were moving and needed more tea.

At the maid's reluctance to be seated, Caro said kindly, "Please join us, Lettie, and have a cup of tea. You'll have to explain the situation and I daresay your mistress wouldn't care to have the matter overheard by the rest of the dining room's occupants."

Once Kate had joined them and Lettie was settled with a cup in her trembling hand, Caro nodded. "Now, tell us what brought you here. What do you mean when you say Effie has gone missing?"

"Just that." Lettie clutched her drink with both hands. "She went to the theatre for a fitting of her costume for *Hamlet* this morning. She told me before she left that she'd be back in time to change so that she could come here to Applegate's to meet with the two of you. But when she wasn't home by lunchtime, I went to the door to watch for her carriage and found her young man, Mr. Francis Thorn, in a great heap on the back steps, bleeding from a gash on 'is head."

At the mention of Francis Thorn, Caro felt a jolt of recognition. She'd known Effie was seeing someone but she hadn't realized the Frank she'd referred to was Francis Thorn, the cousin of Lord Valentine—that is, Viscount Wrackham. She knew from town gossip that some of her former beau's paternal cousins were rumored to be disreputable, but she wasn't sure if Mr. Thorn was one of them.

"Why would Mr. Thorn be there?" Caro frowned. "Was Effie expecting him?"

"No, miss." The maid shook her head in emphasis. "Mr. Thorn has taken to escorting my mistress home from the theatre on days when she has to go in for fittings and the like."

"Is there some particular reason for that, Lettie?" Kate asked, her gaze sharpening. "Or did he simply wish to spend more time with her?"

"I can't say for sure, my lady." Lettie frowned. "She did say she felt safer when he was with her. But today both her and the carriage is missing." The maid raised her brows, as if to state just how wrong her mistress had been to put her trust in Francis Thorn.

"And what had he to say about the matter?" Caro asked, exchanging a worried glance with Kate.

"That's just it, miss," the maid said miserably. "He hasn't waked up yet and there's still no sign of my mistress."

Lettie continued, addressing Kate. "Mrs. Spencer remembered how you helped with that business in the Lake District a couple o' year ago and thought you or your husband might know best what we should do."

Kate's husband had made a name for himself by solving the high-profile disappearance of a socialite before he and

Kate had captured the Commandments Killer. So Effie's companion was correct—even if Caro and Kate were unable to untangle what had happened, Eversham would be able to open a proper investigation.

Still, Caro hoped it wouldn't come to that and they'd find Effie unharmed before the day was over.

Lettie broke into her thoughts. "Will you come, Miss Hardcastle? And will you summon your husband, Lady Katherine?" She pressed a closed fist against her sternum. "The footman we sent to see if she was still at the theatre said she left at the usual time in her own carriage with Mr. Thorn right beside her. Now she and the carriage is missing and he's hurt bad."

Caro didn't like the sound of any of this. Especially the fact that whoever had taken Effie and her carriage hadn't been afraid to use violence against Francis Thorn.

"Of course we'll come," Kate was saying to Lettie. To Caro she said, "You go to her house with Lettie and I'll see if I can find Andrew. He should be at Scotland Yard today unless he's been summoned away. Either way, I'll meet you there with or without him as soon as I'm able."

With a farewell to her friend, Caro settled their bill with Annie and turned to Lettie. "Come, Lettie. We'll go and see if Mr. Thorn has regained consciousness yet. Perhaps he'll remember something that can help us find Effie."

"I hope so, miss," the maid said as they left the tea room. "I do hope so."

"You said Effie felt safer when Mr. Thorn was with her," Caro said once they were inside the carriage. "Did she have a reason to feel frightened?"

"She said she seen a man watching her," Lettie admitted,

twisting her hands in agitation. "She was used to stares from gents, of course, but she said this was different. She was scared, Miss Hardcastle. And now I think she were right to be."

Caro didn't want to tell her so, but Lettie's words were setting her own inner alarms clanging like the bell on the fire brigade's carriage. Instead, she mustered her most reassuring tone and said, "It's likely she's already safe and sound back at the house by now. But if she's not, we'll sort it out, Lettie."

When she reached for the girl's hand, she wasn't sure if she was comforting Lettie or herself.

Berkeley Square, London, 1867

"He is barely in the ground, sir. It's far too soon to speak of marriage and getting an heir." Valentine Thorn—Viscount Wrackham—had suspected the impetus for his father's summons might involve his duties as new heir to the Thornfield dukedom, but that didn't keep the distress from his voice. He'd only in the past week begun to stop looking over his shoulder for Piers whenever someone addressed him by his late brother's title.

"It's been over a year, Valentine," the Duke of Thornfield said impatiently. "I realize none of us are reconciled to the loss yet, but it cannot be helped."

A glance at his father's face, so like his late brother's as to be unsettling, was enough to make Val look instead at the fine scrollwork on the desk before him. It was the pater's preferred location from which to deliver pronouncements to his children. Val and Piers had endured many a lecture from across that desk. Val glanced at the empty chair beside him and wished for the hundredth time his brother hadn't gone riding that fateful day.

"It's time for you to find a wife and do your duty by this family," the duke continued, his voice not unkind, but implacable nonetheless. "If anything, the loss of your brother should make it clear to you just how imperative it is for you to do so with all haste."

Val knew his father had been just as deeply affected by the loss of his eldest son as the rest of their family had been, but the duke had always had a stern streak when it came to the continuation of the family line. Of course, the man had inherited the dukedom when he was just a child and had barely known a time when duty didn't inform his every decision. Still, though he'd had months to adjust himself to the change in his own circumstances, Val couldn't help but mourn the freedom his new role curtailed. He'd given up his work at *The London Gazette*, where he'd covered sporting matters. He'd also moved to Wrackham House from his bachelor rooms, which meant he could no longer come and go without the whole of the *ton* eying him.

Not for the first time he felt the infringements like a too-tight neckcloth.

Unable to maintain his calm and remain seated, Val rose and walked to gaze out the window facing the back garden. "It's not that I don't know my duty, Father. I've thought of little else since the news came about the accident. I suppose I thought there would be more time."

Unbidden, the image of Miss Caroline Hardcastle's heart-shaped face rose in his mind. Once he'd thought they'd make a love match of it. That had been before she realized that however *he* might reject his class's inherent snobbery, the same didn't apply to his family. He'd fumbled to find a balance between his divided loyalties, and she'd broken things off between them a mere three weeks after their betrothal, claiming she could never endure a lifetime spent under the judgmental watch of the nobility. Though he'd understood her frustration and hurt, even now he was resentful of her inability to understand his position. He might have been born into the aristocracy but he'd thought himself different enough from the rest of them.

When he'd seen her last, he'd been surprised to realize the same spark of attraction that had brought them together four years ago was still there. Yet if Caroline thought him too loyal to his aristocratic family as a younger son, she would certainly find his position as first in line to the dukedom objectionable in the extreme.

"Here, drink this."

Val startled at his father's voice. Turning, he took the glass of whisky, grateful for the show of care if not the reason behind it.

"I know you never thought to be in this position, Valentine." The duke took a sip from his own glass. "But you've had time enough for sowing your wild oats. There is no sense in delaying the matter. Especially when, if something should happen to you, the dukedom would pass to Reginald's ne'er-do-well son, Lawrence. We both know what a disaster that would be."

As children, Val and Piers had not been close to the

son or daughters of their uncle Reginald. Instead, they'd preferred the company of their cousin Francis, son of their father's youngest brother, who'd been closer to them in age. As adults, they might have forged a friendship with Lawrence, but his penchant for dissolute behavior made that unlikely.

The very idea of that man holding in his hands the wealth and livelihoods of everyone employed by the Thornfield estates was unthinkable.

"I do know," he said aloud. "Of course I do."

Downing the rest of his whisky, Val set the glass on the desk. "Do not mistake my reluctance for an intention to shirk my duty. If nothing else, I owe it to Piers to see to it that the estate remains in our direct line. He, after all, did his years ago by marrying Cynthia. It was no fault of theirs that they weren't blessed with offspring."

"Then get on with it, man," the duke said with a pointed look. "It matters not why your brother didn't sire a son. What matters is that you stop dawdling and find a bride. Your mother would be happy to help."

Val blanched. He loved the duchess, but the notion of choosing a wife from among a selection of ladies she found suitable was enough to put him off the notion of marriage itself, much less the marriage bed.

Perhaps reading Val's expression, the duke tried another tack. "If you dislike the idea of your mama's input, perhaps you can ask Cynthia for suggestions. I seem to recall you were quite taken with one of her school friends at her wedding to Piers."

If anything, Val grew more uncomfortable, though this time he was able to mask his feelings.

"Miss Hardcastle," he said tersely. Neither his family nor Caroline's had known anything of their brief understanding, and he had no intention of revealing their broken betrothal to his father now.

"Yes, Miss Hardcastle." The duke nodded. "That's right. She was a pretty little thing. If a bit odd. From what I recall the chit's father was not at all the thing. Terribly wealthy, of course, or how could they have paid for the schooling, but still, a bit coarse. What does Hardcastle do again?"

Val bit back an instinct to leap to the Hardcastles' defense. England was changing, and men like Charles Hardcastle, who could buy and sell the Thornfield estate ten times over, wielded more power than the duke would comfortably admit. And moreover, it was disingenuous to behave as if the Thornfield family were somehow more worthy than the Hardcastles simply because they'd had the good fortune to inherit their wealth rather than earn it themselves.

"He is in manufacturing, I believe," Val responded, careful to keep his emotions from his voice.

"Of course," Thornfield said with delight. "Tinned food or the like, correct? And the daughter was a writer. Cookbooks?" He laughed heartily. "I can just imagine you married to a girl like that. Ink-stained fingers and very likely scarred from kitchen mishaps as well."

Val, who before his elevation to the viscountcy wrote sporting columns for *The London Gazette* and authored a biography of the noted boxer Gentleman Jim Hyde, held up his ungloved hands to reveal his own ink stains. He might have agreed not to write for the newspaper anymore, but he was currently at work on another biography, this one of celebrated jockey Billy Rooney, and he had no intention of giving up the project, whatever his family's wishes. "That's hardly the sort of thing I would hold against her."

Some imp of mischief prompted him to add, "And she no longer writes cookbooks. She is a rather celebrated crime columnist these days, along with Lady Katherine."

But if he'd hoped to put his father in his place, Val was mistaken.

"Oh! I hadn't made the connection. Of course, that's the same girl. Regardless, she's entirely unsuitable as far as potential brides go. However, as I suggested, you can speak with Cynthia. Her years of marriage to your brother have, I'm sure, introduced her to a higher quality of friends far more appropriate for the Thorn name."

It took every bit of self-control Val possessed to keep from telling his father to go to the devil. He might not be interested in marrying Caro anymore, but he'd be damned if he would listen to the duke speak of her as if she were a foxhound of inferior pedigree.

"Enough," he said sharply. "You've made your point. It's unlikely that I will even meet Miss Hardcastle again in the near future, much less ask for her hand."

He wanted to decry his father's snobbery, but like always, he knew it would be as helpful as asking the sun to shine at night.

"But you *will* ask for the hand of some suitable young lady," the duke said firmly. "And the sooner the better."

"It's not something that I can accomplish in a day," Valentine argued, feeling his collar tighten at the thought of being forced to marry the sort of woman his parents would find worthy of the Duke of Thornfield's heir. "Wooing and wedding take time."

"We don't have time," Thornfield said curtly. "I wish to dandle my grandchildren upon my knee before I'm too decrepit to do so comfortably. And since your sister, Genevieve, seems more interested in writing her novels than marrying, it's up to you. Whomever you choose for your wife, you'll need to wed her and bed her with all due haste."

Leave it to his father, who had just dismissed the Hardcastles as being uncouth, to put the matter so bluntly.

Val pinched the bridge of his nose. "What has Mother to say to any of this?"

"I thought you wished to keep her out of it." The duke arched a brow.

"I meant I didn't wish her to choose a wife for me," Val argued. "Not that I don't value her opinion on the matter."

The duke's blue eyes, which were mirrors of Val's own, brightened with affection. "She is even more intent upon hurrying along the getting of grandchildren than I am. Though she would not be so vulgar as to state it that way. But do not think her absence from this meeting indicates a lack of interest on her part. In fact, she asked me to have you go up to her sitting room once we're finished. She, ah, has a list of potential brides to discuss with you. And you'll want to prepare yourself. She's decided our annual ball this season will be a celebration of your betrothal."

Valentine didn't bother to hide his groan.

"It doesn't have to be a trial, my boy." His father clapped him on the shoulder. "I know young men make much of avoiding the state, but when all is said and done, you may pick and choose those parts of your life you wish to alter upon your marriage. You may keep a mistress if you wish."

"And we both know," Val reminded his father, "that I'm not the sort of man who would do that to a wife—no matter how much or how little affection I hold her in."

"No, you would not." The pride in the duke's tone dissipated Val's frustration somewhat.

His father hadn't thrust this situation upon him out of some wild whim, after all. It was the system into which they'd both been born. And for all his faults, the duke was simply trying to do his best for his family and their dependents.

"You're a good man," he continued. "And despite your dabbling in pursuits not quite worthy of a duke's son, you have always behaved with honor. I have every faith that whomever you choose to marry, you will treat her with respect. And I hope, in time, affection will grow between you. It is your mother's dearest wish, too."

If Val's heart rebelled at this as-yet-unnamed bride who would put paid to any possibility of the love match he'd hoped for with Caroline, he reminded himself firmly that she'd already rejected him once before and dismissed the emotion as nothing more than misplaced longing for a simpler time.

He was about to take his leave when a brisk knock sounded at the library door. A footman appeared. "Your grace, we've just had a messenger for Lord Wrackham."

At a nod from his master, the young man handed the note to Val, then took his leave.

Frowning, Val looked at the letter. It was unusual, but

not unheard of, for his servants to contact him at the duke's residence rather than wait for his return. Especially given how much time he spent going over the various business holdings and estate books with his father's secretary. But Val dreaded every unexpected messenger ever since the day they'd learned of Piers's accident. He bit back a curse.

"Is something wrong?" the duke asked, his expression clouded when Val glanced up.

Val realized that the duke probably felt likewise.

"Nothing dire," he assured his father once he'd read the note. "Francis has been in some sort of altercation and has asked for me, apparently. His man assures me it's nothing serious."

The duke scowled. "He's not still mixed up with that actress, is he? I vow the last time I spoke with Theo, he assured me he would cut the boy off without a penny if he didn't stop trying to marry every opera dancer or performer he became infatuated with."

Since the note had stated that his cousin awaited him at the Half Moon Street address of Miss Effie Warrington, the actress, Val made a noncommittal noise rather than answer his father's query. He certainly had no intention of informing the duke that Frank and "that actress" were betrothed to be married. That news would prompt a much longer conversation than he could afford at the moment.

"Thank heavens neither you nor your brother ever gave your mother and me pause on that score," the duke continued. "You might have been taken with Miss Hardcastle, but you weren't so foolish as to ask the chit to marry you."

Val didn't bother to correct him. "I know my duty,

Father. But surely Frank should have more leeway in choosing a bride than I do."

He certainly envied Frank his independence at the moment.

Before the duke could respond, he went on, moving toward the door as he spoke. "But much as I'd like to continue this discussion, I must be off and ensure my cousin isn't hurt too badly. Please let Mama know I will have to see her another day."

As soon as he'd given his coachman orders to take him to Half Moon Street, Val gave an exasperated sigh. "Dear God, Frank, what have you got yourself into now?"

Chapter Two

When Caro alit from her carriage on Half Moon Street, she noted that another was already there. With a sinking feeling, she recognized the coat of arms as that of Viscount Wrackham. It wasn't entirely surprising, but she did wish she'd arrived first, if only so that she could have questioned Mr. Thorn before Valentine could protect him. But it wasn't to be helped.

Lettie had gone around to the servants' entrance to see if there was any news of the coach, leaving Caro to knock on the front door of Effie's townhouse alone and prepared for battle.

Effie's butler, Woods, sagged with relief when he saw her. "This way, Miss Hardcastle," he said, leading her through the simply but elegantly furnished entrance hall toward the sitting room. As they drew closer, Caro could hear raised male voices, but when Woods rapped on the door, the din ceased.

She'd never met Francis Thorn before, but his resemblance to his cousin was enough for Caro to tell who he was. He was slumped against the cushions of an overstuffed chintz sofa and had a hand pressed to his head as if in pain. On seeing her in the doorway, he attempted to stand up, but when Caro quickly gestured for him to sit back down, he all but collapsed back onto the seat. It was clear that he wasn't feigning his injury. Or if he was, he was just as good at acting as Effie.

Valentine had his back to the window, arms crossed over his chest, the aristocratic lines of his face tight with annoyance. He looked remarkably fit, damn him.

He'd always been handsome, with his dark hair, light eyes, and cheekbones that could cut glass. But the responsibility conferred by his new title had etched new lines around his eyes and mouth. And his year of mourning, and the months since, had left him looking more serious than she'd ever seen him, even if physically he was broader and more imposing.

When she'd last seen Val, before the death of his brother, during that case in the Lake District, she'd thought they'd parted on civil, if not friendly, terms. If she'd hoped for a welcome from her former beau now, however, she was doomed to disappointment. When he saw her, his brows snapped together. "What are you doing here? Didn't you have enough of detecting after that business with the Commandments Killer? Though I suppose there's no predicting what you'll do when the notion strikes you."

"I might ask you the same question, Lord Wrackham," she retorted, stung by his mockery. "I should have thought you'd be too high in the instep now for such plebeian matters as missing actresses. Doubtless you consider Effie unsuitable for a duke's nephew."

From the other side of the fireplace, a female voice rang out. "I sent for her, my lord. And Lady Katherine." Mrs. Thomasina Spencer, Effie's companion, was a handsome woman in her middle years whose late husband had left her without the means to support herself. Caro had met her when calling on Effie in the past and had seen firsthand both how Mrs. Spencer saw to it that Effie was properly fed and how Effie in turn had treated Mrs. Spencer more like a favorite aunt than an employee. Now, the older woman's eyes were red rimmed from crying. Her hands reached forward to squeeze Caro's while still addressing Wrackham. "They are both dear friends of my mistress. And since you've done nothing but accuse Miss Effie of faithlessness since you arrived, I think it's high time we had someone here who will take her side."

Caro's gaze shot to Valentine's but he only narrowed his eyes. It wasn't like him to suspect every woman of treachery. But if it was a matter of blaming his cousin or Effie herself for her disappearance, she had little doubt he'd try to acquit Mr. Thorn of any wrongdoing.

"Of course, you must invite whomever you like, Mrs. Spencer." Valentine gestured generously with his hands. "But I wasn't accusing your mistress of anything of the sort. I simply asked whether the kidnapping might have been staged."

Mr. Thorn, who had until this point kept his silence, spoke up. "And I told you, Val, that it wasn't her doing. She was terrified. And I saw them strike her."

Mrs. Spencer opened her mouth to speak, but Caro

placed a hand on her arm. "Perhaps we should wait for Detective Inspector Eversham to arrive before Mr. Thorn tells his story. While we wait, could you please call for a tea tray, ma'am? I suspect we'd all appreciate a cup just now."

The older woman nodded. Giving one last glare at Valentine, she left. Caro suspected she also wished to recover her temper.

She was moving to take a seat across from Thorn when Valentine spoke up. "Might I have a word with you in the hall for a moment, Miss Hardcastle?"

She glanced at him in surprise, but his blue eyes were unreadable.

"Perhaps you can lie down for a moment while we chat, Mr. Thorn," she told the other man, who was looking rather pale. "I'm sure you'll feel better after a cup of tea."

Once she and Valentine were out in the hall, she echoed his earlier stance, crossing her arms over her chest, ready to do battle. "How can I help you, my lord?"

His dark hair was mussed, as if he'd been running his hands through it. Perhaps he was not quite so calm about matters as he'd at first appeared.

"Are we back to using formalities with one another, then, Miss Hardcastle?" he asked, brow raised in challenge. "I thought perhaps we'd managed to forge a friendship of sorts during that business in the Lake District. Or is it my title that's made you skittish? I can assure you my suggestion regarding Miss Warrington's whereabouts was to raise possibilities, not besmirch the woman's character."

"Whatever friendship we might have forged hunting the Commandments Killer was born of necessity, Lord

Wrackham," Caro said coolly, making sure to use his title. His attitude at her arrival had been a stark reminder of where his loyalties lay. "And in my assessment, when it comes to protecting your family from those of us outside the nobility, you will do whatever it takes. But let's not dwell on bygones, my lord. Why did you call me out here?"

She noted that his mouth had tightened. No doubt he disliked being reminded of the way in which he'd once chosen to side with his family over her. But she wasn't concerned with keeping their conversation comfortable for him. He was the one who'd wanted a private word.

Now he did thrust a hand through his hair. She felt a little thrill at having discomposed him. Especially this new version of him, whose anger had seemed too cold for such gestures, despite all evidence to the contrary.

"I know you think I'm here to interfere," he said grimly, "but Frank sent for me. It's not as if I have someone watching every member of the family to see they don't shame the Thorn name, for God's sake. He's convinced whoever attacked him and took Miss Warrington means to do her real harm."

"Then why suggest she staged it herself?" Caro wasn't quite ready to believe him. He wasn't only here as an ally for his cousin; he was now the heir to the Thornfield dukedom. She knew all too well how his family felt about misalliances such as that between Mr. Thorn and Effie. "That speaks of a suspicion that, from what we know so far, is unwarranted."

He raised his hand, then dropped it, as if stopping himself from disordering his hair again. Instead, he clenched his fist at his side. "When we were younger, and first on the town, there was an opera dancer."

Caro was bemused to see color appear on his cheekbones.

"She was hoping to parlay her beauty into a marriage with a wealthy but green young admirer. She hired some street toughs to stage a kidnapping so that her young man could come to her rescue. The thought was he'd be so overcome with relief and his own pride at rescuing her he'd propose."

"And did you?" Caro asked, making an educated guess. She'd never supposed him to be a virgin, of course. But the notion of him raking about town as a young man gave her an unwelcome burn of jealousy. Which was patently absurd, she told herself.

"It wasn't me." Valentine smiled wryly. "Though I was just as wet behind the ears. It was my brother. And he didn't, as it happened. The dancer, Sally Bright, lost her temper and cried and confessed the whole plot. Piers had been on the verge of marrying the girl, but her scheming scared him as no lecture from our father could have. He settled handsomely with her and offered to help her retire to the country if she wished, but she declined."

"It's not an easy life," Caro admonished gently. Through her work with Kate, she'd learned all too well the dangers a woman who made her living with her body could face. Even for the ones who could demand a higher quality of clientele, the inherent risks in giving up control over one's body to a relative stranger didn't change. "I daresay the girl was faced with a number of demands that made marriage—however deceptively arranged—to a young man she might be able to manage seem like heaven."

"I blamed her back then," Valentine admitted. "But over time I came to realize that she was a product of a system that forces women to trade their youth and beauty for monetary gain. And Piers and I were no better than any other men who took advantage of their vulnerability."

Caro blinked at his honesty. She'd spent a great deal of time since she and Kate began writing together considering the ways in which their world was weighted in favor of men at the expense of women. But she hadn't expected to hear some of the same ideas they'd discussed come out of Valentine's mouth. She wouldn't have been attracted to him if he were a misogynist, of course. Only, she couldn't let herself think he was some sort of new man. He was clearly still of the opinion that his aristocratic pedigree elevated him above the people in his orbit.

"You think Effie is trying to perpetrate the same sort of scheme on your cousin Mr. Thorn?" she asked, trying not to betray how moved she'd been by his words. "They're already betrothed. Why would she risk everything by doing something like that? It makes no sense."

"I didn't say it was staged by Miss Warrington," Valentine pointed out. "I said perhaps the kidnapping was staged."

"Explain," Caro demanded, intrigued in spite of herself.

"The relationship between my cousin and Miss Warrington has hardly been a state secret," he said reasonably. "Any number of people at the theatre, for instance, might have heard about it. It would take little enough to enact an elaborate hoax in order to extort money from my family."

Caro bit back a sigh. "Not everyone is as obsessed with your family as you are, Valentine."

"I'm not suggesting obsession, Caro." His vehemence belied his use of the shortened form of her name. "Just a cold-blooded decision to extract money from a logical source."

"And what of Effie? If she didn't come up with the idea, then what role do you suggest she played?"

"If she was indeed as frightened as Frank says, perhaps she played no role at all." He gave a slight shrug. "Indeed, if she's as enamored with my cousin as he says she is, I'd say she was an unwilling participant, if she participated at all."

"If this is what happened," Caro said, her fists clenched at her sides, "then you realize there should have been some sort of demand for money by now."

As if on cue, a knock sounded at the front door of the house.

As it happened, the summons to the front door heralded not the arrival of a ransom note, but instead Lady Katherine with her husband, Detective Inspector Andrew Eversham of Scotland Yard.

"I apologize for taking so long," Kate said as she hurried toward Val and Caro and gave them each a quick hug. "It took me a little while to track Andrew down. But here we are at last. Any news?"

Val shook hands with Eversham, whom he'd befriended shortly before the detective's marriage to Kate. He'd found the man to be thoughtful during the one investigation he'd observed and his presence now gave him confidence that they'd soon resolve the matter of Miss Warrington's disappearance.

"Nothing yet," Caro said, leading the newcomers into the parlor, her back ramrod straight and chin held high. He wasn't vain enough to think her defiant posture had anything to do with him, but there had been a definite edge in their conversation. He'd felt damned vulnerable telling her about his youthful indiscretion, even if Piers had been the one to nearly fall prey to that marriage scheme. But even though she'd reacted with empathy, her studied distance had stung. Yet he could hardly blame her for her continued distrust of his family.

That she claimed a friendship with Miss Warrington did not come as a surprise. Caro had always gathered an eclectic group of people from all walks of life around her. And indeed, he'd seen firsthand at the offices of *The London Gazette* just how many women in particular had flocked to meet both Caro and Kate after the success of their column. Her ability to mix easily with every sort of person was one of the things that had first attracted him to her during their betrothal.

And yet, her appearance on Half Moon Street raised an unforeseen complication to his cousin's ordeal. If he was to be honest, Val had supposed Frank had been in a brawl and needed him to act as his second. Dueling was illegal, of course, but his cousin had always been hotheaded. What he'd discovered instead could endanger Frank's future much more severely if his father learned of the betrothal and cut him off entirely.

"We asked Mr. Thorn to hold off telling the tale of what happened until you could be here," Caro continued as they filed into the parlor, followed by Mrs. Spencer and a footman carrying a laden tea tray. "That way he won't have to repeat himself."

Once they were seated around a trestle table and Caro had personally ensured Frank had a cup of heavily sweetened tea in his hand—an act of kindness for which Val was absurdly grateful—Eversham spoke. "Perhaps you can start by explaining what happened from the time you left the Lyceum Theatre until you arrived here at the house, Mr. Thorn."

Val noted that his cousin seemed to have regained some of his composure—whether that was because he felt the pressure of an audience or he was feeling better, he could not say. It was a relief to him, however, to see an indication that there would be no permanent damage from his injuries.

In a clear voice, Frank explained that he'd taken to accompanying Miss Warrington to and from the theatre on those days when she was meant to attend fittings, rehearsals, or any other meetings required of her as one of the players.

"And why was that?" Kate asked, her gaze on Frank assessing. "Surely it was something a footman could have done so that you might be free to go about your business during the day?"

Val watched with amusement as his cousin looked sheepish. "We are that fond of one another, Kate," Frank said. Both Val and Frank had known her since childhood and felt comfortable using her more familiar name. "But it wasn't that. It was the fact I'd seen someone watching her from the street a few weeks ago."

Frank hadn't mentioned such a thing when he'd arrived and Val was understandably annoyed. His cousin had made it sound as if the attack had come as a complete surprise. But if someone had been watching Miss Warrington, there was good reason to believe they might have been involved in her kidnapping.

"Where was this?" Eversham asked sharply. "Here outside her townhouse or elsewhere?"

"Both here and outside the Lyceum Theatre." Frank's jaw was tight. "I knew I should have done more to ensure her safety. But I had no notion the bastard would bring two brutes along with him to take her from her carriage in broad daylight. I thought just me being there would be enough to frighten anyone off." He set his cup down so hard the remaining tea sloshed onto the table.

"Did either of you know who it was, Mr. Thorn?" Caro's gentle tone belied her grim expression.

"No," Frank bit out. "Otherwise, I'd have searched him out as soon as I came back to and demanded the fellow tell me where he took my Effie."

"How was he dressed?" Eversham asked. "Were his clothes shabby or new looking? Did he wear a livery of some sort?"

"What has that to do with it?" Frank's frustration rang out through the room.

"If he was able to linger in this part of Mayfair for a long period of time without having someone call the watch on him," Eversham explained calmly, "then it stands to reason he must have blended in. Gentlemen and servants are the most frequent visitors to this area."

Understanding dawned on Frank's face. "No, he was

dressed well enough. The colors were dark except for his shirt, but then what gentleman doesn't wear black or gray these days? And he definitely did not wear livery."

"So, he was dressed as a gentleman?" Caro asked before Eversham could comment.

"I suppose so," Frank said. "He didn't strike me as a servant, though I couldn't tell you why. Maybe the way he held himself."

"Was she having a problem with admirers at the theatre?" Eversham continued. "Someone too eager? Perhaps someone didn't like the fact that she had chosen you over them?"

Frank suddenly looked exhausted. "Of course, there were some who cut up rough. It's part of that world. Especially for a performer as beautiful and talented as Effie. But she knew how to handle them. She's been on the stage for nearly a decade now. There are quite a few men who frequent the greenroom that I would just as soon see transported to the other side of the world for their insolence."

"Is that how you met?" Caro asked, not quite keeping the censure from her tone. "In the greenroom?"

"What does it matter?" Val didn't bother to soften his exasperation. He knew well enough she held a low opinion of men who dangled after actresses without a care for their situation, but Frank was betrothed to Miss Warrington, for heaven's sake. He'd already proven his honorable intentions. Caro's criticism, while well-meaning, was misplaced. "We can save the story of how they met and what their favorite tune is for later."

"It matters because he might be able to link one of those men at the theatre to whoever who took her today," Caro said tightly.

"What of the man's accomplices who attacked you in the carriage?" Eversham asked, getting them back on subject. "Did you recognize them from the theatre?"

"No," Frank said firmly. "If these men ever go to the theatre, it's not to lavish gifts on actresses. They were rough. Their clothes were dirty and they smelled of"— he closed his eyes as if to recapture the memory—"grease and onions."

"My poor Miss Effie." Mrs. Spencer was weeping openly. "To be violently torn away from her own carriage. Why would someone do this to her?"

Caro placed a comforting hand on the older woman's arm, and Val was reluctantly relieved she was here. Her fierceness masked a deeply caring nature, and it was moments like these that made it impossible for him not to be drawn to her all over again. Even as common sense and past experience warned him against it.

"We're going to do our best to find out, Mrs. Spencer," Eversham assured the companion. To Frank, he said, "Tell us what happened in the carriage in as much detail as you can remember."

"We were discussing her fittings," Frank said, his eyes closing momentarily, "and her argument with one of the other actresses earlier today."

Caro's brows drew together. "What did they argue about?"

"Julia was saying that she's the one who should be playing Ophelia in this production—not Effie."

"Julia Todd has been jealous of Miss Effie ever since she began working at the Lyceum," Mrs. Spencer said sourly. "She's a nasty young woman with no more manners than the good Lord gave a goat."

"Could this Julia have something to gain if Effie disappears?" Caro exchanged a look with Kate that Val couldn't interpret. Perhaps they knew something about their friend's dealings in the theatre they weren't ready to share yet. He reminded himself to press them for more details later. If Miss Warrington had something to hide, then his cousin should be informed of it. "Is she Effie's understudy perhaps?"

Frank sat up straighter. "Yes. She is."

"Before we go down that road," Eversham interjected with a lifted hand, "please finish telling us precisely what happened in the carriage, Frank."

Looking only slightly chastened for taking them off course, Caro clutched her hands together in her lap.

"When we were nearing Half Moon Street, the carriage came to an abrupt halt," Frank said. "Effie knocked on the panel and asked if there was some problem, and Johnny, the coachman, said all was well. We took off again, but I could have sworn we'd made a turn that we weren't supposed to make. Turns out the villains had steered us into the mews behind the house."

"And then?" Val prompted when his cousin seemed to lose himself in memory.

"Then it happened faster than I could have imagined. The carriage door was wrenched open and two ruffians were dragging us both from the carriage. When I tried to fight them, one coshed me in the head with a club.

They threatened to kill me with it if she didn't go quietly."

He stared into the distance, as if seeing the scene again in his mind. Then he said with excitement, "There was someone else. Outside the carriage. Where they dragged me. He had a more cultured accent than the other two."

"Did you see his face?" Kate asked.

But Frank shook his head. "No. I was near to passing out by that point. But I heard him." Turning to Val, he scowled. "It had to be the one Effie and I saw before."

"It seems plausible," Val agreed. "Though we can't know for sure until we learn all of the men's identities."

They were all quiet for a moment, taking in the gravity of the situation. Men who were willing to beat a duke's nephew were either too stupid or too reckless to fear the hangman's noose.

"Next thing I knew I'd been brought into the house," Frank concluded. "I sent for Val as soon as I was able to form a coherent thought."

"Why Val?" Caro asked. "Why not the authorities?"

"Because the authorities would alert my family to the fact that Effie and I are betrothed," Frank answered. "I know I can trust Val to be discreet, but if my father gets wind of the engagement, he'll do what he can to see to it that, even once Effie is back safely, we'll never be able to marry."

"The aristocracy does dislike seeing its ranks sullied by common blood, doesn't it?" Caro asked in a biting tone.

Her question cut a bit too close to the bone after his earlier conversation with his father, and Val answered more sharply—and more defensively—than he might have otherwise.

"However misguided he might be, my uncle merely wishes to protect Frank. I'm here to see to it that we find Miss Warrington without exposing either her or my cousin to scandal."

Chapter Three

He realized his error almost as soon as the words left his mouth. A fact made clear by Caro's little exhalation before she said, "How fortunate that Kate and Eversham and I are here to do the hard work of finding Effie, then, Lord Wrackham, while you see to protecting the Thorn family name."

"I never meant to imply—" Val began, only to be interrupted by Caro.

"I don't believe there's any other way to interpret—"

"That's because you're determined to—"

"The only matter I'm determined about—"

A piercing whistle from Eversham brought their bickering to a halt.

The rest of the room's occupants stopped speaking to stare at him.

The detective shrugged. "A skill learned in my patrol days that comes in handy now and again."

Val felt a pang of guilt at having provoked the other man's response. He'd been brought up to be better behaved than to engage in arguments with ladies. Even those who were hell-bent on thinking the worst of him.

A glance at Caro told him she was feeling every bit as chastened.

"Thank you, my dear," Kate said, patting her husband on the arm. She turned to Mrs. Spencer and Frank. "Are either of you in contact with Effie's family? They might know of others who wish Effie ill will."

Mrs. Spencer twisted the handkerchief in her hand. "I don't believe she has much family. She said a foster couple raised her in Sussex, but they passed some years ago. She was never more specific than that."

"It wasn't a particularly happy upbringing," Frank said miserably.

After a glance at Eversham, Kate said briskly, "Now, I think there are two directions in which to take our search for Effie. First, we should speak with Julia Todd at the Lyceum Theatre. If she was as jealous as you say she was, Frank, then it stands to reason that she may have hired someone to see to it that Effie misses her opening night tonight."

From Val's perspective, this was the most palatable—and probable—of the possible reasons to abduct Miss Warrington. A rival would have no reason to permanently harm the other woman. He didn't say so aloud, however, because he didn't wish to belittle his cousin's very real fear. He'd known a similar fear, when Caro had come in contact with a killer at his Lake District estate. Though the situations were not nearly the same, he reminded himself.

"The other possibility is that Effie has been taken by an overzealous admirer, I suppose?" Caro asked, her eyes shadowed with worry. Everyone there knew the dangers a woman might face at the hands of a man unwilling to take no for an answer.

"I hope to God not," Frank said grimly. "Some of those chaps are obsessed to the point of madness."

"If you were so concerned about them, then I wonder you didn't warn them off," Val said.

Frank frowned at him. "I did, but they're deuced determined. Ask Langham if you don't believe me, Val. He'll tell you."

Val and his cousin had known the Duke of Langham since they were boys, though the older man had been closer to Piers than Val and Frank. "What has he to say to it?"

"He's in the greenroom as often as I am. Ever since he—" Frank reddened and broke off before continuing. "That is to say, he is a great admirer of the theatre."

Caro gave a familiar exasperated sigh. "If the duke is the protector of one of the actresses at the Lyceum, Mr. Thorn, you need not curb your tongue. We all know very well how such arrangements work. Effie was never missish about things like that with us."

Frank, looking slightly scandalized, turned to his cousin with his eyes wide.

"I'm not foolish enough to set foot in this quagmire," Val said, raising his hands.

"Never mind the reason the duke was in the greenroom, Miss Hardcastle," Frank said, soldiering on, "but there are a number of men without honor who linger there. It's them I'm speaking of."

"And you believe if one of them has taken Effie, then she's in real danger?" Kate asked.

"I'm more afraid than you can imagine, Kate." Frank swallowed. "If only I'd not let myself be overpowered. What kind of man lets the woman he loves get snatched right out from under his nose?"

"The kind who is human," Caro said softly, and to Val's surprise, she sat beside his cousin, taking his hand. "You did the best you could. You weren't expecting to be assailed in broad daylight. And certainly not so near your destination."

As much as he resented how cold-blooded Caro had been when ending things between them, Val had to admit that she had an usually generous heart. Others might have lashed out at Frank for not protecting her friend, but instead she was offering him comfort. If only she'd shown as much generosity of spirit with his ill behavior. He'd been in the wrong, of that there was no question. But perhaps if she'd made an effort to understand why he'd acted so poorly, they might be together even now.

"My dear, since you're organizing everyone so splendidly," Eversham said to his wife, "why don't you tell us what our next moves should be? Though I suggest that I go back to the Yard and get some men searching for Miss Warrington's missing carriage." Turning to Frank, he asked, "Are there any distinctive marks on the vehicle, Mr. Thorn? Something that would make it easier to distinguish?"

At his question, Kate giggled.

Eversham frowned. "What's so funny?"

"It's just that Effie's carriage is a bit, er—" Frank broke off, smiling for the first time Val had seen that day.

"It's a 'gilt-covered monstrosity,'" Caro said baldly. "Those are Effie's words, not mine. She said if society was going to treat her like a harlot for making her living on the stage, then she'd dash well play the part in one respect at least."

"She thought it was a grand joke," Frank said fondly. With a sideways look at Val, he added, "I did, too. Especially given my father's likely reaction to our betrothal. Might as well be hanged for a sheep as for a lamb."

Val had the good grace to feel ashamed of his family's snobbery. What had Frank done that was so very terrible, after all? He'd fallen in love with a woman who made an honest living. He hadn't cheated at cards or sired an entire family with his mistress as their Uncle Reggie had done. Confronted with Frank's damning, if true, assessment, it was impossible not to think of his family's snide remarks about Caro. He might have been too much of a coward to fight back all those years ago, but if faced with the same situation again, surely he'd react differently.

Then he remembered his conversation with his father only just that afternoon, and he flushed.

"That should make it easier for my men to locate Miss Warrington's carriage, then." Eversham nodded. "Unfortunately, I cannot set them to searching for her without my superiors hindering our investigation. Though *we* all know she hasn't simply run off with another man to the Continent, there is a prevailing attitude that ascribes only the most selfish and flighty motives to any women but their own wives and daughters. And sometimes even them."

"And the men who write to us about our column wonder why we're always so angry," Caro said, her tone more tired than anything else. "Are you really saying the Yard cares more about a missing carriage than a missing woman, Eversham?"

"The carriage is private property, so…" The detective shrugged. "I don't condone it, Caroline. I simply wish to be as candid as possible. By the time I might convince my superiors that Miss Warrington did not disappear of her own accord, we'll have lost valuable time. It will be much more expedient to conduct our own investigation first, and if we find the culprits, bring them to the Yard's notice."

"Then we'd better get started." Caro looked them over. When she reached Val, her assessing gaze arrested him. *Can we trust you?* her eyes seemed to ask.

When he'd arrived here this afternoon, Val wouldn't have known his answer to that question. But for his cousin's sake—and for the actress's own sake—he wanted to know what had happened to Effie Warrington. And for once he didn't give a hang about what his family might think.

Kate thought it best for them to split into groups so that they might cover more ground. Eversham would go back to the Yard and send some men searching for Effie's carriage, while Val would take Frank to the Wrackham townhouse to be seen by a physician.

"I'm grateful you are so good at managing things, my dear," Eversham said wryly. "Otherwise, I might not know why I was summoned here to begin with."

"Oh hush." The twinkle in Kate's eye belied any real pique. "You love it when I take charge."

Turning back to the others, Kate continued. "Caro and I will visit the Lyceum and see if we can learn something about this enmity between Julia Todd and Effie. And we'll, of course, let them know that Effie won't be appearing in tonight's performance."

"Do you think that's a good idea for you to go to the theatre alone, Miss Hardcastle, Lady Katherine?" asked Mrs. Spencer. "I know Miss Effie wouldn't wish you to endanger yourselves on her behalf."

Caro had grown fond of the older woman over the months of their friendship with Effie and she was touched by her very real, if unwarranted, worry. But she felt it was clear that Effie's abduction hadn't been happenstance. Which meant that Caro and Kate should be relatively safe.

"I suppose I could go with them," Val said. "That is, if Kate and Caro don't mind."

"We don't mind at all—" Kate said.

"—we mind very much," Caro said at the same moment.

She and Kate stared at one another. Kate's steely eyes said that she should stop being so stubborn, but Caro shook her head to remind Kate that she wasn't precisely Val's greatest champion.

"What I meant," Caro said, finally, "is that your presence might hinder our ability to glean helpful information, my lord."

Val's raised brow told her how unbelievable he found that excuse, but rather than argue, he simply nodded. "If you think so. I daresay I should wait to see what the physician says about Frank."

"I'm not a child, Val," muttered his cousin from where

he still slouched on the settee. "I should be out looking for Effie, too."

But it was clear from the way he then tried and failed to rise from his position that he was barely well enough to remain upright.

"Mr. Thorn," Caro assured him, "you must know that Effie would not wish for you to do yourself an injury in your attempt to locate her. Let your cousin call the physician. Then as soon as you're feeling better, you will be able to join the search."

Frank grumbled but he allowed himself to be helped to his feet by Val, and soon they were all—with the exception of Mrs. Spencer, who had elected to remain in the townhouse in the event Effie returned—piling into their various vehicles.

Caro's sigh of relief once the door to Kate's carriage shut behind her was louder than she'd intended.

"I'd suspect you were overset by Effie's disappearance," Kate said wryly, "if I didn't know that your relief has everything to do with the fact that a certain viscount did not join us."

Caro considered protesting the unfairness of her friend's words, but they'd always been honest with one another. "I have to admit that I did not look forward to sharing a closed carriage with Lord Wrackham."

Kate's eyes shone with sympathy. "I thought the two of you had moved past your mutual resentment during our investigation in the Lake District. What changed?"

"Just that he's become the heir to his father's dukedom and gained the requisite self-importance to go with it," Caro said with bitterness.

"I haven't noticed any great change in him." Kate frowned. "He has been a bit more somber, though it's to be expected, given that he's lost his brother. I know they were very close. And he's had to stop writing for *The Gazette*. Though I know he resents having had to do so, I doubt there would be time for it with all of his added responsibilities."

"I'm sure you're right." Caro stared out the carriage window, unable to endure her friend's gaze. She knew that Kate and Val had been close since childhood, and she didn't wish to say anything that would endanger that relationship.

"Caro," Kate said in a gentle voice. "I've never asked before because I thought you'd come to trust me enough to tell me on your own, but this enmity you have for him is more than just casual dislike. It's almost as if—"

"As if we were once betrothed until he so disappointed me that I had no choice but to break things off?"

Caro let the words hang in the air, terrified of how Kate would respond to her confession. But she should have known better than to doubt her friend. She'd barely turned to face Kate before she found herself being hugged.

"My dear," Kate said as she pulled away, "I was afraid it might be something like that. But you must have been very discreet indeed, because though I suspected after we met, I never heard any rumor of it before then."

"We told no one," Caro admitted, relieved to finally have her secret out in the open. Even if Kate was now the only one who knew besides her and Val. "As it turns out, that was for the best. Otherwise, I'd have been labeled a jilt."

Sympathy was evident in Kate's tone. "How long ago was this? You were critical of him when I first mentioned that he worked for the paper."

"Four years ago," Caro confirmed. "We met at his brother's wedding to my school friend Cynthia."

"Of course. I remember your mentioning the wedding when we learned of Piers's death." Kate's husband at the time had forbidden her from attending or she'd have met Caro then instead of years later.

The funeral had been a private family affair, and Caro had sent her condolences to both Cynthia and Val. She knew he'd been very close to his brother, and unlike many so-called "spares," he'd never wanted to take his place as heir to the Thornfield dukedom. But when she'd received a response from Cynthia only, she'd taken that to mean any thawing of relations between them during the events at his Lake District estate had been supplanted by his new title and responsibilities.

"After a few weeks of seeing each other clandestinely about town, we were foolish enough to think we might suit." It *had* felt foolish, but in the most intoxicating way.

"We hadn't said anything to our parents yet," Caro continued. "I knew that my mother would not be happy at my falling in love with a younger son. She wants more than anything for me to marry a title, you see. And Val suspected his own family would have objections to my lack of aristocratic pedigree."

Caro laughed softly. "And indeed, he seemed genuinely embarrassed at what he feared the duke and duchess's reaction would be."

"Then what was it that made you break things off?" Kate asked. "If, that is, it's not too personal."

Since her friend had confided some of her most painful secrets from her relationship with her abusive first husband, Caro could hardly refuse to reveal her own, mild by comparison, reason for her broken betrothal. But finding the words wasn't easy.

"Because we were eager to see one another, while still keeping our understanding private, we tried to attend the same society entertainments," Caro began, realizing this was the first time she'd told the tale to anyone aloud. "Naturally, I was pleased when Cynthia invited my family to the first ball she hosted as Lord Wrackham's bride."

"And?"

"And I foolishly went searching for Val and stumbled upon him having a conversation with his brother," Caro admitted, remembering the way the glow of the fire in the antechamber had ensconced the Thorn brothers as they shared a drink. She could still recall the glint of the lamplight on the cut crystal of their glasses. "It was not a pleasant one."

"Oh no." Kate raised a hand in horror.

"Piers was so proud that Cynthia had managed to pull off such a crush, given they'd only been married little more than a month. And then he said she'd made only one misstep, but he chalked it up to her softheartedness." Caro remembered each of those awful words. "'Once she learns what is what, she'll realize that people like the Hardcastles are not our kind of people. Especially that daughter. She's trying so hard to be an original she's on the verge of making a spectacle of herself.'"

"What did Val say?" Kate asked, her lips pressed tightly together.

"He said nothing," Caro said, unable to keep the hurt from her voice. "He changed the subject. He had a chance to defend me and my family from his brother's snobbery and chose not to do so. I'd had a lifetime of my mother trying to mold me into a perfectly behaved social paragon, and suddenly I could see the future stretching out before me where I would be found wanting by my husband's family while he sat by and let them criticize me. It was too much. I broke off our betrothal that very night."

"Did he have anything to say for himself?"

Caro smiled sadly. "He tried to explain—he knew the moment he saw my face that I'd overheard—but my mind was made up. He said he was trying to honor our decision to keep the betrothal just between us, but how could I believe him? Surely in such a moment, the impulse to defend me should have outweighed secrecy. Besides, I'd already seen how I'd be treated by the Thorn family if I dared to marry him. I said something about realizing we came from two different worlds and rushed back into the ballroom before we could argue more. Then I asked my parents if we could leave early, which Papa, at least, was happy to do."

"I'm so sorry, Caroline," Kate said to her. "Both for what Piers said and Val's failure to defend you."

Caro hesitated, then continued. "I'm not one to nurse regrets after I've made a decision, but I sometimes wonder if I was harder on him than he deserved."

"You've had second thoughts?" Kate raised her brows.

"I wouldn't go that far," Caro said. "Especially not since he's inherited. Even if he didn't openly agree with his brother, the fact that he didn't argue signaled tacit approval. Now that he's to be the next Duke of Thornfield, he probably thanks fate for his lucky escape. I know I do."

"I understand now why the two of you have been at such loggerheads," Kate said, just as the carriage began to slow. "And why you resisted having him come with us to the Lyceum. It must be painful for both of you to be around each other."

"That wasn't because of me," Caro said, correcting her. "For all of his faults, he's a handsome devil and I doubt we'd get a word of sense out of any of the actresses if we'd brought him along."

Kate laughed, as Caro had intended. While their conversation had been uncomfortable, she felt better for having finally told Kate the truth. But after such a heavy topic, she badly needed a change of subject.

"Good point," Kate agreed as the carriage drew to a stop. "Now, let's go see what we can learn about Effie's mysterious watcher."

"We should also find out what we can about Effie's relationship with Frank," Caro said, steeling herself against a tendency to think the best of her friend's betrothed. "I can't help but think that in most cases, when a woman is harmed, the culprit is either the husband…or the lover."

Kate paused before taking the step the coachman had just let down. "Do you really think Frank might be to blame? He *was* injured. And I don't believe he was feigning illness."

"We can't rule it out," Caro said. "Even though we both know how enamored Effie is of him. He could easily have instructed the men to strike him so as to make his innocence seem more plausible."

"Another reason for us to come here without Val," Kate said as she waited for Caro to reach the pavement.

"I hope we don't learn anything to implicate his cousin," Caro said, "because if you think Val and I are at odds now, I fear you will see outright war between us if I accuse his cousin of kidnapping."

Chapter Four

Despite Frank's protestations that as soon as he'd had a bit of rest he'd be ready to go out and search for Effie, it was clear to Val that his cousin's injuries had left him more ill than he was willing to admit. The physician proclaimed Frank also had several bruised ribs and a sprained wrist.

"Your cousin is lucky to have escaped with only minor injuries, my lord," Dr. Woolford told Val in the hallway outside of the guest room where Frank had been persuaded to lie down. "If they'd not been in such a hurry, I feel sure the ruffians who attacked him could easily have broken his bones or worse. As it is, he has suffered no more than many young men who do a bit of sparring."

Rounding the corner toward the stairs, Val placed a hand on the physician's arm. "Woolford, I hope I can count on your discretion about this. I would like to keep my cousin's name out of the papers for as long as possible."

The two men knew one another from Jim Hyde's boxing club, where Val was a frequent observer and Woolford acted as house physician. He counted the man as a friend from his time spent writing Hyde's biography. Woolford was a competent physician, but the primary reason Val had asked for his assistance was the doctor would not disclose that he'd been urgently called upon to treat a member of the Thorn family.

"Of course, my lord," Woolford assured him. "No one will learn of this from me."

The doctor made to leave, but Val stopped him again. "I have a delicate question. And again, I'd ask that you please exercise discretion in the matter."

When Woolford nodded, Val continued. "Do you think it's possible that my cousin could have caused his own injuries?"

To his credit, the doctor didn't bat an eye at the question. Either he'd heard far worse in his career or he had learned over the years to keep a strong control over his reactions. "I don't think so, no. There were very clear finger marks on his upper arms where one of the men grabbed hold of him. Is it possible he gripped himself into that position?" The wiry man's lips twisted so that his thick salt-and-pepper moustache bristled comically. "It's possible, but most men would stop before causing any kind of bruising."

Val had argued silently with himself all the way from Half Moon Street to his townhouse. Merely thinking that his cousin might have caused his own injuries had felt like such a betrayal that he'd chastised himself for even considering the possibility at all. But he'd read enough of Caro and Kate's column to know that the most common culprit when a woman went missing was her husband or lover. And as much as he wanted to believe Frank, they weren't as close now as they'd been in their youth. It was not inconceivable that he might regret a hastily made betrothal when faced with the prospect of being cut off from his allowance. It wasn't as if he had some profession that would help him earn a living.

Biting his cheek to keep from voicing his relief at the news, Val clapped the doctor on the shoulder instead, then said, "Thank you for coming so quickly, Woolford. Give my best to your wife."

Once Val heard the sound of the door closing below, he sagged against the wall, grateful his suspicions had been wrong.

When he made his way back up the hall and around the corner, he was startled to find Frank waiting for him just outside the door of the guest room.

"How could you have thought such a thing?" his cousin demanded, his face—as familiar as Val's own—pale with fatigue. "And why did you not just ask me? You didn't have to go to some bloody sawbones to see if I was lying or not."

Val knew better than to make excuses. "Emotions run high in the heat of the moment, Frank. I haven't been around the two of you together to gauge whether you have that sort of relationship. She's an actress, after all, and—"

"You'd better stop right there if you don't wish to feel my fist in your face," his cousin said coldly. "You're talking about the woman—the lady—I intend to marry. And you'll speak of her with respect."

Val winced, ashamed of his words. As hard as he tried to

keep from judging people on the basis of their social standing or professions, he sometimes found himself making
snobbish pronouncements that sounded eerily like the sort
his brother had been wont to make.

"You're right." He raised his hands in a gesture of
surrender. "I have no excuse for such disrespect to your betrothed. As for my questions to Woolford, I simply needed
to make sure there was no chance that you'd done any
of that to yourself. Because Kate and Caro and Eversham
will be wondering, even if they haven't yet asked you
outright."

"And you were wondering, too," Frank said flatly. It was
not a question.

"And I was wondering, too," Val agreed, meeting his
cousin's gaze, uncomfortable though it was. "I don't know
you as well as I once did. And even you must admit that
you've the devil's own temper."

"I'd never take it out on a woman, for pity's sake,"
Frank spat out. "Do you truly have such a low opinion of
me, Val? I might have expected it of Piers. He was always
quicker to judge than you were. But I thought we were
better friends than that."

The comparison to Piers stung. Much as he'd loved his
brother, Val knew all too well how scathing he could be. He
regretted that his lack of trust had hurt his cousin, but he
couldn't apologize for his questions to the doctor. If Frank
had, indeed, harmed himself and could be implicated in
Effie's disappearance, then Val needed to know—if only so
that he could protect him.

Before Val could speak, Frank walked back into the
bedchamber and looked around the room. "Where are my

clothes?" He was currently wearing one of Val's robes with an old nightshirt beneath it.

"They've been taken down to be laundered, I imagine," Val said. That seemed like the sort of thing his valet would have taken care of not long after they'd arrived. "I'll send one of the footmen to your bachelor rooms to collect some clothes and toiletries so you'll be more comfortable here."

"I need clothing," Frank said heatedly, walking carefully toward the bed in a manner similar to that of someone who'd overimbibed and was trying desperately not to show it. When he reached the bed, he grabbed hold of one of the oak posts. "Gonna go."

Val stared at his cousin's back. "Go where? You're weak as a kitten. I don't think you can make it downstairs on your own, much less to the Albany."

"I won't stay a moment longer with a man who thinks me capable of harming the woman I love." Frank's tone was mulish. "I'll be right as rain in a few moments."

But even as he spoke, he turned to sit on the bed. Or perhaps collapse would be a better way to describe Frank's fall onto the mattress, Val thought, as he hurried forward to more comfortably situate his cousin on the bed.

"Don't be a stubborn fool," he told the other man. "I won't have you falling unconscious on my doorstep."

"No more than you'd deserve." Frank rested his head on the pile of pillows behind him. His earlier anger seemed gone, but Val suspected that was only because he hadn't the energy for it.

There was a chair beside the bed, and Val sank into it. The emotional turmoil of the afternoon was finally catching up with him. And though Frank was in no condition to demand one of him, he knew he owed him an apology.

"I know you will have a hard time believing me now, Frankie," he said, using the childhood nickname his cousin had abandoned at Eton, "but I'm sorry for what I said about Effie. What's more, I'm proud of you."

"For what?" his cousin asked drowsily.

"For following your heart," Val said. "For proving yourself to be a more courageous man than I was."

"What're you talking 'bout?"

But Frank was losing his battle with fatigue and on his way to falling into sleep.

Val thought back to the night that Caro had broken off their betrothal. She'd overheard his brother's disparaging remarks about both her and her parents. What she'd also overheard was his own silence in the face of Piers's insults. He'd had a chance to defend her and he'd failed her. At the time, he'd thought keeping their betrothal a secret was of primary importance, but he knew now he should have told his brother to stop insulting his betrothed. Just as Frank had just done to *him*, in fact.

Perhaps if Val had told Piers just what a snobbish ass he was, he'd be married to Caroline even now. He'd have become Viscount Wrackham with a viscountess at his side.

But he hadn't had the courage Frank had. He only hoped his cousin's loyalty to his beloved would be rewarded with her being returned to him unharmed.

Val was stepping out of the bedchamber and heading to his study when he heard someone at the door below. At the sound of a familiar voice, he hurried downstairs.

"Eversham," he said as he reached the entrance hall, "what news?"

The grim expression on his friend's face told Val that whatever he needed to say would go down easier with a whisky, as well as away from where Frank could overhear.

Once they were safely ensconced in Val's study with drinks in hand, Eversham said, "We found Miss Warrington's carriage in Whitechapel."

"And Miss Warrington?" Val asked, dreading the answer for Frank's sake.

"She wasn't with it," the detective said. "Nor was she in the vicinity. We asked our informants in the neighborhood and they confirmed the vehicle was abandoned not more than an hour after your cousin was attacked and Miss Warrington was abducted."

"Did they see who left it there?" Val set his glass atop his desk, too agitated now to drink it. "Was Miss Warrington with them? Did she seem well?"

"She wasn't with them," Eversham said tersely. "And they'd never seen the man who left the carriage in that neighborhood before."

Val cursed. "Then that's it? There was nothing else to be learned from it? Frank is going to be wild with worry." He ran a hand through his hair.

"I didn't say that." Eversham's voice was placating. "We found something in the carriage. We'll need to ask your cousin if he recognizes the item, however, to know if the kidnappers left it."

He reached into his coat and handed a crumpled paper to Val.

Moving closer to the lamp, Val saw that it was a playbill announcing the opening of *Hamlet* at the Lyceum Theatre, dated for that very night, and starring Miss Effie Warrington as Ophelia. There was a line drawing of a young woman in the middle of the page, her hand clasped to her cheek. Val had never seen his cousin's fiancée before, but from the wording on the advertisement, this was her.

"How do we know this wasn't simply a souvenir Miss Warrington took home from the theatre to commemorate her role?" Val asked, unwilling to let this item symbolize more without additional concrete information. He didn't wish to give his cousin false hope, especially not after seeing just how anguished he was by her disappearance.

"Look at the back." Eversham lifted his chin.

Wordlessly, Val did so and saw a delicate feminine hand had written:

For Richard, my most devoted admirer
—Effie Warrington

Val stared down at the page in disbelief. Then, he thrust the paper into Eversham's hands and pulled the bellpull. This was just the opportunity he needed to make things right for both Caro and Frank. He moved behind his desk, pulled out a sheet of paper and a fountain pen, and began writing.

Once he'd sealed the note, Val handed it to the footman who'd answered his summons. "Deliver that to 19 Belgrave Square. Wait for a response if there is one."

When the young man was gone, Eversham asked wryly, "What was that all about?"

"If my cousin's fiancée was taken by one of her admirers, we'll need to attend tonight's performance and ask the hangers-on in the greenroom who is conspicuously absent. Or suspicious."

The detective laughed. "There is no 'we' about it, my friend. This part of the investigation is just the thing for a viscount about town."

"You don't seriously believe Kate and Caro will permit me to go there by myself. Or that Kate will allow you to escape with some flimsy excuse."

"Where did you send that note?" Eversham asked, his eyes narrow with suspicion.

"To Caro's parents," Val said with a shrug. "I think it would be best for us all to watch the performance from my family box. You and Kate included." He didn't say aloud that he also hoped the invitation could serve as a renewed apology of sorts for his allowing Piers to speak so disparagingly of both her and her parents that evening years ago. What better way to prove that he had no qualms about being seen with them than by having her family join him in the duke's private box?

Eversham's eyes widened. "And now I will have to save my wife's best friend from the gallows because you're simply too much of a coward to invite her to the theatre like a rational person. Instead, you send the invitation to her marriage-minded mama, who will take it as a sign of your interest in her daughter. You have a death wish, my lord."

"Don't be so fatalistic." Val waved his hand, though now he was rather concerned that what he'd thought was a clever idea would only backfire. "I'm sure she won't murder me."

He wasn't quite so sanguine inside. It was entirely possible Caro would be livid at him for his high-handed behavior. But damn it, Frank's courage in standing up for Effie had shown him he needed to prove to Caro that he wasn't the coward he'd once been. Not because he wished to win her back, he told himself firmly. It was the principle of the matter.

"I suppose it will be worth kitting myself out in evening gear to watch you get your comeuppance from a woman who barely comes up to your shoulder," Eversham said thoughtfully.

They stood in companionable silence for a moment, but neither man had forgotten the real reason Eversham was there. Val only hoped that tonight's foray into the greenroom would give them some much needed answers.

When Caro and Kate alit from the carriage in the alleyway behind the Lyceum Theatre, they headed straight for the players' entrance, which Effie had shown them once after a performance. The actors and actresses couldn't come and go via the same doors as the public—not only to preserve the theatrical illusion, but also to protect them from those admirers who might assume more familiarity with them than was warranted.

Now, a few hours before the curtain was to go up, the area was deserted with the exception of a few workmen milling about.

Caro had learned long ago that the secret to gaining

entrance to an establishment where one wasn't sure of one's welcome was to simply behave as if one had a perfect right to be there. Therefore, she and Kate strode forward, heads held high, opened the door and walked inside.

If the alley outside was calm, the backstage area of the theatre was anarchy. A series of hallways led out in three directions from the large open space before them and was clogged with people coming and going. Here, a woman carried lavish costumes, and there, a burly man hauled a gilded chair that must have been meant for the set. There was a feeling of controlled chaos, and Caro was reminded of what Effie had once said about the excitement and energy she felt before a performance. She sent up a hope that her friend would be back soon to immerse herself again in such a scene.

"What we need," Kate said, glancing around them, "is someone in authority. To let them know that Effie won't be here for tonight's performance."

"Not yet," Caro said in a low voice. "I want to gauge Julia Todd's reaction when we tell her Effie is missing. If she had something to do with her rival's disappearance, then surely her response will be muted."

"I'm not sure she's going to be as revealing as you think," Kate said in an equally low voice. "She is an actress, after all."

Caro winced, but before she could respond, a stunningly beautiful statuesque blonde in an elaborately patterned silk dressing gown, trailed by a plainer woman carrying a stack of dresses, crossed from one hallway to near where they currently stood.

"Pardon me." Caro stepped in front of the beauty. "I

wonder if you can tell me where we might find Miss Julia Todd?"

Releasing an impatient huff, the woman stopped and glared at them. "This area is for theatre staff only. We can't have people wandering in from the street." Her words, coupled with a dramatic toss of her golden ringlets, told Caro they'd found the woman they sought.

Deciding a little flattery wouldn't hurt, Caro clasped a hand to her chest and asked breathlessly, "Oh my heavens, never say *you* are the famous Miss Julia Todd? I apologize for not recognizing you. It's just I've never seen you off-stage before."

Actresses weren't the only ones with a flair for the dramatic, she thought with a little thrill of satisfaction.

Beside her, Kate coughed into her hand, but Caro suspected it was a laugh in disguise.

In no hurry to leave now that she'd discovered the intruders were admirers, Julia Todd turned to the costume-laden woman behind her. "Take those to my dressing room. I'll be there in a moment."

To Caro and Kate she said in a far sweeter tone, "It's always a delight to meet a theatre aficionado. How can I help you?"

"It's an honor to meet you, Miss Todd," Kate said with an easy smile. "I'm Lady Katherine Eversham and this is my friend Miss Caroline Hardcastle." Despite her marriage to Eversham, as the daughter of a marquess, Kate held the courtesy title of "lady" for life. Though Kate didn't always choose to use it, Caro supposed this was an instance in which it might be a help rather than a hindrance to their investigation.

"We're here to speak to you about Effie Warrington," Caro continued.

Gone was the syrupy sweet actress greeting her public. At the mention of her rival, Julia's striking green eyes turned cool and her mouth tightened. "What about her? Other than how she's an hour late for rehearsals on opening night." The last she said with an added degree of complaint. As if she personally had been harmed by Effie's absence.

"She was abducted just a few hours ago." Caro didn't attempt to soften the news. "Do you know anything about that?"

The actress's eyes widened in obvious fright. "What?"

"It's true," Kate said in a gentler tone. "She's a dear friend of ours and we were asked by both her fiancé and her companion to see what we could learn from her friends here."

Julia glanced around them suspiciously. Then, apparently coming to a decision, she gestured at them to follow her. "Let's take this conversation away from where anyone might overhear."

After she'd turned, Caro exchanged a wide-eyed look with Kate.

When they stepped into a small but comfortably furnished room off the nearest hallway, Julia's companion was there arranging gowns on a rack. At a word from the actress, she slipped out of the room and shut the door behind her.

Collapsing into a comfortable-looking chair covered in pink chintz, Julia gestured for Caro and Kate to take a seat on a low sofa in the same fabric. "Now, are you saying that Effie won't be playing the role of Ophelia tonight?"

"I suppose that's part of what we're saying, yes." Caro was not sure whether she was disappointed or relieved at Julia's behavior. She supposed she'd hoped the actress would show such naked glee at learning Effie wouldn't be here tonight that they'd know at once they'd found the person responsible for her absence.

"Don't look at me like that," the actress said crossly. "I'm her understudy. I have a job and this is information I need in order to do it."

"Are you saying you knew nothing about Effie's disappearance before we told you?" Kate asked. Caro recognized her tone as the one she used to calm witnesses when they interviewed subjects for their column.

"Of course I didn't, for God's sake." If Julia was lying, Caro had never seen anyone better at it.

"It's just that we heard that you and Effie didn't get along at times and that you were disappointed that she'd been cast instead of you," Caro said carefully. "I understand competition among actresses can get quite vicious."

"Yes, we're competitive." Caro noted Julia's slight emphasis on the first syllable of "competitive." It was indicative of someone who hailed from the north of England, rather than upper-class London as her enunciation otherwise indicated. Was Julia so alarmed that she'd allowed her pronunciation to slip? "We're of a similar age and are frequently up for the same roles. But I wouldn't have had her *kidnapped*. We're friends." The actress bit her lip at this last pronouncement.

Standing, she began to rummage around her cluttered

dressing table. Finally, she found a cigarette holder from which she withdrew one and lit it from a silver box of matches. "Filthy habit," she said, biting her lip again. "And I only indulge rarely."

As the smoke began to gather near the high ceiling of the room, Julia's shoulders began to relax.

"You seem overset by Effie's abduction," Caro said. "I have to admit I was expecting a bit more glee from you, Miss Todd."

Her composure regained, the actress glared at Caro. "I already told you I wouldn't have done something so devious. I'm not flush enough in the pocket to pay for the removal of my every rival, and I quite respect Effie. If I didn't, I wouldn't be so bloody upset when I lost out to her."

"You seemed afraid just now," Kate said carefully. "Can you tell us why?"

Julia stubbed out her cigarette in a glass tray on the dressing table before perching on the edge of her chair. "I've read your columns, you know. I should think if anyone in London understands the fears actresses have about the men who admire them, it would be you."

"So you're saying you expected something like this to happen?" Caro frowned.

"Not necessarily," the woman responded. "But you have no idea what sort of men show up in the greenroom after a performance. We have guards there to ensure that the most egregious are removed without incident, but that's no guarantee. I've experienced everything from proposals of marriage to men who thought nothing of openly fondling my breast in a room full of people. I can assure you that Effie has endured much the same. Until Mr.

Thorn began appearing at her side after performances, that is."

"There was a change after they became involved?" Caro's heart accelerated. That could mean that whoever had abducted Effie had done so because she was no longer available in the greenroom as she'd been before.

"Certainly. And I'm not sure what prompted it, but he also began escorting her to and from the theatre." Julia frowned. "How was Effie taken if he was with her? I saw him when she left earlier today."

Quickly Kate explained what had happened.

"And you've no idea where they took her?" Julia asked, concern shadowing her green eyes.

"No," Kate said. "Scotland Yard is looking for the carriage now and we're hoping they'll find Effie unharmed with it."

"But that's not likely, is it?" Julia was clever, Caro thought. She was well aware that if robbery had been the motive, then the men who'd stopped the carriage would have left both its occupants behind when they fled. The fact that they'd taken Effie indicated they had plans for her.

"Have you noticed anyone in particular watching Effie lately?" Caro asked. "Either in the greenroom or outside the theatre. Perhaps someone simply behaving oddly?"

"My dear Miss Hardcastle," the actress said dryly, "this is a theatre. There is always someone about who's behaving oddly."

They laughed a little, puncturing what had become a very somber mood indeed.

Julia continued, "As I said, since Mr. Thorn began

accompanying her, Effie has seemed to be free of the more undesirable sort of admirers. Do not ask me to name any of them, however, for I've no such protection and must keep my attention on my own coterie."

"And what about outside the theatre?" Kate asked.

Julia's eyes lit up. "I never saw the man, but I did hear from Nell Burgoyne, who's playing Gertrude, that Effie had seen some strange man outside both her house and the theatre at different times. Neither of us had seen the fellow, though, so I didn't think any more of it."

A knock sounded at the door, followed by the dresser from earlier poking her head through. "I told Rupert that Effie isn't here yet, Julia. He's on a rampage. I thought I'd better warn you." She excused herself and ducked back out.

"You'll have to excuse me, ladies." Julia rose from her chair. "I really must prepare for tonight. Do let me know if there's anything more I can do to help."

"Thank you for speaking so frankly with us, Miss Todd." Caro offered the other woman her hand. "And please don't hesitate to be in touch if you recall anything else."

Caro and Kate were silent as they retraced their steps back to where they'd entered the building.

As soon as they were in Kate's carriage, Caro said, "How much of what she told us was truthful, do you think?"

"I'd say there's a kernel of truth in all of it," Kate said thoughtfully. "I don't think she was lying about being innocent from having Effie removed. She didn't strike me as the sort who would willingly admit to being poor. Especially not given how hard she's worked to rid herself of her Manchester accent."

"You heard it, too!" Caro whooped. "I'm glad I didn't imagine it."

"It was faint but definitely there," Kate confirmed. "But she most certainly dislikes Effie intensely."

"Intensely," Caro repeated. "She has a way of biting her lip when she's feigning sincerity. She did the same when she said smoking was a filthy habit. Which she clearly doesn't believe because I've read of her expressing how much she enjoys it."

"One thing is certain," Kate said firmly. "We need a list of the regular admirers who hover around Effie after performances."

"And we need to attend tonight's opening so that we can see their reactions when it's announced she won't be playing Ophelia as expected." Relief filled Caro that they were finally getting somewhere in their investigation.

"I can't help but hope I'll get home to find that Andrew has found both Effie and her carriage while we were speaking with Julia." Kate's smile was rueful, as if she knew such a wish was doomed to be fruitless.

"You know I wish the same." Caro reached out to grip her friend's hand. "But you heard what Julia said. I can think of nothing that would infuriate a man obsessed with a woman more than to have all access to her denied to him unexpectedly."

She only hoped that such a man would also value the object of his obsession so much that he'd refuse to harm a hair on her head.

But Caro was all too aware that she was the one indulging in wishful thinking now.

Chapter Five

After Frank confirmed with Eversham and Val that the advertisement Effie had autographed had not been in the carriage with them, the two men went back downstairs. He'd been all too eager to leave earlier, but from Frank's easy acceptance of Val's suggestion to rest, it was clear that his cousin had reconciled himself to the fact that his injuries precluded such activity for the time being.

"Where are you off to?" the detective asked Val suspiciously when they left the house together. Or perhaps he wasn't suspicious at all. Now that he considered it, that was the man's usual expression. "I should have thought you'd wish to keep watch over your cousin."

Settling his hat upon his head, Val, stepped out onto the street beside Eversham. "I can hardly sit by his bed and stare at him for hours, can I? I'd like to keep busy. So, I thought I'd head to my club and see if I can run down Langham. I'd like to get a perspective on the greenroom from someone other than my cousin."

Eversham looked at him sharply. "You don't believe him?"

Thinking of his earlier lack of trust in Frank, Val grimaced. "I do, actually. We will, of course, confer with him afterward, but it occurs to me that Frank might see all of Effie's admirers as threats since he's a man in love. Langham might be able to give a more even-handed list of names."

"Because he's only there for a mere mistress?" Eversham asked wryly.

"Because, aside from you, he's the most rational fellow I've ever met," Val corrected.

Eversham laughed as they reached the edge of the square where they would part ways. "I suppose I'll see you tonight at the theatre."

Bidding him goodbye, Val continued on before catching a cab to St. James's Street and getting out at White's.

He didn't spend a great deal of time at the club since it was a place he still associated with his father and brother rather than himself—though his elevated standing necessitated him spending more time there now than he liked. He still preferred a more relaxed atmosphere. But like most gentlemen of rank, he had memberships at all of the usual places and was greeted by several friends as he entered the reading room to see if he could run down Langham. He was often to be found there with a stack of the day's papers and a glass of brandy in the afternoon.

Sure enough, he saw the man's large frame slouched in

a burnished leather chair with a coil of cigar smoke rising above the open newspaper before him.

Adopting a similar pose in the seat opposite Langham's, Val gestured for a waiter to bring another glass of brandy for Langham and a whisky for himself. He didn't usually drink more than one dram in an afternoon, but he could hardly put the other man at ease while sipping tea.

Langham lowered his newspaper—*The London Weekly*, to Val's disappointment—just enough to show his eyes and nose. "Wrackham." The duke nodded. "What can I do for you?"

Joshua Fielding, Duke of Langham, had never been one for small talk. He said what he meant and meant what he said. And he didn't waste time with trivialities. It was a measure of his good looks and impeccable wardrobe that he was as popular with the ladies as he was, Val thought, because it was assuredly not his charming personality.

"I've a matter of some delicacy to discuss with you, your grace." Val accepted his glass from the waiter, who'd also returned with Langham's brandy. "I know I can count on your discretion."

Sighing, as if he could have been enjoying the execrable writing of those hacks at the *Weekly*, Langham lowered that inferior rag enough to see that Val had been courteous enough to order him another drink. Wordlessly, he folded the paper and put it down on the table. Then taking up his glass, he said, "Discretion might cost you more than one brandy, Wrackham, but I'll decide after I hear your story."

Despite himself, Val barked out a laugh. "You always did drive a hard bargain. I'll tell you up front that it involves the Lyceum Theatre, so you may be right."

The duke's golden brows rose at Val's effrontery. "I hope you aren't here to try to persuade me to let you have a go at Nell, because I don't share. Not even with a friend I've known as long as you, old man."

Val wasn't sure whether he should be insulted or amused. Langham well knew that Val was hardly the sort to pursue another man's mistress, even one as lovely as Nell Burgoyne. He raised a brow. "Sharing isn't one of my strong suits either, if you recall." There'd been an incident when they had brangled over the same woman at university, but it had ended badly for each of them when she rejected them for a different classmate altogether.

It was Langham's turn to laugh. "Fair enough, fair enough. What was the wench's name? Maisie? Molly?"

"Millie." Val smiled at the memory.

"Millie! Of course!" Langham took a drink of his brandy before prodding, "So if it's not to poach on my territory, what do you want?"

In as succinct a manner as possible, Val explained why he had come and his need to know who might be of interest among the regulars in the Lyceum Theatre's greenroom.

As Val spoke, Langham abandoned all pretense of lethargy and sat forward, alert. "And you've no idea where she is?"

"None," Val confirmed. "I imagine because of your involvement with Miss Burgoyne you know what sorts of fellows spend time there. Do you think any of them are capable of arranging something like this?"

The duke blew out a breath. "I wish I could say it's impossible, but you know as well as I that if you have enough money, you can make anything happen."

"And the men who flock to Effie Warrington are wealthy?" Val asked, his heart sinking for his cousin's sake.

"Not all of them, though they're mostly rich enough. Fortune hunters spend their evenings at balls, searching for heiresses. They certainly don't have pockets deep enough to afford someone of Miss Warrington's calibre. She's got eyes for no one but that cousin of yours, but even if she were on the hunt for a protector, she has the beauty and talent to command more than some pockets-to-let younger son can afford."

"Can you give me the names of some of the ones who reacted badly to my cousin's arrival on the scene?" Val asked. "Or who disappeared soon afterward?"

"It's not as if I spend all my time watching the crowd around Miss Warrington, you know," Langham said, raising a brow. "Nell's possessive enough as it is without me ignoring her in favor of another woman right under her nose."

"Of course. Just the ones who stood out even from your place kneeling at Miss Burgoyne's feet." Val kept his expression deliberately grave.

The hand gesture Langham displayed in response was accompanied by a dramatic roll of his eyes. "Wise arse," he said without rancor.

Then, his expression turning serious, he rattled off four names. All of them known to Val and none of them the sorts he imagined would become unhinged enough to have an actress kidnapped.

"I see you're surprised." Langham's lips twisted. "You never know what a man will do until he wants something he can't have. Unfortunately, there are far too many of our sex who believe themselves entitled to whatever takes their fancy. And if that happens to be a woman, with thoughts and preferences of her own, well, some of them are willing to take without permission."

"You sound as if you've been reading *A Lady's Guide to Mischief and Mayhem*," Val said, unable to keep the astonishment from his tone.

If he was expecting the other man to look sheepish, he was to be sorely disappointed. "Of course I have." Langham shrugged. "So has everyone else in this town. And they're smart to do so. They've been given a whole new understanding of just what sorts of nonsense women have to put up with from men. You're friends with Lady Katherine, aren't you? I'd forgotten that."

"Indeed." Val nodded, feeling a new appreciation for the man. He'd assumed, wrongly it seemed, that an aristocrat like Langham would consider columns like Caro and Kate's to be beneath him. But the conversation had reminded him that not all peers were cut from the same cloth as his father and brother. And perhaps that was a good thing. "And Miss Hardcastle as well."

"Ah, the pocket Venus with the glorious—" The duke made a gesture with both hands this time and it wasn't nearly as amusing as the other had been.

"I know we're old friends, Langham," Val said coldly, "but if you ever speak of Miss Hardcastle in such a disrespectful manner again, I'll have to put a bullet in you and I'll enjoy doing it." Even before he'd uttered the words, anger had clouded his vision. He summoned every ounce of willpower to stop himself from grabbing the duke by his neckcloth and shaking him like a dog with a squirrel.

Rather than draw back in dismay, the duke's eyes

widened as he leaned forward. "I never thought I'd see the day." He shook his head in apparent disbelief. "My apologies, Val. I had no idea it was like that. I have nothing but admiration for Miss Hardcastle. Indeed, she's a witty writer. I've even enjoyed her cookery books and you know I don't give a damn about how to make the perfect sponge."

Val barely heard the other man, other than noting he'd made his apologies. He'd never felt that sort of rage before. The sheer magnitude of it unsettled him.

Before he could embarrass himself further, he bid Langham a good afternoon and made his way back into St. James's Street.

"What the devil was that?" he muttered, staring sightlessly as the carts and carriages passed before him.

He'd never come so close to striking a man—a friend, even—like a damned hothead. Such lack of control was unacceptable for any gentleman, much less the future Duke of Thornfield. He'd always prided himself on his restraint, but suddenly he was in danger of coming to blows with a friend, and he couldn't even say why.

That wasn't true. He knew exactly why—or rather who—and she would not thank him for his behavior. She loathed him so much that she hadn't even wanted to share a carriage with him for a brief ride to the Lyceum. He could only imagine how she would react to his little tantrum just now.

Then he remembered the invitation he'd sent to her parents earlier and cursed.

"I am a colossal clodpate." He pinched the bridge of his nose. "What was I thinking?"

It had seemed like an inspired notion at the time. A way to prove that he didn't give a hang what his father or anyone else said about his friendship with her. But they weren't friends, were they? And he'd just proven to himself, if not Langham, that his emotions where she was concerned were still entirely too ungovernable for comfort.

"I don't know, mate," said a clerk who was trying to get around him, "but I'd be obliged if you considered the matter somewhere else so the rest of us can go about our business."

Shaking himself out of his reverie, Val apologized and hurried down the street in search of a cab. If he was going to attend the theatre tonight with a snarling Caro and her fawning parents, the least he could do was bathe first.

Once they left the theatre, Kate instructed her coachman to stop at her townhouse so that they could see if Eversham had left any word about the search for Effie's coach. The news about the autographed advertisement was conveyed directly by Eversham, who met them at the door.

"We should definitely attend tonight's performance so that we might survey the men in the greenroom," Caro said once they'd discussed the likelihood of a connection between Effie's disappearance and her work at the theatre.

"Wrackham has kindly invited us to join him in his family box," Eversham said, an inscrutable expression on his face. "It's all been arranged."

"It's unlike you to willingly agree to attend the theatre, my dear," Kate said, turning to him with wide eyes.

"It's related to an investigation." Eversham shrugged. "Besides, I've never been in a private theatre box before. It should be entertaining."

There was something suspicious about his smirk, but if Caro was to have time enough to wash and dress, she needed to get home. Bidding her friends adieu, she climbed back into Katherine's carriage and was soon handing her hat and gloves to the Hardcastle family butler, Newton.

She'd barely made it past the entry hall when she heard her mother's voice hurtling toward her.

"Caroline! Caroline!" Lady Lavinia Hardcastle cried, waving a piece of paper in the air, as she hurried down the thickly carpeted stairs. "You'll never guess what's happened. It's as if the heavens have opened up and rained down good fortune upon us."

Unaccustomed to her mother exhibiting such enthusiasm—which she considered unseemly most of the time—Caro stared up at her. "It must be a summons from the queen herself to have you in such raptures, Mama. I don't believe I've seen you this pleased since Lady Altheston invited you to co-chair the summer fete in the village."

Further surprising Caro, her mother clasped her to her bosom in a rare show of affection. She never doubted her mother's love. But she'd never been what Caro would consider demonstrative. And she'd certainly never been one for impulsive embraces or giddy displays of glee. Indeed, if Caro ever dared behave in such a manner, she was roundly scolded. Pulling back from the cloud of her mother's lily-scented perfume, Caro reached for the note clutched in her hand.

"Lord Wrackham has invited us to join him this very evening in the Duke of Thornfield's box at the Lyceum Theatre," Mama interrupted before Caro had even finished reading the hastily scrawled note.

"I will strangle him with his own neckcloth," Caro muttered while her mother continued to chatter happily about the honor the viscount had done them. Had she not noticed that the invitation arrived only a few hours before the performance began? Or perhaps she had but then decided the condescension Wrackham had shown was far too fine a gift horse to look in the mouth.

Whatever imp of mischief had inspired Val to include her parents in his invitation when Caro could have easily attended tonight with Kate as her chaperone and the Hardcastles none the wiser, he deserved every bit of the tongue-lashing she intended to give him. She might be prone to impulsivity, but he certainly wasn't. He would have known that sending the invitation directly to her parents would ensure that she'd have no choice but to spend the evening in his family box—which he likewise had to know would be abhorrent to her.

His brother might be gone now, but what he'd represented—the scorn heaped by the aristocracy upon families like hers—was still very much alive. The possibility of Val's parents being in attendance filled her with dread. If they dared to utter a word of derision about the Hardcastles, Caro would not be held accountable for her actions.

"Mama, I don't think—"

"You will wear the ivory Worth with the Hardcastle diamonds," her mother said as they made their way upstairs, "and I will make sure Talbot takes extra pains with your hair. You are far too likely to rush her and the result always falls only moments after you leave the house."

"Mama, you mustn't think this indicates any sort of romantic intent on Wrackham's part," Caro warned once she was able to get a word in, as they reached the door to her bedchamber. "Kate and Eversham will be attending as well and I daresay the viscount was merely being polite by inviting us. Indeed, I shouldn't think this sort of entertainment would be to Papa's taste at all. Perhaps you should consider staying ho—"

"No, Caroline," her mother said, interrupting her. "I will not let you dissuade me. I've begun to despair of ever finding a man willing to overlook your eccentricities. You know I love you, but you must admit that the way you cavort around town with that ill-behaved cat and insist on writing about matters of which no proper lady should ever speak aloud makes even the most adventurous of men shy away."

Caro had heard all of this before, so she listened with half an ear as she went to find Ludwig, her mama following determinedly behind.

The enormous Siamese cat was curled up in the window seat in the sitting room adjacent to her bedchamber. On seeing his mistress, he stood and stretched, greeting her with a cry that sounded unsettlingly like a human baby's.

"I do wish you could train Amadeus to behave like a normal cat, Caroline." Her mother shuddered as she sat, uninvited, on the long sofa where Caro liked to nap occasionally. "It's not natural for him to caterwaul like that."

"His name is Ludwig, Mama, as you well know. And it's characteristic of his breed. I can no more train him out of it than you can train Papa out of dropping his *h*'s."

As Mama disliked being reminded that her husband hailed from less-than-elevated beginnings, she simply ignored Caro's statement. It wasn't that she was ashamed of her husband. Theirs was a love match and Caro had—to her everlasting dismay—stumbled upon enough affectionate moments between them to know that their fondness had not dimmed with age.

Even so, her mama had never made a secret of her wish that her only child would make a brilliant match with a member of the aristocracy. Caro wasn't sure if it was because she wanted to regain the standing she'd lost when she married her father, or if she wished to prove to her relatives that their daughter was just as worthy of marrying an aristocrat as anyone else. Though her mother's family had never cut them off entirely, they had looked down on her ever since her marriage. Invitations from them were few and far between and Caro had never been close to her maternal relations.

"Your papa is quite enthusiastic to attend tonight, as well," her mother continued as if Caro hadn't even spoken. "He is keen to see Lord Wrackham again. Especially since the viscount is showing an interest. Though it's too late for you to be choosy, Caroline. You're nearly nine and twenty now. Far too long in the tooth to turn down an offer from the heir to a dukedom."

"Mama!" Caro held up her hands to stop her. "There is no offer from Lord Wrackham. You mustn't jump to conclusions all on the basis of one invitation to the theatre.

My goodness. Your mind leaps with a speed that threatens my coiffure with its gust."

"Do not be such a contrarian, Caroline." Mama frowned. "I know you don't like to hear it, but I want to see you settled and happy. I thought perhaps Lady Katherine's marriage would encourage you to look toward finding someone, but there has been no indication of that."

Her mother's words made Caro regret her harshness. She knew Mama was sincere in wishing to see Caro settled. It wasn't Lady Lavinia's fault that Val had a cruel sense of humor where she was concerned. No doubt her fractiousness at Effie's house had inspired his little joke. But the damage had been done now and no amount of arguing would convince her mother that he wasn't dangling after her.

"I apologize, Mama," she said, patting her mother's hand. "I know you mean well. But I want the kind of love you and Papa have. And I won't find that with one of the pampered aristocrats who look down their noses at Papa."

It was the first time she'd confessed this wish to either of her parents. As a debutante, Caro had been so frustrated with her mama's insistence on securing the most impressive match possible that she'd never bothered to explain why she was so against the idea. She'd been so successful in her efforts at thwarting Mama's matchmaking, in fact, that for the year before they'd left for the Continent, Mama had stopped trying to marry her off altogether.

But once they'd returned, her none-too-subtle hints had resumed.

Val's invitation couldn't have come at a worse time.

As if sensing her discomfort, Ludwig leapt down from his

window seat and stretched his feline body in his customary gesture that meant he wished to cuddle. Moving to the chair opposite her mother's, Caro sat down and allowed the cat to jump into her lap. Resisting the urge to hug him against her chest, she ran a hand down his sleek coat as he settled, and let the rumble of his purr soothe her.

"You mustn't be too hard on the nobility," her mother said with a gentleness Caro was unaccustomed to hearing from her. "They do work in their own way. At least the honorable among them. And those who don't would never pass muster with your father. I simply want you to rise as high as you can. Not only because I will be assured you're taken care of, but also because I know it would assuage some of your father's fears."

Caro frowned, startled at the openness in her mother's voice. "What do you mean? Is he afraid I'll never marry, too?" It had been her own choice not to marry, and she'd thought her parents understood. It was one matter for society to think she was incapable of making an acceptable match, but the thought that both her parents believed her too disagreeable to tempt anyone to the altar was just too much to bear.

"Not that," Mama said softly. "He is perfectly content for you to remain independent for the rest of your life. Indeed, since you will inherit everything in due time, he would like to discuss more managerial aspects of the business with you. It's only because of me that he stopped when we returned from the Continent."

Caro gasped. Her father's silence on business matters these past months had stung, but the knowledge he hadn't stopped out of his own doubts with her came as a relief.

She had always assumed her father would simply arrange for everything to be managed in a trust by his man of business. Though she knew he valued her intelligence, it had never occurred to her that he would wish for her to have a hand in the day-to-day operations of Hardcastle Fine Foods. She was touched. And more than a little concerned. She wasn't sure that she would ever be ready to take on such a monumental endeavor on her own.

"But why did you ask him to stop?" she asked. If her mother wished for her to be kept away from business matters, then Caro deserved to know why.

"Because I could see that as much as he enjoyed your talks, they raised fears that weighed heavily on him."

Caro's heart clenched at her mother's tone.

"He would not like me sharing this," Mama said, her eyes troubled, "but he's had it in his mind that in spite of his money, his upbringing will be a detriment when it comes to finding a husband worthy of you. And the more he's shared with you and realized how clever you are, the more…fearful he's become. He wants more than anything for you to be happy. And to his mind, that means securing a husband who won't hold your father's lack of a pedigree against you."

"Why would he think that?" Caro asked, aghast. The very idea that her papa would question his own worth in such a manner crushed her heart. He might have a reputation for ruthlessness in business, but he was the kindest, gentlest of men when it came to his family. "Any man would be lucky to have him for a father-in-law. And anyone who turned their nose up at him wouldn't be someone I'd want to marry."

Unbidden, she remembered the way Val had stood by while his brother cast aspersions on both her parents. Yet another reason to wish him to the devil for his foolish invitation. He might not say such snobbery aloud, but if he exposed them to so much as a blink of derision, Caro would flay him alive.

"He's always had it in his head that if not for him, I could have married royalty—and the same for you if you wished," Mama said fondly. "It's silly, of course. Royals marry other royals for one thing, but also he reckoned without the reality of you, Caroline. You have always done as you please and you've never given a fig for social standing."

"So you believe if I were to marry someone like Lord Wrackham, for example, Papa would be able to forgive himself for taking you away from your place in society?" Her mother's logic made an odd sort of sense, though Caro was sure her father would never wish for her to decide upon a husband based on his own insecurities. It wasn't his way to impose his fears on the ones he loved.

"I do," Mama said. "Though he would be quite angry if he knew I'd told you any of this. He's a proud man, your father. I simply wished to explain why I suppose I seem inexplicably eager to marry you off to someone of high rank. But ultimately, I want you to marry someone who cherishes you."

Touched by her mother's words, Caro hugged her impulsively. When Mama pulled away, she was dabbing at a suspicious brightness in her eyes.

"If this wonderful man," she said with a pointed look, "happens to also be the handsome heir to a dukedom who is kind enough to invite us to the theatre in his family's private box, well, so much the better!"

Caro laughed out loud at her mother's declaration. Really, she was shameless.

But it was impossible for Caro to let her go on thinking this invitation had to do with tender feelings on Val's part. "Mama, about tonight. Lord Wrackham's invitation is—"

"No." Mama rose from the settee. "I will not let you spoil my pleasure in this, Caroline. Whatever you might suspect is the reason behind the viscount's invitation, you will keep it to yourself until tomorrow. Tonight, we will dress in our finest gowns and Papa in his finest evening suit, and we will go enjoy sitting in a duke's private box."

Recognizing that even if she were to explain the real reason for tonight's trip to the Lyceum her mother would quite likely still romanticize Val's motive for inviting them, Caro decided to give up. Besides, a glance at the clock reminded her that she needed to bathe and dress.

She intended to greet him looking her best, even if her reasons had more to do with making Val squirm than pleasing him.

"I'll send Talbot in to assist with your hair," her mother said before hurrying off to see to her own toilette.

"Ludwig," Caro said, lifting the cat close to her chest, "what are we going to do with him?"

As if Ludwig knew she was speaking of his mortal enemy, the cat hissed and jumped down.

Clearly, Caro thought with exasperation, all the men in her life were determined to be as troublesome as possible today.

Chapter Six

Since his invitation had included an offer to convey the Hardcastles to the theatre, Val was there to help Caro into his carriage after her parents had climbed in.

"You won't know when it's coming, Valentine," she said under her breath as she took his hand, "but I will have my revenge."

Deciding his best course of action was blithe ignorance, Val pretended he hadn't heard her and set about making himself agreeable to Caro's parents.

They'd met before, at both his brother's nuptials and various social functions, so there was no discomfort on his part, and however annoyed Caro might be, she didn't seem to wish to discomfit her parents. The quartet passed a pleasant interval on the drive. When they disembarked before the theatre, they were met by Eversham and Kate.

Once greetings had been exchanged all around, they made their way through the throng of ladies in their finery and gentlemen in evening dress toward the Thornfield private box.

Val was surprised to find an attendant from the theatre already waiting in the private antechamber outside the box. He'd requested refreshments earlier but generally wait staff wasn't sent up until after the guests had settled in their seats.

"The duke and duchess are already inside, my lord," the young man said with a bow.

Though in his mind he was uttering a list of curses that would make even the saltiest of sailors blush, Val kept his reaction as bland as he could muster. "Ah, excellent. Thank you."

"I believe the phrase is 'hoist with your own petard,' is it not?" Caro asked pleasantly as he escorted her on his arm into the alcove overlooking the stage and the ground floor of the theatre. "Or is it 'boiled with your own pudding'? Whatever the saying, I must say it was worth my own discomfort to see your face lose all color for that barest moment. Though really, you're quite good at maintaining your composure. Well done."

He was saved from responding by the necessity of presenting his guests to his parents.

"My dear boy," the Duchess of Thornfield said as Val bent to kiss her cheek, "I had no notion you'd be here tonight. And who are your guests?" It was clear from the way her eyes had lit up that she'd drawn exactly the wrong conclusion from the Hardcastles' presence here.

"Mama, you will remember Mr. Charles Hardcastle and his wife, Lady Lavinia, from Piers's wedding. And, of course, their daughter, Miss Hardcastle, is a school friend of Cynthia's." He had no doubt that his mother recalled exactly who the family was. Her pretending not to recognize them was her way of putting them in their place.

"Of course." The duchess allowed Mr. Hardcastle to bow over her hand, then nodded as his wife dropped a short curtsy. To Caro, his mother said, "Miss Hardcastle, how do you do? It's a pleasure to see you again."

Val took that moment while everyone exchanged greetings to get a good look at Caro for the first time that evening. With her father seated beside him in the carriage, he hadn't been able to take in the exquisite totality of her appearance. Her gown, a gauzy confection constructed of layer upon layer of a silvery metallic fabric picked out with blue flowers, emphasized her tiny waist and the soft curve of her hips and made him long to pull her close and explore the way the bodice gently cupped her ample bosom. She'd also done something different with her hair. The Caro he'd known wasn't much for elaborate hairstyles, but tonight her tresses were gathered up on the crown of her head with a cascade of ringlets dipping down to kiss the nape of her neck.

Reminding himself that her father was with them—and that his own parents had been added to the mix—Val steeled his mind against further appreciation of her attire and turned his attention back to the conversation.

"We are always happy to welcome a friend of Valentine's, my dear," Val's father said, bowing over Caro's hand. "Indeed, we were just discussing how—"

Before his father could finish, Val broke in with what he hoped was an easy laugh. At the same time, he tried to convey a message saying *stop talking* to the duke with his eyes. The last thing he needed was for his father to remind them of Val's prior infatuation with her. "My father is always encouraging me to bring more guests to the theatre."

Caro looked from Val to the duke and back before saying in a puzzled tone, "How nice of him?"

He was saved from further uncomfortable conversation by Kate, who stepped forward to introduce Eversham to his parents. Giving Caro his arm, he led her to a pair of seats in the row behind where her parents now sat.

"What were you thinking?" Caro hissed once they were seated. This close to her, he could feel the warmth of her skin through her gown and smell the clean floral scent of her perfume. What had she asked?

"Val." She glared. "You know how much my mama wants to see me married into the aristocracy. She might not go so far as to force me into marriage but she will remind me about this invitation every day until the end of time. Have you forgotten that we tried this once before and decided we would not suit?"

"I acted impulsively," Val hissed back, the confession of his capriciousness filling him with shame. "Once Eversham and I saw the signed advertisement, we knew we needed to come here tonight and keep a watch on the greenroom."

He turned to face her, knowing that he should be looking her in the eyes. "If you must know, I was afraid you'd refuse to attend in my box unless I sent the invitation to your parents. I knew your mother was unlikely to turn it down and that she'd persuade you to come even if I couldn't."

Fortunately, there was enough ambient noise around them that their conversation was relatively private. A circumstance for which Val was grateful. He suspected Caro was about to give him the sort of setdown that would leave his ears blistered for years to come.

But rather than anger, he saw chagrin, followed by some other nameless emotion in Caro's eyes. It was all the encouragement he needed to speak the words that he knew he must if they were ever to move forward from their past.

"It was no doubt silly to do so without discussing it with you first," Val said, his usual aplomb all but deserting him, "but your anger today reminded me of what my brother said that night."

Her eyes narrowed and he realized he'd been clumsy. "Not that I agreed with him but that I wished to make amends. To truly prove to you that I don't agree with him, nor have I ever."

Caro stayed silent, but Val was relieved to see that her expression had softened.

"I thought having you and your parents here in my family's private box," he continued with a slight shrug, "would demonstrate to you—and the rest of the world—that I don't give a hang about where your father was born or where his money came from."

Caro looked away and Val felt every second until she turned back to him. "Thank you," she said, her brown eyes dark with emotion. "Your gesture is"—she paused—"appreciated."

He hadn't realized he was holding his breath until he exhaled at her words.

"I'm not your enemy, Caro," he said softly. "I don't hate you."

Their discussion was becoming uncomfortably personal. "And I want to find Miss Warrington, too." He hoped moving it back to their shared goal of finding Frank's fiancée would dissipate the emotions brewing between them.

"You don't even know her." Caro frowned. "I'm still not sure you approve of Frank's betrothal to her. My first thought when I saw you today was that you were there to spirit Frank away before he could bring scandal down on the family name. Tell me I'm wrong."

"Not entirely," he admitted. Before she could argue, he continued, "But I didn't even know why Frank had summoned me. Once I knew she was missing, I was ready to help. My father and uncle may not approve of the marriage, but I have no objection. Once we find her."

Her mouth twisted in suspicion, but he'd pleaded his case with her enough for one evening.

She was silent for a moment before changing the subject. "Your parents are encouraging you to marry, then?"

Val fought the urge to pinch the bridge of his nose. Caro was the very last person on earth he wished to discuss his marriage prospects with.

"It's been over a year," he said. What interest, if any, could Caro have in the matter? She'd certainly shown herself unwilling to take on the role of his wife. "My father is quite eager to see the succession secured. Especially given how unexpectedly we lost Piers. I know he and Cynthia certainly weren't expecting to remain childless forever."

Caro's eyes softened. "Poor Cynthia. She's lost both her

husband and any chance at his child. It seems doubly cruel, somehow."

Caro had always been loyal, and that she could find it in herself to show sympathy for his brother's widow given how cruelly dismissive Piers had been of her only proved how generous she could be.

Kate and Eversham came and sat beside them then, so there was no further chance for private conversation.

It felt to Val as if an age had passed before a man came onto the stage and announced that the role of Ophelia would be played by Miss Julia Todd rather than Miss Effie Warrington as previously scheduled.

A cry went up from several men in the pit and one even shouted, "Blasphemy!" as if having anyone besides Effie perform was a crime against Shakespeare. It was clear that Frank and Mrs. Spencer hadn't exaggerated about Effie's popularity.

Once the play began, he tried to settle back and watch, but concentrating was difficult after his conversation with Caro. He hadn't intended to tell her the whole of his reason for inviting her parents. Not tonight, anyway. But his parents' presence and her close proximity in a pretty gown had thrown him off balance, weakening his resolve, and he'd confessed all. He'd never behaved with more rashness in his entire life than he had today.

Perhaps he was sickening with something. He should have asked Woolford to examine him after looking over Frank.

She'd been just as annoyed as he'd predicted, but her understanding at his attempt to make amends for his past sins had been gratifying. He wasn't sure what she would think about the motive he *hadn't* shared—the simple fact that he wanted to spend more time with her. He'd only just realized that desire within himself.

Beside him, Caro sighed. "Will you please be still?" she whispered. "You're jumpier than Ludwig with a bit of string."

Of course she'd compare him to her damned cat. He grimly concentrated on quelling his nervous energy.

When the interval arrived, he was more than ready to stretch his legs.

As Eversham, Kate, and the Hardcastles rose and made for the door, he got up with the intention of following them but was waylaid by his father.

"I thought we'd agreed Miss Hardcastle wasn't a suitable candidate to become Lady Wrackham," his father said discreetly. "However lovely she might be, and she is that, we are not in the sort of dire straits financially that we expect you to sacrifice your title for a fortune."

"I don't recall any agreement of the sort," Val said coldly. He loved the duke, but he was long overdue in needing to set him straight on this one matter. "You have made your wishes clear as to my needing to marry sooner rather than later. But you will find me much less pliable than Piers was when it comes to your involvement in my choice of bride. I'll thank you to remember that."

He might have let his father and brother get away with disparaging remarks about Caro and her family in the past, but no more.

Rather than abashed, however, the duke seemed amused by Val's sharp words.

"Don't tell me you actually have feelings for this girl."

His brows rose in a familiar display of ducal hauteur. "When you were the younger son, such a mésalliance might have been acceptable, but you are my direct heir now. You owe the family a lady of impeccable lineage. Not the daughter of a tin can merchant. Do your best to forget her and let your mother introduce you to—"

"Miss Hardcastle is also the granddaughter of the Earl of Leith, and her father, who is one of the most successful businessmen in London, is currently my guest. If you wish me to take my guests elsewhere before the end of the interval, I will do so, but know that Mama would not wish to be embarrassed in that way."

Val saw the moment his father realized he'd gone too far. The duke's expression turned from one of disbelief to puzzlement, like that of a pampered spaniel chastised for the first time. As the younger son, Val had enjoyed a somewhat more casual relationship with him than Piers. But it seemed that their easy rapport was at an end, and Val couldn't say he was sorry. Whether he'd intended it or not, his refusal to stand up to his father in the past had led the duke to assume that Val would bow to his wishes. But it was high time to prove himself to be his own man. And if that meant a change to their easy relationship, then so be it.

"There's no need to leave," his father said at last, his tone defensive. Val would hardly call the man repentant. He was far too full of his own importance for that. But perhaps he'd recognized that he'd crossed a line. "Of course your guests are welcome. We will discuss Miss Hardcastle at another time."

Like hell we will.

But concluding that he'd already demanded enough concessions for one evening, Val simply nodded.

The subject at a close, the duke waved a dismissive hand. "Go and find that policeman Lady Katherine married." There was an unspoken complaint buried in his words about Kate's choice of husband, but that was a battle for another day.

Satisfied that he'd made his point, Val left the box.

Once he was in the hallway, however, he saw no sign of Eversham, Kate, or Caro.

Uninterested in making conversation with the acquaintances in the corridor, and in no mood to return to the box and further brangle with his father, he decided to see if he could find the greenroom from here.

On a hunch, he made his way in the opposite direction from where the throngs were headed. At the end of the hallway, he found what he was looking for, a door cleverly hidden in the wallpaper. He'd once kept company with an opera singer who had told him about all the little ways theatres hid their inner workings from the patrons who came to watch the performances. Similar to the great houses with their hidden staircases to mask servants' comings and goings, theatres held corridors within the walls for the ushers and various other workers so that they didn't mingle with the upper-class patrons of the boxes.

He tapped the wall in an effort to find the mechanism that would open the entrance, but before he could manage it, the door opened from the other side. The usher who emerged quickly attempted to mask his surprise. "I apologize, my lord, but this is for employees of the theatre only."

But once Val had pressed a few coins into the young man's hand, the usher was willing to let him through with a cry of thanks.

The other side of the door revealed a far more utilitarian decor. No wallpaper hung on the wood-grain walls, and the sconces that lit the way were of a cheaper quality than those in the public areas. Clearly the owners had no concerns for the aesthetic tastes of their workers.

He followed the short hallway to a stairway, which should lead, according to his mental picture of the theatre's layout, to the area behind the stage.

Then he heard a man shouting.

"Where is Miss Warrington? I demand to see her at once! She made no mention of being absent tonight."

A female voice that sounded oddly familiar followed his words. How had Caro managed to get down here so quickly?

His surprise turned to alarm, however, when he heard her scream, followed by a loud crash.

Every nerve on high alert, he took the steps two at a time and rushed forward into chaos.

Grateful for the opportunity to remove herself from Val's distracting presence, Caro followed Kate into the corridor as soon as the performance broke for the interval.

His admission that he'd invited her family tonight out of a desire to apologize for his actions four years ago had nearly taken her breath away. She'd assumed, wrongly it seemed, that he'd coerced her into his family's private box in order to manipulate or humiliate her. It had never occurred to her that he might have done so for altruistic reasons.

Caro knew she was prone to making rash judgments, but she'd thought she knew Val well enough to safely guess his motives. That she'd been so utterly mistaken came as a blow to her own faith in her powers of discernment.

"The cast seems to be managing well with the casting change," Kate said as they worked their way into the throng crowding the corridor outside the Thornfield's box. "I had supposed there would be at least a bit of disarray with Julia in the role, but I could detect none."

"Having met Julia, I'm unsurprised she's making the most of this opportunity to shine." Caro had to raise her voice in order to be heard over the din.

Caro saw Eversham reply, but by this point Caro could barely hear herself breathe. She tried to stay close to her friends, but she was soon forced to watch helplessly as more and more theatregoers pushed into the gap between them. And because of her small stature, she was unable to view them from above.

Deciding that it might be best to stay close to the edges until the crush thinned out, she made her way to the lavishly papered wall and tried unsuccessfully to see over the crowd by going up on her toes. But she'd never had any great fondness for waiting. Perhaps she should use this time to do some investigating on her own.

Soon, she was in the marble-tiled reception at the theatre's entrance. Spotting an usher, she asked him to direct her to the greenroom. He frowned. "There won't be anyone there now, miss. You don't want to go."

Belying the usher's words, however, was a man of middle

years carrying an elaborate bouquet. He crossed from the main entrance to slip through a carved door just opposite from where she and the young man now stood.

Could one of Effie's admirers have skipped the performance, thereby missing the announcement that she'd been replaced by her understudy? Or could the admirer responsible for her disappearance be coming to the greenroom—without bothering with the play—in an effort to make himself appear innocent of the crime? She had to find out.

Moving past the usher, she started for the door, only to have him step forward and bar her entry. "It's not a proper place for you, miss."

Biting back a curse, Caro decided she needed to act quickly. Adopting what she liked to think of as her "helpless waif" expression, she grasped the man by the arm. "Oh, sir, please. You see, my poor brother was headed there. He's drunk again and I simply must get him home before he importunes that poor actress once more. She's already told him a dozen times or more that she's not interested, but..." She made a vague hand gesture that could mean anything from "c'est la vie" to "my poor nerves."

The young man, who was possessed of a guileless face—and, Caro hoped, a gallant streak—pulled back to look at her with suspicion.

She wasn't sure if it was her plaintive tone or the appeal of her person, but he finally capitulated. His boyish countenance reddened a little as he sighed and gestured toward the door the bouquet-carrying gentleman had disappeared behind. "But you mustn't tell anyone I let you in. We've been instructed not to let ladies in the greenroom ever since Lady Broadwhistle accosted her husband with a pistol while he was visiting his—"

He broke off, clearly trying to find a polite way to say "mistress."

Taking pity on him, Caro put a finger to her lips. "I'll tell no one, Mr. . . . ?"

"Alf, miss. It's Alfred, really, but me friends call me Alf and it's been that way ever since me mum and—"

Before he could further open the floodgates to his, no doubt amusing, tale of how he came to be called Alf, Caro interjected. "I'm so sorry but I must hurry. My brother. You understand?"

Having no wish for him to follow her, Caro touched him lightly on the arm. "Thank you so much, sir—" She corrected herself. "Alf. I'd best go inside on my own. I don't wish to embarrass him. And you'd better get back to work. I don't want you to lose your position."

At the mention of his job, Alf paled a little.

"You be careful, miss," he said before turning to leave.

Slipping through the coveted carved door, she noted the hallway beyond was dimly lit. And just to the right she saw what must be the greenroom.

When she pushed through the entryway, however, she found it was far from empty. Quite the opposite.

"There she is!" shouted one of the half-dozen or so men gathered in the chamber. Another aggrieved voice quickly followed—no doubt when they realized she was not any of the actresses they'd come here to pay homage to. "Who the devil are *you?*"

"My apologies, gentlemen." Caro kept near the exit on the chance that she'd need to make a hasty escape.

"I was hoping to ask you some questions about Miss Warrington."

"Where is she?" demanded the well-dressed gentleman she'd seen go in moments before, flowers in hand. His watery blue eyes were narrowed with ire and his fair complexion was flushed with emotion. "I came here to see her opening night, only to find she's been replaced for no good reason with that Julia Todd. Is this Thorn's doing?"

Since the man had arrived after the interval, Caro very much doubted that seeing the play had been foremost in his mind.

A chorus of agreement went up among the others.

"She's the only one worth seeing, if you ask me," said a young man who still bore the puppyish face of youth. "We want Effie back!"

This led to a spontaneous chant among the men of "We want Effie! We want Effie!"

If it weren't so astonishing, it would be amusing, Caro thought. She'd known, of course, that Effie was popular with theatregoers, but she had never actually witnessed their adoration in action.

She was trying to determine how best to calm them so she could ask her questions when a tall man with red side-whiskers and a receding hairline stumbled forward. "You're working with Francis Thorn, aren't you? What did he do with her?" he demanded, stepping closer to Caro than she would have liked. She fought back a wave of panic as she tried to move back. "What. Did. He. Do. With. Her." He punctuated the question with a wag of his finger, coming dangerously close to her face.

"He's done nothing with Miss Warrington, sir, and neither

have I." She made sure to enunciate her words carefully and loudly, since the others hadn't stopped their chanting and this newcomer was clearly drunk as a lord. She didn't have a great deal of experience with intoxicated men, but if he felt this strongly about Effie, then surely he'd be able to give her some useful information about his rivals for her affection. Aside from Frank, that was. She'd underestimated how strongly Effie's admirers would resent him.

But the inebriated man only swayed closer. "Where is she? She was supposed to be here tonight. What have you done with her?"

Perhaps recognizing that one of their number had crossed a line of sorts, the other men stopped their chant. Only, rather than coming to Caro's rescue, they shuffled back from them both.

"Where is Miss Warrington?!" he cried, his spirit-soaked breath exploding into Caro's face in a fetid burst of humidity. She nearly gagged as she pushed against his chest in panic. She had to get away from him. "I demand to see her at once! She made no mention of being absent tonight!"

"Sir, you must calm yourself!" Caro leaned away from him as best she could.

As he spoke, he continued to gesticulate, the motion throwing him off balance. So much so that he launched his arm forward so hard that his entire body soon followed.

Caro, recognizing the danger too late, screamed in dismay as the man's body carried her down to the floor with him.

She was attempting to push him off when a familiar voice rang out.

"Get the hell off of her, you brute!" Valentine shouted.

Chapter Seven

"A re you hurt?" Val demanded once he'd lifted the drunken oaf off of Caro and helped her to her feet.

Having experienced inexplicable rage on her behalf once already that day with Langham, he wasn't quite as surprised by it this time—especially given she'd been in physical danger in this instance. Even so, he was unaccustomed to the role of hothead. He'd always been the one to keep his wits about him while others lost theirs. Clearly the renewal of his acquaintance with Caro was affecting him, and not for the better. Still, if the impulse kept her from further harassment, then he supposed he could be grateful for now.

"I'm fine," she said, though he noted a tremor in the hand waving him off. The gown he'd been admiring earlier was sadly crushed and one of the puffed sleeves had been torn. "I was merely surprised—that's all."

As if feeling his gaze on her, she raised a hand to her disheveled hair. "I'm not too much of a fright, am I?"

A groan drew their attention back to the cause of Caro's disordered state.

Her coiffure forgotten, Caro scowled down at the man with the unfortunate hairline. "He was shouting about Effie," she told Val. "Demanding to know what I'd done with her. They all were."

She turned to look behind them and gasped. There was no one else there.

"Where did they go?" she demanded of Val, as if he'd personally helped the others make their escape. "First they let this fellow accost me, and then they turn tail and run at the first sign of trouble? Men!"

Val forbore from pointing out that he himself was a man and had come to her aid. That would only anger her further. And he was fond of his nose in its current location, thank you very much.

"Who were they?" he asked instead.

"There was a whole passel of Effie's admirers," Caro said with disgust. "I suppose they were waiting for the play to end so that they could demand to know Effie's whereabouts from Julia and the rest of the cast."

"Anyone you recognized?" he asked.

"No. Not even the one who knocked me down."

They both turned to look at Caro's accoster, who hadn't attempted to rise from where Val had tossed him aside moments before.

"Lift him up," Caro said to Val. "I wish to ask him some questions."

"I'm not some footman for you to order around," Val groused even as he moved to do as she asked. He hauled the man onto an overstuffed velvet sofa.

"Effie." The man sighed as his head dropped back against the seat. "Where is Effie?"

"What's your name, sir?" Caro asked him in an overloud voice.

"He's not deaf." Val barely disguised his amusement. "Only drunk."

The look she gave him could have curdled tea, but Val shrugged. If she was going to conduct investigations in his presence, she'd have to endure his input. And he had far more experience with sots than she did.

"Not deaf," the man repeated forlornly. "Only drunk."

Dropping to his haunches, Val looked the man in his bleary eyes. "What's your name, old fellow?"

"Thom's Har'son," the man enunciated very carefully.

Val shot Caro a sidelong glance of triumph. She rolled her eyes, which only amused him more.

He was clearly losing what little grip he had left on his sanity if he now actively wished for her derision. But damn it, if this reminded her that he wasn't the humorless society toff she now thought him to be, then he'd take it.

"Mr. Harrison." Caro leaned down to his level. "Who are the other men who came to ask after Miss Warrington?"

Unfortunately, her stance gave Harrison an excellent view of her impressive bosom and his eyes fixed there. Val physically lifted the man's chin. "Her face is up here, Harrison," he growled.

Caro's face turned pink and she stood up straight again. She mouthed her thanks to Val, who nodded.

"Ask him again," he told her.

"Who are the other men who came to ask after Miss Warrington, Mr. Harrison?" she repeated.

At the mention of the actress, Harrison, now focused on Caro's face, brightened. "Effie? Is Effie here?"

"I doubt we'll get sense from him in his current state," Val said, exasperated. "He's clearly beyond focusing on much besides Miss Warrington and your bos—" He caught himself. "Apologies . . . besides Miss Warrington."

But Caro waved away his correction. "I'm not ready to concede defeat yet."

To Harrison she said, "No, she's not here just now, Mr. Harrison. But we'd like to ask you some questions about her. Do you know—"

"Uncle Thomas, there you are!" A young man rushed toward them, his expression one of relief.

"I'm so sorry if he's been bothering you," he continued as he moved to his uncle's side. "He becomes a bit of a handful when he's in his cups. And he was quite distraught when Miss Warrington didn't appear onstage. I turned my back for only a moment, and he'd disappeared from my side. But I don't know why he came here."

"I believe he hoped to find out the reason for her absence from some of the other cast members." Val offered his hand to the young man. "I am Lord Wrackham. And you are?"

The youth's head shot up, stopping his inspection of his uncle. "My apologies, my lord," he said, bowing deeply. "I'm James Harrison and this is my uncle, Thomas Harrison. I'll just get him out to our carriage and back home."

But before he could lift his uncle, Caro spoke up. "Please don't go just yet, Mr. Harrison. I'd like to ask you a few questions first."

Val wasn't sure what the nephew of Miss Warrington's

most intoxicated admirer could tell them, but Caro had been thwarted so many times in her quest for answers tonight he didn't have the heart to discourage her.

"Oh, I am doubly sorry now. I beg your pardon, Miss...?"

Val didn't miss the way the younger Harrison's eyes widened. Whether at her beauty or her disheveled appearance, he couldn't tell. "This is Miss Caroline Hardcastle," he said. "Caro, this is Mr. James Harrison."

Once she'd offered her hand and he'd bowed over it, Caro pressed on. "Do you often accompany your uncle to the theatre, Mr. Harrison?"

"Fairly often." He shrugged, glancing down at his uncle, who was now softly snoring with the side of his face pressed against the sofa. "My mother is concerned that he'll get into trouble on his own. And since he's got no wife and family, and I'm his heir, it's up to me."

"So, you'd be familiar with the usual men who come to see Miss Warrington here in the greenroom?" Caro asked.

"There are always newcomers when the play changes," Harrison said thoughtfully, "but there are several who come back no matter what."

"And who might they be?" Caro asked.

His previously easy expression turned guarded. "What's this about?"

Before Caro could respond, Val said with a confidential air, "We're friends of Miss Warrington's and she's asked us to speak with her most loyal admirers to let them know how sorry she is to have missed tonight's performance." He didn't want the young man to stop sharing information with them, and since he could hardly reveal Miss Warrington was missing, this seemed the best excuse.

To his relief, Caro went along with the ruse, though she shot him a look of exasperation. "She's too ill to tell us the names of the gentlemen herself."

"She won't be back for the rest of the week?" Harrison asked, an odd bit of hope in his voice. Perhaps seeing their puzzlement, he continued. "It's just that it gets tiresome following my uncle here night after night."

He leaned forward and said sheepishly, "I'd much prefer a bit of light opera to all this Shakespeare folderol. Give me dancing girls and—" He colored. "That is to say, this sort of play isn't my forte."

"We aren't sure when she'll return," Caro said, ignoring the young man's disclosure. "It depends on the duration of her illness."

She returned to her earlier question. "Are there any of her coterie who stand out in some way? Someone overly attached to Miss Warrington, perhaps?"

Harrison rubbed his chin. "Well, aside from Uncle Thomas, there are only a handful who appear week after week. When Francis Thorn started keeping guard over her, a few of them stopped coming. There's the Duke of Langham—he was here just last week for the final performance of *Othello*. A bit intimidating, if you must know. Langham, I mean. Especially when he just sits there and glowers at everyone. I thought at first he was here for Nell Burgoyne but he didn't take his eyes off of Effie the whole night."

Val muttered a curse. Unless young Harrison was mistaken, Langham had lied right to his face this afternoon. Could he be involved with Miss Warrington's disappearance? He'd seemed so damned sincere about Nell, though.

He hoped the man hadn't taken the opportunity to go underground before Val could question him in the morning. Because he definitely needed answers from him, duke or no duke.

"The only other man I've seen focused on Effie," James Harrison continued saying, "is Lord Tate. I've only crossed paths with him here once before tonight. I don't know that he's an admirer, though. He really upset her. Thorn wasn't there, so she had no one to put him in his place. I suppose he brought all those roses tonight to apologize."

"When was this?" Caro demanded. "Recently?"

"Just last week," the young man said. "As I said, whatever they discussed truly overset her."

Clearly it hadn't seemed alarming enough for either of the Harrisons to come to her rescue, Val thought grimly. What a useless passel of fools these men were. Aloud, he asked, "Where was Langham that evening?"

"Oh, he wasn't here that night either. Poor Effie was on her own."

"You're sure that was Tate here with the roses tonight?" Caro asked.

"Absolutely. He seemed to be in just as sour a mood, though. I suppose because she wasn't here to accept his apology."

"Any others who stand out?" Val asked. He was growing impatient to leave. Perhaps he'd track down Langham tonight while his annoyance was fresh.

But young Harrison shook his head. "I don't really think any of them had a chance even before Thorn bagged her. You know how actresses are. They're looking for the wealthiest protector they can find. It's why

I tried to dissuade Uncle Thomas. But he would have none of it."

"What do you mean 'bagged her' and 'how actresses are'?" Caro asked, her voice quiet. Val could have warned Harrison her tone did not bode well for his continued good health. He suppressed the urge to teach the fellow a lesson for his insulting words. Caro was more than capable of dispatching the man without his help. "Are you suggesting that they are at fault for the fact that men see them as—"

A nearby clock tower chimed the hour. Good Lord, the interval was long over. They had to get back to their box at once.

"Thank you very much for your help, Mr. Harrison," he said, interrupting Caro's admittedly warranted scolding. "Best wishes to your uncle."

Pulling her out into the corridor, he said in a low voice, "Do you know how long we've been gone? Your parents are probably frantic."

Caro gasped, lifting a hand to her torn sleeve. "My gown."

He looked at the unseemly amount of creamy skin revealed by the ripped seam and cursed. The unexpected desire to run his tongue along her exposed skin did not improve his temper. "Don't you ladies carry pins in your reticules for such things?" he demanded crossly.

"At balls," she snapped, trying to hold the two edges of fabric together. "Where there is an expectation of dancing with gentlemen prone to treading on my hems. I hardly expected to be accosted by a drunkard tonight."

Val looked away from her shoulder, but his eye fell on her bosom, which was no better for his attitude.

"Here," Caro said, touching his chest. Val almost leapt away in surprise, until he realized she'd been reaching for his cravat pin. "This should work."

He stood stoically, staring at the wall behind her, trying his damndest not to think about how she was performing an act that was usually a prelude to undressing.

"There," she said, having worked the jeweled stick free from its mooring. Handing it to him, she continued, "You'll have to do the honors."

Ignoring the brush of her hand as she gave him the pin, Val turned his attention to the torn sleeve. He bent his head to see, which meant inhaling the sweet floral scent of Caro's warm skin as he tried to tamp down his inconvenient desire. Of course, the sleeve had ripped away from the bodice, which meant he also had to touch the soft curve of her collarbone. He was going to get roaring drunk tonight, he promised himself.

"What's taking so long?" Caro asked impatiently. "Is it not working?"

"It's working," he said more harshly than he intended. His task finally completed, he stepped back.

He watched as she reached up to test the sleeve. "Well done," she said with a shy smile, her cheeks flushed. Then, as if recalling their predicament, she squared her shoulders. "Let's go."

But as they stepped through the door leading from the corridor into the main lobby, Caro gasped.

Not only were both sets of their parents before them, but a group of theatregoers Val didn't recognize had also crowded into the wide chamber. No doubt they saw before them a damning picture: a young lady whose gown was much the worse for wear, and whose once-elegant coiffure had escaped more than a few of its pins, accompanied by a gentleman who was neither her betrothed nor her husband and in whose company she had been alone for far longer than propriety dictated.

"Hellfire and damnation," Caro said in a low tone.

Val could not argue with the sentiment.

After a moment's rally, however, she called out with a false brightness that set his teeth on edge. "Mama! Papa! There you are!"

Caro desperately hoped that her merry smile and calm demeanor could forestall the coming storm. Because one look at her mother's shocked face was enough to tell her the situation was grave indeed. Anything less than her best performance and Mama would calculate how to turn this very scene into a marriage between Caro and Val.

The degree to which Mama's usual inclination toward matchmaking had been replaced with alarm told Caro all she needed to know.

Still, she had to try to convince both their parents and the rest of the onlookers to reject what they saw before them with their own eyes.

"It was the most amusing thing," she said cheerfully. "You know how clumsy I can be, of course. Well, I entirely misjudged my footing and if it hadn't been for Lord Wrackham—"

Val squeezed her arm, no doubt in warning, but he was too late.

A tall older man with bushy white side-whiskers had stepped forward. He said, in a scandalized tone, "This is the daughter you were speaking of, Hardcastle? I don't know if I can continue to do business with a man who isn't even able to manage his own children."

Though her father's expression quickly turned from amusement to clear anger, Caro—who had spent her whole life learning this man's moods—caught his fleeting look of disappointment just before he turned to his customer.

"Yes, this is my Caroline," Charles Hardcastle said hotly, "and I'm sure she has a perfectly reasonable explanation for this commotion. Don't you, my dear?"

His face was so full of trust and love that Caro felt her heart sink. She knew that no amount of explaining would make these people—for now everyone in the room had their eyes firmly fixed upon her and Val—believe that she'd torn her gown and mussed her hair simply by missing a step. No matter that they had not been engaging in the sort of activities these oh-so-respectable onlookers were themselves visualizing, it was the appearance of impropriety that mattered with polite society. No, there would be no talking her way out of this predicament.

Caro admired her father more than any person in the world. But it had never occurred to her that her behavior might make matters difficult for him with the more narrow-minded of his customers, unfair as that was. Her mother's earlier confession only made her feel worse about how her lack of concern for her actions must have affected him.

If she'd been born a boy, she could have sown as many

wild oats as she pleased, and no one would dare threaten to stop doing business with Hardcastle Fine Foods. But she hadn't.

There was one step she could take now to make this right. She'd always faulted Val for his rigid adherence to his family's expectations, but for the first time she recognized that perhaps his behavior had come not from a place of aristocratic snobbery, but family loyalty. His actions hadn't always been right, but here and now, faced with a chance to protect her own family's reputation, she understood him far better.

She only hoped that he still retained enough affection for her to forgive her when she sacrificed both of their future happiness with her next words.

Almost as if he sensed her hesitation, she felt Val slip his arm around her and pull her to his side. The gesture gave her the courage she needed to go through with her impulsive plan.

"If you'd only waited until I finished, sir," she addressed the bewhiskered man in a playfully chiding tone. In hope of warning Val, she reached across her abdomen to cover his hand where it clasped her waist, squeezing it gently. Then, taking a deep breath, she likened herself to Lady Macbeth and made it "done quickly."

"I did lose my footing," she told her parents. "And Lord Wrackham did keep me from falling. But only because when we had a moment to talk alone, he asked me to be his wife and I accepted him."

There was a beat of stunned silence before the room erupted in chaotic conversation.

Rather than denounce her for a lying jade, Val turned to

his father, who'd just stepped forward. "I hope you'll wish us happy."

Caro wasn't sure what it was that passed from father to son, but it wasn't well wishes. The duke's expression was stony, as was Val's. Her heart swelled as she realized that, however silently, he was standing up for her.

Aloud, the duke said, "Caroline, may I be the first to welcome you to the family." And rather than kissing her hand, the duke gave her a brief hug.

She didn't hear his words to Val because next she was pulled into the arms of the duchess. To Caro's surprise, Val's mother had tears in her eyes when she stepped back. "My dear." She took Caro's hands in hers. "You must forgive an old woman her excess of emotions. But I lost one son not too long ago and it does my heart good to see my other child so soon to be settled."

Caro wasn't sure what to say since she wasn't sure how settled Val would be when—or if—they did marry. But touched by the duchess's words, she said truthfully, "I will try my best to make him happy. I can promise that, your grace."

Caro then found herself facing her father, who enveloped her in one of his bearlike hugs. "What a sly minx you are, Caroline." He smiled fondly, keeping his hands on her shoulders. "I should have known the two of you were up to mischief when you dragged me to the theatre with not so much as a by-your-leave." In a quieter tone, he said, "I'm sorry for Gates. I'll have a word with him tomorrow. A man shouldn't make accusations like that in public. Especially before there's been a chance to get a grasp on the truth of the situation. I reckon he feels like a clodpate, and don't he deserve it?"

"What a horrid man." Mama pressed forward to kiss Caro on the cheek. "I'm so sorry he caused a scene, my dear. Especially when you wished to share such happy news. We should have known when the two of you didn't come back after the interval that Lord Wrackham was unable to hold back his feelings any longer. I told you his invitation wasn't as innocent as you thought."

"Indeed, you have seen through me, ma'am," Val said, stepping up beside Caro and slipping her arm through his. "I had thought to save my proposal for a more romantic occasion, but when she fell literally into my arms, I could not let the occasion pass without declaring myself. I was only lucky that Caroline decided to put me out of my misery and make me the happiest of men."

"I speak the truth, my lord," Caro said, smiling slyly at his outrageous words, "when I say that it has long been my fondest wish to put you out of your misery."

Her betrothed was suddenly seized by a coughing fit that sounded suspiciously like laughter.

"You should see a physician about that cough, my lord," said her mother with concern. "We want you to be in your finest fettle for the wedding."

When he'd recovered himself, Val said with a suspiciously sincere tone, "Ma'am, I can assure you, I will only ever endeavor to show your daughter my finest fettle."

Mama seemed satisfied with that nonsensical statement, but Caro had had enough. Once her mother had turned to speak with the duke and duchess, she gave Val a none-too-gentle elbow to the ribs.

"Stop that," she said in a low voice.

"But, beloved"—he patted her hand—"I have it on

the highest authority that my fettle is among the best in London. Modesty keeps me from saying all of England, but really, if I'm being honest—"

She was saved from further teasing by the appearance of Kate and Eversham. Caro pulled Kate aside and left Val to entertain Eversham.

"My dear." Kate's eyes were wide with disbelief. "What happened?"

"We went to the greenroom," Caro explained, keeping an eye on the rest of the assembled gathering over Kate's shoulder. Quickly she described seeing Lord Tate with his flowers, followed by her encounter with Thomas Harrison and their discussion with his nephew. "I'd forgotten about the time until the bell rang and then it was too late."

"I assume that horrid man was one of your father's customers?" Kate asked, her brow creased with sympathy.

Caro nodded. "I simply couldn't let Papa suffer for my carelessness. Especially not when he's so worried that my unmarried state might be due to his own birth. And now this awful man, Gates, has tried to shame him through me. I never realized, Kate, just how much gossip both he and Mama have withstood without complaint over the years."

Then, remembering who she was talking about, she amended, "Perhaps Mama wasn't *entirely* without complaints."

"Perhaps not." Kate squeezed her shoulder in reassurance. "But I sincerely doubt men of business spend their time discussing the latest gossip. I know the ones at the paper don't." At the reminder that Kate herself was a business owner, Caro realized her friend would be an excellent confidante for the news that she'd one day be in charge of Hardcastle Fine Foods.

But that discussion would have to wait until later.

"I suppose," Caro said, "but even if they didn't complain to Papa openly about me, who knows how many of his business contacts chose to sever ties—or worse, never do business with him at all—because of me?

"I can't hold Val to this, of course," she continued. "I was just so angry when Gates spoke out that I said the only thing I knew would make him feel horrid for his hateful words."

Kate blinked. "I'm not sure this is something that can be easily undone without—"

But Caro was in no mood to hear reason. "I'm sure Val will agree with me once we've had a chance to talk. He's no more eager to marry me than I am to marry him."

Though she'd been angry when she'd first learned of his invitation to the theatre, his explanation and subsequent apology had cooled her temper. And even had she wanted to punish him, only a ninnyhammer would consider an invitation to the theatre and a surprise betrothal to be of equal consequences.

Kate glanced over to where Val was laughing with Eversham. "He doesn't seem to be particularly upset to me."

"He's good at hiding what he feels," Caro said dismissively. "You know that."

But her friend only smiled. "Not where you're concerned, Caro."

Chapter Eight

Val was in no mood to sit through the rest of Hamlet's string of bad decisions, and to his relief, the Hardcastles were amenable to his suggestion that they leave early.

He'd been thrumming with nervous energy ever since he and Caro had stepped out of the corridor and onto their own stage of sorts. He'd gone through the scene with a sense of unreality, though at no moment did he feel the urge to object to Caro's announcement. Indeed, if she hadn't been the one to speak up, he would have. It had been clear from the gathered crowd that she'd be ruined if he didn't offer for her.

And though he had begun the day without any notion of seeing her again, let alone marrying her, he couldn't say he was altogether upset by how events had turned out.

"It's not every day my little girl gets betrothed." Hardcastle clapped him on the back with a smile.

Lady Lavinia chattered about wedding plans the whole

drive back to Belgrave Square and didn't seem to notice Caro's monosyllabic responses to her queries.

But Val did.

When the carriage finally pulled to a stop in front of the Hardcastle townhouse, he climbed out to hand out Lady Lavinia, then waited until Mr. Hardcastle had disembarked before placing a hand on Caro's arm to stay her.

"I'd like a few words with my betrothed, if I may." He spoke loudly enough for Lady Lavinia to hear.

Caro's eyes widened but she did not demur.

Lady Lavinia gave him an indulgent smile. "I suppose I can allow it. Do not be too long, Caroline. We'll have lots to plan tomorrow."

After instructing his coachman to drive around the square until he signaled, Val climbed back in and faced Caro. She seemed remarkably unrepentant for one who'd blithely announced their betrothal only an hour ago without an actual proposal. He didn't mind the fact of it, but her brazenness amused him.

"You needn't lecture me," she began, her chin held high. "I got us into this debacle and I shall find a way to get us out. I simply could not let that awful man shame my father. He's done nothing wrong. Why should his business suffer because I was foolish enough to be caught in a compromising position? I know your father will be relieved. Even though he was polite enough, it was evident that he would have preferred you with nearly any other young lady. Indeed, I suspect—"

"Caro," Val interrupted when it became clear that if left unchecked, she would keep talking until they were both old and gray. "Take a breath. I have no intention of reading you a scold. Indeed, I would have announced our betrothal if you'd not done so first."

"That's just what I expected you to—" She broke off, her hand frozen mid-gesticulation. "You...what?"

In the dim light through the carriage windows, her skin was luminous. And her mussed hair and gown gave her the look of a woman who'd been freshly bedded. Val had always thought her alluring, with her lush mouth and dark hair and eyes, but in the years since he'd first met her, she'd gained a confidence that made her almost irresistible. A confidence that urged him again and again to share how he, too, had changed—because of her. But just below the surface, he saw a vulnerability—from a hurt he'd caused?— that likewise tempted him to wrap her in his arms and tell her everything would be well.

It took every ounce of his will to stop himself. They'd avoided difficult conversations in the past and their relationship had fallen apart. This time, however their match had come about, he was determined the betrothal would end not just in a marriage, but a happy one.

"It doesn't matter how innocent we are of indiscretion," he said. "Honor demands that I offer you the protection of my name. I should have realized as soon as I rescued you from Harrison how it would look when we left the greenroom. If I'd been thinking, I'd have spoken to you before we even stepped out into the lobby."

If he thought Caro would thank him for riding to her rescue, he was to be sorely mistaken.

"I might have known you'd find a way to twist yourself into a knot like a Covent Garden contortionist to do the honorable thing," she said with disgust. "There's no need to sacrifice yourself, Val. I'll find a way out of this that will leave you free to marry some meek little thing who will hang on your every word."

Given how many times she'd thrown his noble actions back at him today, Val should have known by now that she had no interest in his protection unless she asked for it. But though he might have changed since their first betrothal, some parts of his personality simply remained essential.

Still, her words surprised a laugh out of him. "You truly must think me a self-important ass."

"I think you are a man." Caro shrugged. "So, perhaps?"

"I'm not perfect, Caro," he said, his composure slipping in the face of her scorn. How could he show her that in this instance, his inclination and duty aligned? "I may be as fond of my own opinions as the next man, but I have no wish for a wife who does nothing but parrot my own ideas back to me."

Her lush mouth was set defiantly, but the glimmer of interest in her eyes gave him hope. Perhaps his cause was not so lost as he'd feared.

"That is the sort of wife your father wants for you." The undisguised hurt in her voice cut him to the bone. "Or at the least, he wants someone other than me. I could see how displeased he was with our announcement, though he was well-behaved enough to disguise it."

Val had never wanted more to strike his own father. But the duke was not the true problem here. His own failures in the past were what kept Caro from trusting him now.

"My father's wishes don't come into it." He took her hand in his. "I won't let him dictate my behavior."

"No," she said bitterly, pulling her hand away. "You will

simply let him denigrate your choices without argument while pretending to be your own man."

Her words hung in the air like smoke from a fire that had long ago destroyed all in its path.

"We've never really discussed how I failed you four years ago," he said softly, the hurt in her eyes making him ache with remorse. "I think it's time, don't you?"

He was committed to saying what clearly needed saying, but dear Lord in heaven, would this be dashed uncomfortable. For them both.

"I don't know what you're talking about." Caro turned to gaze sightlessly out the window. "I think you should take me home now."

Val stared at her. "I'd never have taken the fearless Caroline Hardcastle for a coward."

Glaring at him, she said hotly, "Perhaps I simply have no wish to discuss a relationship that ended long ago, Val. We should leave all that in the past. I've moved on. You should, too. Indeed, we need never see one another again once we end this fictional betrothal."

But he wasn't going to let her hide from him—from them—without a fight.

"Moved on?" he asked with a bark of laughter. "You can barely stand to be in the same room with me without stripping the flesh from my bones."

"I had no idea you were so sensitive, Lord Wrackham," she said coldly. "I shall endeavor to be gentler with your aristocratic feelings in future."

"I hurt you that night," he said, ignoring her defensive posture. "By not defending you when my brother insulted you. But we both know that if you'd been surer of me, you wouldn't have been so ready to break things off. Indeed, I think I gave you reason to doubt my loyalty to you long before you heard my brother's hateful words."

Her eyes welled with tears.

Wordlessly, he handed her his handkerchief.

"What's this for?" she demanded. "I'm not crying."

But just then she gave a little sob and raised the cloth to her eyes. Val could have no more stayed on his side of the carriage than flown to the moon.

Moving to sit beside her, he said softly, "Let me hold you, Caro. Please."

She turned and wrapped her arms around him, burrowing her head beneath his chin.

"I'm so sorry," he murmured as she wept against him. "I'd always known my view of the world was different from my father and brother's, but I managed to get along with them by letting their remarks pass without engagement. When Piers spoke about you and your family, I was stunned. I hadn't even had a chance to speak to your father. I was torn between ripping into him and keeping the betrothal secret like we'd agreed."

He took her by the shoulders and dipped his head to look her in the eyes. "And truthfully, it shouldn't have mattered whether he was speaking of my betrothed or a stranger in the street. I had my own convictions but not the courage to fight for them. I made the wrong decision, Caro. I knew it as soon as I saw your face when you came to dissolve our understanding."

"I thought you were different from them." Caro's voice was hoarse from tears. "But you were just the same sort of disdainful aristocrat we'd laughed at together. How could I possibly have gone through with marrying you? Your brother would have made my life as part of your family a misery. Not to mention what your father would have said."

His chest squeezed at the realization that she'd very likely been correct. He'd loved his brother, but he knew all too well how pompous he could be. Though Val liked to think he would have done his best to shield Caro from the worst of his family, he also knew that at the time he'd lacked the maturity necessary to do a proper job of it. Caro had been right not to trust him entirely.

"Is it fear of my father that makes you reluctant to go through with our betrothal now?" He thought back to his conversation with the duke earlier that evening, before bedlam had descended upon them all. Caro hadn't been wrong when she'd found his warm welcome suspect. Val had been mistrustful of it himself. "Because I can assure you that however I might have failed to do so in the past, this marriage is my choice and I expect him to treat you with the respect you deserve as my wife."

Val was a different man now. The loss of Caro had forced him to recognize letting his father and brother run rough-shod over him without argument *was* tacit approval of their views. It was a mistake he'd not make again.

"Is there a betrothal?" Caro looked fixedly at the jeweled pin in his neckcloth. "I wasn't jesting when I said we could find a way out. There's no reason for you to go through with it because of my recklessness."

"You weren't reckless," Val said softly, lifting her chin with a gentle finger. Her eyes, still shiny with unshed tears, met his with a trust he wasn't sure he deserved. "You were trying to find your friend. That's one of the things I most admire about you, Caro. You're loyal to a fault. If there's something to be done to protect those you love, you'll do it without thought for the consequences for yourself."

She smiled wryly. "Or consequences for those around me."

"I know what I'm getting myself into." He grinned. "This is one of those rare occasions where my honor and inclinations are perfectly aligned."

As they spoke, they moved closer to one another, as if being pulled by an invisible thread. "May I kiss you, Caroline?" Val asked.

She touched her lips to his.

And stole a march on him for the second time that night.

She'd forgotten how soft his lips were.

They'd only managed a few stolen kisses over their brief abandoned courtship. She'd collected so many details of him from those days—his warm bergamot and lime scent, the feel of his strong arms, the firmness of his muscled chest against her bosom—but the wonder at that first touch of their mouths she'd forgotten.

There was no hesitation or unfamiliarity or newness. Though they'd spent the past few years apart, it was as if no time had passed at all.

Except that wasn't quite right, Caro thought as she brought her hands up to cup his face, rough with evening stubble. She opened her mouth over his and reveled in the feel of his breath mingling with hers. She'd been shy about taking what she wanted back then, but she'd long ago given up that sort of wavering. She still longed for happy endings, but she knew now that they didn't just happen—they were made.

Four years ago, they'd both been too impetuous and immature to talk through their differences. But if Val could learn from his mistakes, then so could she. This second chance was a gift and she would grasp it with both hands.

She returned every touch of his tongue with one of her own, a conversation without words. But when she gasped at his hand tugging at her bodice, the spell was broken. Val gave a low curse and laid his forehead on her bare shoulder.

"It's late," he said at last, setting her gown back to rights. As much as one could with a frock that had already been through the wars earlier that night. "Your mama will think we've eloped."

He rapped on the roof of the carriage to signal the driver to take them back.

She was pleased to see he was just as breathless as she was, and for a moment, they smiled at each other like children who'd just carried out an elaborate prank.

Once the carriage came to a stop a few moments later, he kissed her quickly on the lips before hopping down. But instead of lowering the steps, he lifted her down himself.

Caro was quite sure she'd still be feeling the impression of his hands at her waist when she fell asleep.

"I'll come by tomorrow to speak formally with your father," he said, holding her loosely.

She frowned. "Did we decide to go through with this, then?" Caro knew they'd cleared the air between them, but was she truly ready to marry him? She swallowed, unused to the sudden rush of nerves that filled her at the notion. Before today, they hadn't even seen one another in more than a year. She wanted him now, but how would she feel about him tomorrow?

He raised a brow. "Do you kiss men you have no intention of marrying like that?"

She rolled her eyes. "You know I don't. Not that it should matter. Purity is a concept conceived of by men to control women, and if this were a just world, women could take lovers as men do—as often as they liked with no fear of shame."

Another man might have complained, but Val nodded. "A good point. I'm not sure I'm up to a discussion of political philosophy at the moment, but remind me later."

His kiss this time was sweet but brief, soothing Caro's earlier doubts. They might have spent most of the last four years apart, but he was a good man. She could find happiness with him, she decided.

Val was smiling when he pulled away from her and said, "Now, go inside before I kiss you again. We both need sleep, and we still have to search for Miss Warrington tomorrow."

With a pang of guilt, Caro realized she hadn't properly thought of Effie since the theatre. At least she'd come to believe that Val was sincere in his wish to find her friend. He might also have his cousin's interests in mind, but she no longer feared that he would do so at Effie's expense. Perhaps once Effie was found, they could all sit down to dinner together and laugh over these adventures.

"Good night, my lord," she said before hurrying up the steps.

"I like it better when you call me by my name," she heard him say behind her. When she turned to look back, he was watching her from next to his carriage. "Sweet dreams, Caro."

Chapter Nine

The next morning, Val found Frank in the breakfast room, looking far better than he had the day before.

"What did you learn at the Lyceum?" his cousin asked once he'd filled a plate and taken a seat across from him. A full night of sleep had clearly done Frank good. He still sported some unsightly bruises and moved with the carefulness of a man in pain, but his eyes seemed clearer and more alert.

Val filled him in on what they'd learned, placing special emphasis on Lord Tate and the argument James Harrison had overheard between him and Miss Warrington. He decided to keep what the young man had said about Langham to himself until he had a chance to confront the duke. He couldn't be sure that Frank, in his current mood, wouldn't search out Langham and beat the man to a pulp. Or try, given that his grace frequented Jim Hyde's boxing club and was a head taller than Val's cousin.

At the news about Tate, Frank cursed. "I knew I should have gone with her that evening! Father demanded I come for dinner with the family or I would have done."

Val knew all too well how difficult it was to extricate one-self from a parental summons. He nodded in sympathy.

"Why wouldn't she tell me about her encounter with the man?" Frank continued, his jaw clenched. "I could have ensured he left her alone."

"We can't really know until we speak to Tate and learn what he wanted." When Frank put his napkin down and began to rise, Val raised a hand. "I think it would be better if you let me speak to him."

"But if he knows what's happened to Effie—" Frank began.

"Tell me the truth, Frank. Can you speak to the man and keep a civil tongue in your head? Or will you threaten him with bodily harm if he doesn't tell you what you wish to hear?"

His cousin glowered.

"I promise you I won't let him weasel away before I've learned everything about his dealings with Miss Warring-ton. It's entirely possible the incident has nothing at all to do with her disappearance."

"It's also possible the scoundrel has her locked away somewhere and in fear for her life, Val." Frank pounded a fist on the tabletop, making the cutlery clink against the china.

It was clear that his cousin was in no fit state to search for Miss Warrington. He'd either attack the wrong man and land himself in jail or get himself killed.

"I know you're frightened for her," he said in a calm

voice. "But I promise you we will leave no stone unturned until we find her. Eversham is a good man and a gifted detective. And Kate and Caro care about Miss Warrington, too. They won't let her disappearance go without putting everything they have into the search."

Mentioning Caro reminded him of the news he needed to share. He'd considered holding off on telling Frank, but as he'd sent off the announcement for tomorrow's papers, there was little point in hiding his betrothal. The timing wasn't the best, but it couldn't be helped. And if Val were honest, he hoped the news would distract Frank a little.

"Speaking of Caro," he said, feeling slightly uncomfortable, "we became betrothed last night."

Frank gaped. "What?"

"We had a brief understanding several years ago but it came to nothing and—"

"Caroline Hardcastle?" Frank said, as if there were some other Caro they both knew. "The dark-haired chit who was at Effie's yesterday? Kate's writing partner? The one who despises you? That Caroline Hardcastle?"

It would appear that Val's wish that his betrothal could prove a distraction for his cousin had been answered in spades.

"Yes, that Caro," he said, feeling pettish. "And she doesn't despise me. She's quite fond of me, actually."

At his cousin's raised brows, he amended, "Fond-ish, then. You didn't see us at our best yesterday."

"I sincerely hope not." Frank's voice held more vehemence than the situation warranted, in Val's opinion. "I've seen cats in a bag that get along better."

Val scowled. He didn't have to defend his betrothal to Frank. Or anyone, for that matter.

"I didn't ask for your opinion of the match," Val groused. "I merely thought to let you know, since there will no doubt be talk."

"Talk?" Frank's expression turned serious. "Why?"

Val told him about Caro's run-in with Harrison and the subsequent outcome.

"Oh Lord." Frank ran a hand over his hair. "That happened because you were trying to find Effie."

"Not precisely," Val corrected, feeling compelled to make his cousin understand that however it might have come about, his betrothal to Caro was their choice. Somewhere in between the argument Frank had witnessed yesterday and their goodbyes last night, he'd come to want their marriage more than was entirely rational. "I daresay we'd have argued our way into a betrothal at some point regardless, but last evening's events simply precipitated matters."

Frank raised his brows, clearly skeptical.

Dash it, he didn't need to prove anything to his blasted cousin. Even so, Val said with what he hoped was a cool expression, "We rub along quite well together, in fact."

He suspected his face might be red.

"Is that what you call it?" Frank winked.

"Frank, with all due respect, stow it."

He was saved by the appearance of his butler in the doorway.

"My lord, there is a young lady here claiming to be your betrothed. As it is altogether inappropriate for her to call without a chaperone, I thought it best not to bring her inside."

Good God.

"She is, indeed, my betrothed, Foyle." Val leapt up from his chair and hurried to leave the breakfast room. "You can't just leave young ladies on my doorstep, man."

"If his lordship had informed me of his impending nuptials," his retainer said as he followed at a more decorous pace, "then I should have let her inside. However unusual it might be for her to appear without a maid, the betrothal does add consequence to her visit."

And Caro thought Val's father was high in the instep, Val thought. He would need to have a word with Foyle later.

"I'll just leave you to speak with your betrothed alone," Frank said, rising from the table. "Tell her congratulations from me."

Before Val could tell his cousin he should do so himself, Frank had disappeared down the hall. Mindful that Caro was waiting, Val hurried toward the entryway.

When he pulled the door open, Val found Caro standing there in a very fetching blue velvet driving ensemble with a hat and ribbons to match. At her side, she tapped a driving whip against her leg. Or where her leg would be if young ladies had such extremities, which, of course, propriety said should never ever be acknowledged in public.

"Caro." He felt oddly breathless. "Come in."

She looked up with a quizzical smile. In a teasing tone, she said, "Why are you answering your own door? I feel sure that is not something viscounts do. Does your father know about this?"

He was suddenly very glad she'd called.

"Just come inside." The concentration it took to keep from kissing her then and there made his voice gruff.

She tilted her head in censure and stood her ground. Val sighed, even as her behavior amused him. She'd give him no quarter, and he had better accustom himself to it. "Please, Caroline, won't you let me welcome you into my home?"

"That's better," she said, stepping over the threshold and gazing around with interest.

With a rush of nerves, Val realized she was looking at what would be her new home. Would she approve? Most of the furnishings had been chosen by Piers and Cynthia, and he hadn't gotten round to making many changes. He wanted her to like it. The strength of that want surprised him. Enough so, he realized that he quite possibly would be willing to tear the whole place down and build a new one in its stead should she ask.

"I apologize, Miss Hardcastle," Foyle said with abject regret. "I was not aware that his lordship had taken the significant step of asking you to be his bride. If I had known, I would never have dared—"

"I said I was sorry, Foyle." Val cut off the older man's speech. Foyle had started out in service to the Duke and Duchess of Thornfield as a footman. And as someone who'd known Val since he was in short coats, he understood precisely how to play on his employer's emotions. But Val had no patience for the man's hangdog expression today.

Foyle would not be silenced so easily. "I would like to offer my best wishes upon your forthcoming marriage, Miss Hardcastle. I'm sure the rest of the household would as well, were they aware of the news."

Caro must have found the man's palaver charming because she smiled widely and thanked him with a sweetness that made Val almost grateful for his chiding.

"We'll have tea in the front parlor, Foyle," Val told him as he escorted Caro to the brightly lit room.

He wasn't sure if greeting her with a kiss was entirely appropriate just yet. Especially since it wasn't strictly proper for her to visit his home unchaperoned. So he settled for bussing her cheek, which was really not at all what he wanted, but he wasn't a ravening beast.

"What brings you here?" he asked once she'd seated herself on a chair near the fire. "Not that I don't enjoy seeing you, but I thought I said I'd call on your father today."

"We need to go question Lord Tate," Caro said in exasperation. "Just because we became betrothed last night doesn't mean we're abandoning the search for Effie."

"I didn't suggest that we were," Val said calmly. He eyed the whip in her hand again. Crossing to the window, he saw a gorgeous blue cabriolet with brass fittings and yellow painted wheels parked before his door. He must have been so focused on Caro he'd failed to notice it.

"Is that yours?" he asked, looking from the eye-catching vehicle to Caro and back.

"It is," she said. "And much as I hate to disappoint Mr. Foyle again, I don't wish to take tea with you. I want to go see what Tate has to say for himself."

Val did, too. "All right. Let's go."

He held out his hand to her and she allowed him to pull her to her feet.

"May I drive your carriage, Caro?" he asked as they walked back out into the hallway.

"Maybe after I've seen you handle the ribbons." Caro gave him a sidelong glance.

"You truly enjoy turning the tables, don't you?" He laughed softly.

"I don't know what you mean," she said primly as they reached the entrance hall.

He waited impatiently for Foyle to fetch their hats and coats, not wishing to air this particular quibble in front of his servants.

Once they were safely outside in the brisk morning air with the door firmly closed behind them, he continued, "You know precisely what I mean. First you propose to me, then you kiss me first—"

"I didn't propose to you," Caro corrected. "I announced our betrothal. There's a difference."

"Regardless," Val said, handing her into the carriage, "we've done everything backward."

"Perhaps," Caro said, taking the reins from her groom, "it was never meant to be one way or the other. Perhaps we're finally getting it right."

Before he could reply, Caro urged the horses into the empty street, and he was forced to hold on to his hat to keep it from flying off.

One thing was certain, he thought as a bubble of laughter rose in his chest: Life with Caro would never be dull.

Lord Tate's magnificent townhouse in St. James's Square was showing signs of age and wear.

The entry hall, with its marble floors and expensively papered walls, gave a first impression of wealth, but the sitting room into which Caro and Val had been shown might almost be called shabby. The furniture had gone out of style several decades ago by Caro's estimation, and though the room was free from dust and the carpets clean, what bric-a-brac there was could be cheaply had in any shop around the city.

"Either this is the chamber where our hosts place unwanted guests," Val said, examining a nick in the ear of a chinoiserie statue of a cat on the mantel, "or the fortunes of the house of Tate have not exactly been flourishing." Caro agreed with his assessment, though she wondered if both of their families' wealth was coloring their perception of Tate's apparent lack thereof.

"I suppose we should reserve judgment since we haven't been given a tour of the entire house." Caro came to his side to look at the cat, which to her eye favored Ludwig. She must ask Tate where the piece had come from.

"An unlikely occurrence once we begin our questions," Val commented wryly. Then, he asked, "Was your Ludwig perhaps animated from such an effigy? It would explain his sour disposition."

"Ludwig is an angel." Caro glanced up at him with a raised brow. "And you'd best learn to get along with him if we are to marry. Where I go, he goes."

"There is no if." Val dipped his head, the vibration of his voice against her ear giving her shivers. "Only when."

"If you say so." Caro tried to keep her voice light. She was reluctant to tell him, but she enjoyed their banter. There were few men of her acquaintance who could keep up with the rapid pace of her thoughts. That Val could both do so and share her appreciation for brisk conversation made her optimistic for their future. They were good together.

She could fall back in love with him all too easily.

But part of her was reluctant to fully succumb to his charms just yet. She was impulsive. She knew this about herself. And her whims had gotten her into trouble in the past. The betrothal might be real, but she would not allow herself to feel too deeply until she could be convinced her faith in him was not again misplaced.

"The papers will say so tomorrow, Miss Insolence." He reached down to touch her lightly on the hand. "You'd better make your objection known now if you do intend to make any."

When she looked up, the question in his eyes forced her to acknowledge he was perhaps not as bold and confident as she'd always thought. He'd told her he was no longer the same man as when they'd been together before. Could he also be less arrogant than she'd supposed him to be when she'd first seen him again yesterday? The idea filled her with hope.

"No," she repeated softly. "There is no if. Only when."

He gave her a crooked smile, his eyes darting to her mouth in what she hoped was an indication of a kiss. Before he could do so, however, Lord Tate stepped into the room, and they jumped apart.

He was a handsome man of middle years, with blond hair liberally threaded with silver. Caro was relieved to see he appeared to be in a much better mood than he'd been in last evening.

His expression was open and welcoming until he saw Caro. "You!" he scowled. "You were at the Lyceum last night."

Of course, he made no mention of the fact that he'd

seen Thomas Harrison accost her and done nothing to aid her, she thought. A gentleman, indeed.

Val, perhaps recalling the same incident, stepped forward to stand in front of her, shielding her from the other man.

"Tate," he said with a deceptively friendly tone, "this is Miss Caroline Hardcastle. I don't believe you bothered to wait for an introduction before you fled the greenroom."

The earl reddened at the reminder of his hasty retreat. When Caro stepped out from behind Val, Tate bowed slightly, then pulled back. "Miss Hardcastle, Wrackham. I'm quite busy today. To what do I owe the pleasure?"

"Since you were so kind to remember me from last night," Caro said before Val could stop her, "it will perhaps come as no surprise that we are here to speak with you regarding Miss Effie Warrington. The flowers you brought indicate you have some relationship with her. Is that true?"

She might have been more deferential to his rank, but she hoped her harsh tone would throw him off balance so that he would be more forthcoming.

"I'm not sure what you mean by 'relationship,' Miss Hardcastle," Tate said primly, as if he were a maiden aunt she'd accused of a lurid affair. "I am merely an admirer of Miss Warrington's work. Surely there is nothing untoward in that."

"You were quite overset by her absence," Caro pressed. "What would your wife have made of that, I wonder?"

Tate's lips thinned. "This is a wholly inappropriate conversation. I will not discuss such matters with a lady. No matter how unconventional she may be." He continued, "I read *The Gazette*, Miss Hardcastle. I know all about your ridiculous columns."

She didn't care what he thought of her writings with Kate, but his use of propriety to keep from speaking about Effie annoyed her.

"I can assure you, Lord Tate," she said, "there is nothing you can say to Lord Wrackham that you can't say to me."

"Oh, I very much doubt that." The earl laughed cynically.

Val, who'd seemed willing to let Caro handle things up to now, spoke up while giving her arm a warning squeeze. "If Lord Tate is more comfortable speaking of such matters with another gentleman, my dear, perhaps it would be best if he and I stepped out into the garden for a few moments."

She wanted to argue, but after looking at Tate's flushed face, she realized Val was probably right in thinking Tate would speak more freely if the two men were alone. This wasn't about her own desire to fight back against silly societal restrictions but about finding Effie. If Tate confiding in Val alone would get them information, then she should not object.

"Fine." She nodded. "Go."

"I'll ask the kitchen to send up some tea and cakes, Miss Hardcastle," Tate said, almost pleasant now he'd gotten his way. "Please enjoy the refreshments. We shouldn't be too long."

The two men stepped out of the room, leaving her alone with only the cat figurine for company.

Chapter Ten

What Val really wished to discuss with Tate was his abandonment of Caro to that drunkard Harrison, but that would have to wait for another day. Now he needed to find out what the man knew about Effie.

The Tate garden was pleasantly laid out with a meandering path that led to a small but impressive conservatory with a majestic glass dome pointed at the gray London sky.

The earl's agitation was clear from his inability to remain still.

"What's the meaning of this, Wrackham?" Tate's expression was tight with annoyance. "You know better than to bring questions about a man's paramour into the sanctity of his home. I have a wife who deserves to be shielded from such indignities."

Val was well aware of the frequency with which men of their class kept mistresses their wives knew nothing about. Even in those marriages where the infidelity was known to the wife, a polite fiction was maintained for propriety's sake. It was a silly practice to Val's mind. He knew well enough that any number of marriages were contracted for reasons other than affection. But once the knot was tied, he intended to remain faithful to Caro for so long as they both lived. So, Tate's belated concern for his wife's feelings was particularly grating.

"When Miss Hardcastle and I arrived," he pointed out, "we passed your lady wife leaving. Unless she is able to hear conversations in her home when traveling elsewhere, there is no danger of her learning the reason for our visit."

"She'll bloody well want to know why Miss Caroline Hardcastle was in her parlor," Tate said sharply. "She adores that silly newspaper column. Forever banging on and on about Lady Katherine this and Miss Hardcastle that. I'm surprised she hasn't murdered me in my bed so she can be made famous in the demmed thing."

So Tate did have reason to be overset by Caro's presence in his house, Val thought with reluctant amusement. Still, recognizing that he needed the man to calm down and confide in him, he tried for a placating tone. "Tell her we had a business matter to discuss and I stopped by with my betrothed before escorting her to the park. It has the advantage of being true."

The earl's eyes widened at the disclosure of their engagement, but he didn't comment on it. "I suppose I can do that," he said reluctantly.

"Now," Val said briskly, "despite what you might have assumed last evening, Miss Warrington did not miss the performance because of illness. She is missing. I was told you were seen arguing with her in the theatre last week on one of the nights my cousin wasn't there with her. Can you tell me what that was about?"

But Tate had apparently stopped listening halfway through. "What the devil do you mean she's missing? Where's she gone?"

The man's eyes were wide, and his concern seemed genuine enough.

"I'm afraid I can't say." He watched the other man's face for any slip in his mask. "Miss Hardcastle is a dear friend of Miss Warrington's, and she and my cousin are desperate to learn where she's gone."

"You should ask your cousin what's become of her." He sneered. "He's not as sure of her as he claims. She's been putting out lures for me for weeks. I daresay she's looking for a more experienced man. I can give her things that he can't. I've already found a little house and will set her up in a style your cousin can never match. Why should she settle for a younger son when she can have an earl, I ask you?"

Perhaps because she'd be marrying the younger son for love rather than making a business arrangement to sacrifice control over her own body with an earl who was already married? Since Tate didn't seem willing to share the subject of his argument with Miss Warrington—which, given the man's boasts, Val suspected might have been her rejection of his advances—he decided to change tactics. Sympathizing with the man had certainly gained him no new information. Perhaps an accusation would prod him into talking.

"Do you know anything about a pair of men who were

seen attacking Miss Warrington's carriage near her home in Half Moon Street yesterday?"

Tate gaped. "What? Is that what happened to her? She was taken from her own carriage? Of course I know nothing about that. What do you take me for?"

"A man who might have been rejected by the beautiful actress he'd been pursuing." Val shrugged. "Rejected in favor of a younger son who'd recently begun to curtail her interactions with admirers who were used to seeing her whenever they wished."

"I had nothing to do with Miss Warrington's abduction," Tate said coldly. "Besides, I was in Brighton with my wife yesterday visiting her sister. I almost didn't return in time for the theatre, though in the end it didn't matter, since Miss Warrington wasn't there."

This last he said in a morose tone, like a child denied a treat.

If the earl was telling the truth about being in Brighton the day before, then he couldn't have been the man with the refined voice Frank had heard during the abduction. That didn't rule Tate out, of course, since he could have hired the other man. But if Val were kidnapping the woman he'd been obsessed with for months, he'd want to be there when taking her. Especially if it would offer an opportunity to get in a few blows at his rival. Anyone else, Val supposed, would have stayed as far away as possible.

Tate was just arrogant enough to think his story about Brighton enough to evade suspicion.

Val asked, "Can you think of anyone who might wish to harm Miss Warrington?"

At the very least, if the earl had been observing the actress for a while, then he'd surely seen who else might have been watching her, too.

Tate's expression darkened. "Langham has shown an interest of late."

Val wasn't surprised at hearing the man's name again, but the admission still made him angry. The duke had lied to him without batting an eye. Val was regretting not throttling the man when he'd had only one reason to do so.

"Can you be more specific?" he asked Tate. "Did you learn of this interest at the theatre? Or elsewhere?"

Still frowning, Tate spat out, "I saw him leaving Miss Warrington's townhouse. In Half Moon Street."

Val's head snapped up. "At her townhouse? How?"

"I wasn't watching her if that's what you're thinking." Tate scowled.

Since that was precisely what Val *had* been thinking, he kept silent.

"I have a friend a few houses down," the earl said stiffly. "A mistress, if you must know."

Val tried to comprehend how the man had enough time to juggle interests, however shallow, for three different women. He could barely manage one.

"I saw him leaving early one morning a few weeks ago." Tate's frown deepened. "It was clear because of the hour that he was leaving after a tryst. The smug satisfaction was written all over the scoundrel's face."

Val wasn't sure he trusted Tate, who seemed to be a possessive, petulant sort of man, to have correctly interpreted the Duke of Langham's expression. And while it was unusual for a man to pay an early morning call upon a woman to whom he was unrelated, the duke's actions didn't match what he'd learned of Miss Warrington. For Frank's sake at the very least, he hoped there was an innocent explanation for what Tate had seen.

"Aside from the time you saw Langham," he said, "have you seen anything else suspicious at or around Miss Warrington's house?"

"No," Tate said crossly. "No one but Langham." The man may not consider Francis Thorn much competition, but he clearly did see the duke, who was twenty years younger and outranked him in both wealth and looks, as such.

To no one in particular, Tate continued, "I'm not worried. She'll come around in the end."

"We'll have to find her first," Val reminded him. Tate had become so wrapped up in his mental jousting with his rivals he must have forgotten the lady in question was missing.

Val's words, however, seemed to snap him out of his reverie. "Yes," he said, his expression clearing. "I apologize. Though I can assure you I've nothing to do with her disappearance, I do care about her welfare. Might I be of assistance in the search?"

Considering the possibility for a moment, Val quickly rejected the notion. For one, Tate was still a suspect in Miss Warrington's disappearance. He claimed to be in Brighton at the time of the abduction, but as of now, that was unverified. Secondly, Frank would cut up rough at having a man who was so clearly fixated on Miss Warrington as a member of the search party.

"Many thanks, Tate," he told the other man, "but I

don't believe it's necessary. We also have the assistance of Lady Katherine and her husband, Detective Inspector Eversham of Scotland Yard."

Tate's eyes widened. "It's as serious as that, then?"

For a man determined to win Miss Warrington over, he seemed remarkably oblivious to the danger she was in. "She was kidnapped, Tate," he said flatly. "Only murder is more serious."

Caro stared at the French doors through which Valentine and Lord Tate had just disappeared.

"Vexing creature," she fumed, unsure to which man she referred.

Since she was now in Tate's household, however, she had no intention of allowing this opportunity to go to waste.

Thus, when a housemaid entered the room with a tray laden with a tea service and cakes, Caro engaged the girl in conversation.

"Is there anything else I can fetch for you, miss?" the maid asked once she'd set out the teapot, cups, and several different dainty pastries on a side table.

"No, thank you. This all looks delicious," Caro said in all sincerity. Her weakness was baked goods, and the scents of vanilla, lemon, and cinnamon wafting from the three-tiered server made her mouth water.

Still, she had a job to do, so after biting into one of the iced cakes, she gave the girl her most disarming smile. "I wonder if you might stay with me a moment. One does hate to sit alone in an unfamiliar house."

The girl glanced at the door leading into the hall, but to Caro's relief, she nodded. "I can do that, miss."

Despite knowing that the maid likely wouldn't accept the offer, Caro asked if she'd like some refreshments. Everyone deserved a treat from time to time, and Caro suspected her life in the Tate household wasn't filled with unexpected diversions. When the girl refused, Caro pressed her to at least take a delicately scalloped madeleine. "No one will know," she assured her. "And I won't feel like such a beast for consuming these while you look on."

The maid darted a glance at the lightly browned cakes. Caro gave her an encouraging nod.

"Perhaps just the one," the maid said, taking a madeleine.

"What's your name?" Caro asked conversationally as she bit into another pastry, a flaky lemon tart that burst into flavor on her tongue. Tate might be a boor, but his cook was unparalleled.

"Maisie," the girl said, brushing crumbs from her hands.

"Maisie, I wonder if you would answer a few questions for me."

At the girl's guarded look, Caro set out to calm her. "There'll be no harm in it. My betrothed and I came here to speak to Lord Tate about the disappearance of an actress friend of ours. We hope he might have seen something that will help us find her. Perhaps you did, too."

When the maid's face remained skeptical, Caro tried a different tack. "Do you read *The Gazette*, perchance?"

"Sometimes." Maisie's brow furrowed.

Either the Tate's housekeeper ran an incredibly tight ship, or Maisie was far more cynical than her fresh-faced, open countenance implied.

"Perhaps you've read one of its columns? *A Lady's Guide to Mischief and Mayhem?*"

"Oh aye. It's not as shocking as some others I like, but it's all right."

"All right" wasn't the most fulsome praise Caro had ever received for her writing, but it would have to do. "I'm Miss Caroline Hardcastle—one of the authors of the column," she said. "Lady Katherine—the other author—and I are working to find the actress I spoke of."

Maisie's eyes widened, her mouth forming an O as she clasped her hands to her bosom. "Are you really her? Miss Caroline Hardcastle?" she asked breathlessly. "You ain't shamming me?"

Caro bit back a sigh of relief. She'd been afraid the girl would prove impossible to impress. "I give you my word of honor."

"Do you really think the person wot killed Mary Riley is one o' her customers?" Maisie asked. The murder of an East End shopkeeper was the subject of one of Caro and Kate's most popular editions of their column. The police still hadn't managed to apprehend her killer. "I always thought it must be her man. You ask me, the first place to look when a gal turns up dead is the other side of her bed."

Caro was impressed by the girl's assessment. "While that is most often the case," she said, "Mary's husband was in Manchester visiting family the day she was killed. And Mary often kept the shop open late for some of her more loyal customers. The shopkeeper next door heard her welcome someone that night some half hour past the usual closing time."

Though they would likely have covered the case eventually, Caro and Kate had been encouraged to write about it by Eversham, who'd had the devil's own time convincing his superiors that Patrick Riley had not, in fact, been responsible for his wife's death. When he'd tired of arguing with the upper echelons of Scotland Yard, Eversham had asked his wife and Caro to step in. The Yard might be as difficult to maneuver as a cart with a broken wheel, but if there was one force that the political leaders at the top of the Metropolitan Police bowed to, it was bad publicity. The column had kept an innocent man from hanging, and for that, both Caro and the Evershams were grateful.

Maisie nodded her approval. "That makes sense."

On impulse, Caro said, "Perhaps you'd like to come to one of the salons Lady Katherine and I hold for the more enthusiastic readers of the column. We discuss popular novels, but we also have guest speakers, like experts who teach us how to fight and ways to avoid danger in our daily lives." She liked this young woman. And she had just the sort of quick mind most suited to the group's lively discussions.

"Oh, I know all about keeping safe." Maisie shrugged. "You just make sure to knee 'im in the bal—"

"Yes, quite," Caro interrupted. "That is a most effective technique. But there are others. The salons are a chance for us to discuss our favorite cases as well. You'd be a welcome addition, I think."

"You'd have someone like me?" Maisie's skepticism was back.

"We welcome all women to our salon," Caro assured her. "We don't limit our membership by social class."

"Then if it's on my free day, I'd like to come," the maid said shyly.

The sound of the clock chiming made Caro realize she'd been so engrossed in their discussion she'd nearly forgotten her reason for being here in the first place.

"Maisie," she began, "if you're still willing, I only have a few questions for you."

The maid nodded, clasping her hands before her. Though she did seem much more relaxed than she'd been when Caro first asked to speak with her.

"First, do you know where your master was yesterday?" Caro asked. Tate could be the man with the educated accent Mr. Thorn had heard just before passing out.

"Oh, he and Lady Tate were in Brighton visiting her sister. His lordship's valet brought some of the young ones sweets from a shop there. They got back yesterday around teatime. His lordship went out last evening, but I don't know where. Her ladyship took to her bed with a headache." She leaned forward. "She does that a lot. Her maid swears she's got a delicate disposition, but I think it's to get away from him. He's a good enough master, but they don't get on too good."

The appearance of a narrow-faced woman interrupted Maisie. Her attire and the chatelaine at her waist marked her as the housekeeper.

"I'm sorry to disturb you, Miss Hardcastle," said the woman with a brief smile. "But, Maisie, you're needed back downstairs."

"I beg your pardon, Mrs....?" Caro left the question hanging.

"Mrs. Gooch, miss," the housekeeper supplied.

"Well, my apologies, Mrs. Gooch, for keeping Maisie." Caro hoped the maid wouldn't be scolded because Caro had detained her. "I was lonely since Lord Wrackham and Lord Tate saw fit to abandon me here while they discussed business in the garden. I didn't allow her to leave. Please don't punish Maisie for my selfishness."

The older woman's manner softened. "I understand, Miss Hardcastle. It's no trouble. But we do keep to a schedule and Maisie's needed now. I hope you won't mind."

"Not at all. And it looks as if the gentlemen are returning." To Maisie, she said, "I'll send a note about the salon."

The servants were gone by the time Val and Lord Tate stepped through the French doors.

"I hope you weren't too bored here alone, Miss Hardcastle." Tate's smile didn't reach his eyes.

Whatever the men had discussed hadn't improved the earl's mood any. She tried to meet Val's eyes, but he gave an infinitesimal shake of his head. What that meant she had no idea.

"Not at all, your lordship," she told their host. "I enjoyed the artistry of your skilled cook and a nice cup of tea. What more could a woman want?"

Though there were more tea and cakes available, Tate remained standing, moving to the door. As hints went, it was hardly subtle.

"I hope you'll get in touch with us if you remember anything else, my lord," she said brightly as she took Val's arm. "Any small memory you have might be of use."

"I doubt that will be necessary." Tate followed them

down to the front door, as if to ensure they were actually leaving.

"You drive," Caro told Val as they stepped down toward the cabriolet.

He looked at her with suspicion. "I thought you wanted to test my driving skills first."

"Oh, I know you can drive to an inch." Caro gestured impatiently. "I was deliberately provoking you earlier because I wished to tease you. But now I want to hear everything about your conversation with Tate and don't wish to be distracted."

"I'm glad to hear you admit my driving skills pass muster," Val said tartly as he handed her up into the carriage. "A man must have some proficiencies."

"You're proficient at any number of activities and you know it," Caro retorted, thinking with a flush of how skillfully he'd kissed her last night. But she wasn't quite bold enough to elaborate on that topic just yet. "Stop fishing for compliments or I won't tell you what *I* learned while you were with Tate."

Val, who'd just taken the reins from the groom stationed beside the vehicle, turned back to her. His eyes were wide—with surprise, but also, if she wasn't mistaken, approval. "How did you manage that in a room by yourself?"

"The maid," Caro said impatiently. "I hope you learned more than I did because I suspect Tate might not be the one responsible for kidnapping Effie."

Chapter Eleven

"Why am I not surprised to learn that Tate's obsession is little more than a pedestrian tale of a man of middle years seeking out the favors of a young woman other than his wife?" Caro asked with disgust after Val had finished sharing what he'd learned. "Did he really think *that* was too lurid for my tender ears? There was more intrigue in the play we attended last evening."

Val didn't respond. He was fairly certain Caro didn't need an explanation for how fragile the average man's sense of self-importance could be. Especially when it came to his illicit desires. "At least we know from two sources now where Tate was at the time Miss Warrington and Frank were attacked," he said, deciding a change of subject was in order. "That was clever of you to question the maid."

"I had to do something with my time while you were out hearing Tate's confession." Caro waved a gloved hand in emphasis. "Though there was some truly excellent pastry.

If ever you have the chance to poach the man's cook, you should take it."

Val sent up a silent prayer of thanks that Caro's annoyance at his absence had been mollified by the presence of sweets.

"Are we to call upon the Duke of Langham now?" she asked. "I must confess to some curiosity about the man. His reputation for wildness is rather legendary, isn't it? And he's rumored to be handsome as sin, though I've never laid eyes upon him."

Val bit back a sigh. Of course Caro would be curious about Langham, but he'd hoped to speak with him alone. Especially given that the man had lied to him. The conversation would not be an easy one, and he couldn't afford to be distracted when he made his accusation. Much as he enjoyed Caro's company, he was coming to realize how difficult a time he had concentrating when she was around. "I'll speak to him later this afternoon. I know where he'll be."

"Well, that's hardly fair," Caro complained. "We're supposed to be working together."

"We are," he agreed. "However, I suspect that like Tate, Langham will be more comfortable speaking about his interactions with Miss Warrington when you aren't present."

"Are men really so shy about discussing their romantic attachments?" Caro asked. Absurdly, he wanted to kiss her at the way she tilted her head. If she only knew how loath most men were to talk about such matters—him included— she'd lose what little respect she had for his sex. "Besides, Effie is betrothed to Mr. Thorn. There is probably a very innocent explanation for Langham having left her house at such an early hour. *If* Tate is to be believed at all. I would not be surprised if he invented the story about him in order to cast suspicion away from himself."

Val suspected Tate might have lied as well, but suspicion didn't equal proof. And the earl was not the only one to have pointed to Langham as a man invested in Miss Warrington. "Even so, I think it best if you do not come with me to see him."

Caro made a rude noise. "If it were up to men, ladies would never be present for any interesting conversations."

"I promise," he said emphatically, "that when possible, I will make sure you are there for as many fascinating discussions as I can find." She might think him determined to shield her from those matters society deemed improper for ladies, but he agreed with her that much of the restrictions were insulting to the female intelligence. He'd just have to prove to her through his actions that in this, as in so many other instances, their opinions matched.

"I only ask that you tell me the truth instead of shielding me from it in some misguided notion of chivalry," she said pointedly. "And in that spirit, where will the Duke of Langham be this afternoon and please take me with you."

"You are relentless, aren't you?" Val couldn't help laughing at her tenacity, despite his fear that she was wearing down his resistance.

"Nothing was ever gained by giving in." Caro shrugged. Then, looking around them, she asked, "Where are we going? This isn't the way back to Belgrave Square."

"Half Moon Street." Val was pleased to see her expression brighten. "I thought we might ask Mrs. Spencer if she knows why Langham was at Miss Warrington's house. And since we've both been away from our homes for some time, perhaps she's received word of Miss Warrington."

Caro nodded with approval. "I hope with all my being that you are right and Effie has turned up unharmed. I have to keep reminding myself it hasn't even been a full day." She had gripped her hands together tightly in her lap. "But, Val, the more we hear about these men who were preying upon her—for really, there's no other word for it— the more I fear for her safety."

Val reached over and laid his fingers over hers, holding the reins in his left hand. "We'll find her. There are too many of us determined to do so. And I know Frank won't rest until she's been brought home safe."

"I hope you're right."

He wasn't used to Caro sounding so dejected. Despite her interest in crime and darkness, she was a remarkably optimistic person. He feared how devastated she would be if the worst happened and they didn't find Miss Warrington—or worse, if they only found her body.

Because he knew the revelation would cheer her up, he said against his better judgment, "Langham will be at a boxing match at Jim Hyde's club this afternoon. It's not usually the done thing, but since we are betrothed, I don't suppose it would be too scandalous for you to attend with me."

"Is that all?" Caro demanded. "I thought at the very least it must be a bacchanalian orgy the way you were carrying on."

Val tried and failed to suppress the images his mind conjured at her words. Caro at an orgy would be a sight to behold.

"If you do not wish to attend—"

"Hush," Caro interrupted as the carriage came to a stop. "I didn't say that. I would be happy to watch sweaty gentlemen pummeling one another with you."

"Hence my reluctance to discuss the matter," Val said tartly.

Handing the reins to a waiting groom, he leapt down from the cabriolet and took Caro by the waist, deliberately letting their bodies slide against one another before he set her on her feet.

A little breathless, she asked, "Are you jealous?"

"Of course not," he lied. He tucked her arm into his and drew her up the steps to Miss Warrington's townhouse. He hadn't found his way back to her only to have Langham come along and steal her away. He knew it was an absurd notion, especially given that Caro was nothing if not loyal, but the thought of Caro with someone else was one he wasn't entirely convinced he'd recover from.

Soon they were being welcomed into Miss Warrington's house and ushered into an entirely different parlor from the one they'd been in yesterday.

Mrs. Spencer rushed toward them as soon as the door shut. "Please tell me you've had news," she said, accepting a hug from Caro. "I've barely been able to sit still imagining what my poor Miss Effie must be going through."

"I'm afraid we don't have any new information on her whereabouts, Mrs. Spencer," Val said. "Not since her carriage was found yesterday."

Her face, drawn with signs of a sleepless night, fell.

Caro exchanged a look with Val, then ushered the companion over to the sofa. "When was the last time you ate, ma'am?"

The older woman raised a hand to her brow. "I'm not sure. I had some tea this morning, I think."

"That's not food, Mrs. Spencer," Caro chided. "Effie would be heartbroken if she knew you were sacrificing your health while she was away."

Away was certainly one way to describe Miss Warrington's absence, Val thought grimly.

Before Caro could make the request, he'd pulled the bell and asked the butler to bring up a tray.

Once the food arrived, Caro saw to it that the older woman ate a sandwich and a few biscuits, washed down with a cup of liberally sweetened tea.

Looking calmer, Mrs. Spencer spoke. "I'm glad you came. Though I felt the veriest busybody, I decided to search Miss Effie's bedchamber and study to see if I could find any clues as to who may have taken her."

The older woman's mouth was tight. Whether from shame at having violated Miss Warrington's privacy or at what she'd learned, Val couldn't say. "Did you find anything?"

Going to the mantel, Mrs. Spencer retrieved a saucer.

"I found this in the grate in her study." She pointed to what looked to be the charred remains of a letter.

"May I?" Val asked, and Mrs. Spencer wordlessly handed the plate to him.

He took it to a small table near the window and opened the curtains to let in as much natural lighting as possible. One by one, he lay the paper shards on the surface.

"I can barely tell which way they should be turned," Caro said from where she stood beside him, "much less what they say. I can say that this bit is an impression in sealing wax. Do you know whom the letter is from, Mrs. Spencer?"

Behind them, Miss Warrington's companion said, "No, but my eyes are not what they once were, Miss Hardcastle. I was hoping you young people would have better luck making out the crest."

Removing a quizzing glass from inside his coat pocket, Val handed it to Caro. "Perhaps this will help."

She bent over the table to examine the largest of the pieces.

"Is that a fox?" Her nose wrinkled adorably as she squinted through the glass. "Or a rabbit, perhaps?"

Val would have liked to have given in to temptation and kissed her, but as they weren't alone, he did not. He took the quizzing glass back to look himself. "Definitely a fox," he agreed. "And an arrow."

"Whose seal is it?" She turned to look at him, with far more expectation in her eyes than he was comfortable with. Her next words only confirmed his discomfort. "You're in the aristocracy. You should know such things."

"I don't spend all my free time reading *Debrett's Peerage*," he said defensively. She had to know by now he wasn't so full of his own importance that he'd memorized every crest in the bloody English nobility. "Nor do they require us to memorize it at Eton. Though I daresay one of my aunts would recognize whose family it belongs to easily enough."

"So would my mother." She shrugged. "Perhaps we should take it to her."

If Lady Lavinia really did know the family crests of England's aristocracy, Val thought, then taking it to the Hardcastle townhouse when he spoke with Caro's father made the most sense.

Speaking of the aristocracy, they needed to ask Miss Warrington's companion about a certain duke.

"Mrs. Spencer," he said, hoping he wasn't about to upset the woman, "do you know if the Duke of Langham has ever visited Miss Warrington here?"

"Oh goodness me, no!" Mrs. Spencer laughed. "My heavens, I would surely have remembered if a duke had been here. My lord, it's a grand enough thing that you're here and you're only a viscount."

"Only a viscount, Val," Caro said wryly. "That should puncture your self-importance."

Mrs. Spencer blushed. "I meant no insult, Lord Wrackham," she said hastily. "I hope you know that."

"Of course he does, Mrs. Spencer." Caro patted her on the shoulder. "I was only funning."

"I can assure you, Mrs. Spencer," Val said wryly, "with Caro to keep me humble, there is no danger of your saying anything that will hurt my poor feelings."

"So, you've no recollection of Langham ever having called here, then?" Caro asked, ignoring his complaint. "Or any other nobleman, for that matter?"

Mrs. Spencer shook her head. "I hadn't thought she'd corresponded with any either, but these fragments seem to indicate otherwise. Perhaps if Miss Effie burned the letters, then they weren't important?"

"Perhaps," Caro said, though her tone was skeptical. "Did you find any other notes that might be of help in our search?"

Mrs. Spencer's expression turned to one of discomfort. "I wasn't going to mention…"

"If it is something that paints Miss Warrington in a bad light," Val assured her, "I can make sure Frank learns nothing of it, unless strictly necessary." He didn't like to keep secrets from Frank, but if it meant finding his fiancée alive, he knew his cousin would think the deception well worth it.

"It's not Miss Effie it reflects badly on, my lord," Mrs. Spencer said apologetically.

Val should have known digging around in the lives of his cousin and his betrothed might mean coming across information he would rather forget. Frank was no saint. Nor was he. But he was strangely reluctant to learn whatever the companion was about to share with them. He knew once that knowledge of Frank's character was revealed, he wouldn't easily forget it.

"You may as well show us, Mrs. Spencer," he told her. "If my cousin had some hand in Miss Warrington's disappearance, then the sooner we know, the sooner we'll find her."

With a nod, Mrs. Spencer removed a wrinkled letter from her pocket. Wordlessly, she handed it to Caro, whose face paled as she read.

When she proffered the note to Val, he wasn't certain what to expect.

But not something this damning.

Though only a brief missive, the words alone would be enough to convict his cousin should they find that Miss Warrington had been murdered.

My dearest,

The man has shown himself to be a liar and a hypocrite, but you still choose to go back to him? I can see now all my pleas have been in vain. No matter how I try to convince you otherwise, you will never believe my love is enough.

I have had enough of this. I won't share you.

But know this, my love—if he hurts you, I'll see him in hell.

Yours, if only briefly,
Frank

Val muttered a curse. Frank had lied to him. To them. It was clear from this note that things weren't as blissful between him and Miss Warrington as he'd led them to believe.

There was another man involved. Was it Tate? Langham? He ran a hand through his hair in frustration. He was sick to death of being lied to. It was evident now that his guilt at suspecting Frank had been misplaced. He might have ended this letter on a melancholy note, but jealousy was a motive as old as time. His cousin was temperamental and quick to anger. His moods might blow over as quickly as they arose, but could he have acted in a fit of rage only to regret it later?

"Where did you find this, Mrs. Spencer?" Caro asked, taking Val's hand. However improper, he was grateful for the warmth of her touch.

"It was in the wastepaper basket in her study." Mrs. Spencer sounded almost apologetic. "Since Miss Effie and Mr. Thorn were together for the drive to and from the theatre yesterday, I daresay it was all made up and forgotten."

But it was clear from her earlier hesitation that she wasn't quite so sure.

They left not long after, promising to send Mrs. Spencer notice of further updates. Once they were outside, Caro turned to Val, her eyes bright with sympathy. "Will you go to him now?"

He stood next to the cabriolet and held her hand, needing the comfort of her touch. "I'd ask you to come, but this is definitely not something you should witness." He was angry, true, but also deeply hurt by Frank's betrayal. Perhaps feeling so pained by his cousin's duplicity was silly. They weren't as close as adults as they'd been as children, but with Piers gone, Frank was the closest he had to a brother.

"I understand," she said, with a squeeze of his hand. "I know it sounds odd, especially given how distrustful I've been of your cousin, but it is possible this is just some issue that they've gotten past. Or perhaps we're misunderstanding the matter."

Would she ever stop surprising him? Val wondered, his eyes drinking in her hopeful expression. "I'm not sure how that could be possible," he said, "given that there is obviously another man involved, but I appreciate the sentiment."

"Then perhaps you won't be quite so annoyed by my suggestion that we tell Kate and Eversham about the note?" She looked uncomfortable, but her jaw was set in familiar determination. "I know you wish to speak to Mr. Thorn. And I don't wish to stop you, but if there is a chance he is responsible, they should know. Scotland Yard may not be investigating the disappearance officially, but if Mr. Thorn did hurt her, then they'll have to become involved."

Val closed his eyes. She was right, of course. If Frank had harmed Miss Warrington, then he was a criminal. His kinship to a duke might protect him from some of the harsher aspects of the system—he would likely not hang, even if he had murdered her—but he would suffer the same indignities as the other men were subjected to every day. And it would only be fair.

Unable to speak, he opened his eyes to find Caro watching him. "Shall I drive you to your house?" she asked softly.

But he was in no mood for company. Even hers.

"I'll walk." The chance to collect his thoughts before confronting Frank would do him good. "But thank you for the offer."

She frowned briefly but didn't protest. "Will I see you later?"

He looked at her blankly.

"You were meant to speak with my father this afternoon," she said patiently. "And then we were going to speak to the Duke of Langham."

Damn it. He'd forgotten about both Langham and his

meeting with Hardcastle. But the world didn't stop because he'd learned something damning. "If the discussion with Frank comes to nothing, I'll come directly to your house afterward," he assured her, lifting her into the cabriolet.

He didn't add that if his talk with his cousin resulted differently, then her parents might not be quite so eager to welcome him into the family.

He watched as she took the reins from the groom, then expertly steered her horses into the street. When she glanced back, he raised a hand in farewell.

When he turned to walk in the opposite direction toward home, Val could feel dread nipping at his heels like a vicious cur chasing him into chaos.

Chapter Twelve

When Caro arrived home, the Hardcastle butler, Newton, informed her that Kate and her assistant at *The London Gazette*, Miss Flora Deaver, had called in her absence. They were being entertained by her mother in the lady's favorite sitting room.

After removing her hat and gloves, she hurried upstairs, just in time for the arrival of the tea tray.

"There you are," her mother said with relief. "I told Lady Katherine and Miss Deaver you would be along soon, but I never quite know when you are racketing about in your cabriolet. Though you were with your *betrothed*, so I could not be overly concerned."

Caro supposed she should be glad her mother was too pleased with the engagement to question too closely how or why it had come about. Though it was possible that she would have rejoiced even if Caro had become betrothed at the point of a shotgun so long as the prospective bride-groom possessed a title.

"I left word that I would be back before luncheon." Caro kissed her mother on the cheek. "And here I am, just in time for the morning tea tray."

"Did not Lord Wrackham come in with you?" Her mother looked at the doorway, as if expecting Val to materialize at any moment.

"No." Caro took a seat between her mother's chair and the settee upon which Kate and Flora sat. "He said he'd be back later this afternoon to speak with Papa."

"As well he should," her mother said primly. "He was naughty to ask before speaking with your father, but I suppose you are of age, so there's no harm in it."

"You have my felicitations, Caro," said Flora. She had watched the interplay between mother and daughter with interest from behind her spectacles. She was a pretty young woman with golden blonde hair and a calm manner. Ludwig, Caro's Siamese, had found her soothing from the moment he'd met her when Caro first brought him along with her to the offices of *The London Gazette*. In fact, the cat was so taken with the girl that she was the only one he would tolerate as a caretaker outside of Caro, and now Caro relied on her whenever she had to be away from town. "I understand it was quite a surprise."

Her half smile told Caro that Kate had explained the unusual circumstances behind the engagement.

Beaming, Caro's mother rose. "Now that Caro is here, I will leave you young ladies to chat in private. I have much to do to prepare for the wedding. Once the announcement reaches the papers, we'll have so little time to prepare!"

Caro really should assert herself with regard to the wedding plans, but she would rather speak with Kate and Flora for now. After Val had spoken with Papa, they could discuss their preferences for the ceremony.

Once Mama had shut the parlor door behind her, Caro turned to her guests. "I hope your presence here means Eversham has had news."

"I'm afraid not." Kate sighed. "He was quite right that his superiors would be keener on searching for the carriage's thieves than they'd be to find Effie. But the good news on that score is that they are doing their best to find any witnesses on the abandonment of the carriage. So perhaps we'll have news from that soon."

Caro sighed. "I suppose that's something."

"You and Lord Wrackham went to speak with Lord Tate this morning?" Flora asked.

At Caro's questioning look, the young woman explained, "I asked Kate if I could be involved in the investigation into Effie's disappearance. We've forged a friendship through the salon, as you know. And I simply could not sit by and do nothing while she is missing."

"Excellent." Caro slipped off her shoes and tucked her feet up beneath her. Kate and Flora were good enough friends that she knew they would have no objections, and after witnessing Val's emotional reaction to Mr. Thorn's letter, she badly needed the comfort. "I don't mind telling you, Flora, that we need all the help we can get. Every time I think we've got a handle on this business, something else happens to throw us into chaos again."

"Tell us what you learned from Lord Tate," Kate pressed her. "I've been waiting to hear all morning."

"I'm afraid it was what we learned at Effie's house after our interview with Tate that may be most important at the moment," Caro said, then told them about both the bit of sealing wax and the letter Mrs. Spencer had found from Mr. Thorn to Effie.

"Oh no!" Kate said, understandably focusing on the latter. "What did Val say about Frank?"

"Not much." Caro picked up a scone from the tray. "Though I could tell he was upset. They're quite close, I believe. And with the death of his brother, I suspect he values that relationship even more."

"As many men seem to be in Effie's orbit," Flora said thoughtfully, "I can't see her playing Mr. Thorn false. The few times we've discussed him, she was positively glowing with love. She even hoped they'd be able to marry before the summer. A woman looking to be happily wed wouldn't jeopardize her situation by falling for the lures of a man like Tate, who sounds dreadful, or Langham, who is already involved with her friend at the theatre."

This made some sense to Caro. Mrs. Spencer, who knew Effie better than any of them, had seemed to think Mr. Thorn was mistaken, too.

"Perhaps Frank has the wrong end of the stick." Kate frowned into her tea. "He wouldn't be the first man to misinterpret something he saw or overheard."

"No, he wouldn't." Caro wiped crumbs from her hands. "I hate this. We need more than all these disparate threads and possibilities."

"Do you have the bit of seal with you?" Flora asked suddenly.

"No," Caro said, realizing she'd forgotten to take it with her in the excitement over Frank's letter. "Why?"

"I *am* skilled at research." The secretary smiled. "I might be able to find the family crest in one of our reference books at *The Gazette*. You said it looked like a fox and an arrow were in the design, correct?"

"That's a marvelous idea, Flora," said Kate. "I should have thought of it."

"You've been busy running a newspaper and looking for your friend." Flora shrugged. "Besides, it's my job to think of these things so you don't have to."

"You're missing a friend as well, Flora," Caro reminded the young woman. She was a dear girl, but no matter how Kate and Caro had tried to make her feel welcome, she always managed to keep herself apart. Really, it was no wonder she was such good friends with Ludwig. Flora herself shared many of the same aloof qualities as a cat.

"I know," Flora said with a small smile. "But I find comfort in keeping busy."

Caro could certainly relate to that.

"If you like, I can write a note to Mrs. Spencer requesting she show you the bit of sealing wax," Kate told her assistant.

Flora beamed. "Excellent."

"I know we don't know what to make of Frank's letter yet," Kate said, setting down her teacup, "but were you able to learn anything from Lord Tate?"

Glad for the reminder that they didn't know for sure that Mr. Thorn had hurt Effie, no matter how suspicious his words to her might have been, Caro quickly filled them in on Val's conversation with Tate, as well as what she'd learned from Maisie.

"Do we believe Tate's revelation about the Duke of Langham?" Kate asked when she had finished. "Could he be the man mentioned in Frank's letter?"

"If it's true," Flora said, biting into a macaroon, "then the duke is jeopardizing a three-year-long affair. From what the gossips have said, he and Nell are quite devoted."

At the amazed looks from the other two women, she shrugged. "I enjoy reading about what the *ton* get up to. It helps me know which suitors to avoid when I one day learn I'm the long-lost heir to a rare peerage that only passes through the female line."

"We should introduce you to Val's sister. She's a novelist." Caro laughed, grateful for the needed levity. "It seems a shame to waste such an imagination on managing the mundane details of the paper."

"I'm happy where I am, thank you." Flora's warm smile took any sting out of the rejection. Then, returning to the subject at hand, she said, "I think it's just as likely the man in Mr. Thorn's letter is Tate. Didn't he mention something to Lord Wrackham about trying to lure her away from his cousin?"

"The problem," Caro said with a sigh, "is that because of her profession, Effie was admired by any number of men. Finding the one who so angered Mr. Thorn is like searching for the proverbial needle in a haystack."

They were silent as the difficulty of their task seemed to settle over them.

Then, after they had chatted idly for a few minutes, Kate rose. "We should get back to the paper, I suppose.

I do wish we could run something about Effie's disappearance, but I fear Andrew is right that if she has been kidnapped, such publicity might make her abductors behave rashly."

And, Caro thought morosely, if Mr. Thorn had killed her, it would be unnecessary.

"I'll just go up and say hello to Ludwig, if that's all right," Flora said. Caro suspected she was giving the two women a moment to talk alone.

When she was gone, Kate gave Caro a hard hug. "How are you?"

"I'm fine," Caro said, puzzled. "Why?"

"For someone who became unexpectedly engaged to the man who once broke her heart, you seem remarkably calm. Last night you seemed to think you'd find a way out of it. Have you changed your mind?"

Caro felt heat climb into her cheeks. "We had a chance to talk last night. No declarations have been made on either side, but we've come to an understanding, I believe."

"And are you content with that?" Kate's eyes searched her face. "You can find a way to be happy with him?"

"I believe he's changed since the time of our first betrothal," Caro said. She was telling the truth. She *did* believe he'd changed. She wasn't quite ready to give her heart fully into his keeping, but his words last night had gone a long way toward calming the worst of her fears about the viability of a marriage between them. "And so have I. There are no guarantees, of course, but I have hopes that we can make one another happy enough."

"I would prefer you to say you're certain you can make one another blissfully happy," Kate said wryly, "but I suppose I will have to content myself with 'happy enough' for the time being."

Unsure of her response, Caro shifted the conversation to other, less fraught matters until Flora reappeared and they all said their goodbyes, promising to contact one another with whatever news by supper.

Caro was just at her bedchamber when she heard someone at the door. Thinking Kate and Flora had returned, she hurried back downstairs.

But rather than her previous visitors, it was Val handing over his hat and coat to Newton. When she saw his expression, she gasped. "What is it? What's happened?"

"Frank is gone," he said, his mouth tight with anger. "He's disappeared."

When none of his servants could say when they'd last seen Frank, Val set out for the Albany, where his cousin kept rooms. He'd instructed him not to leave the townhouse, but it was hardly a surprise that his cousin wished to be in his own home—if that was, indeed, where he'd gone. It was the first place Val could think to look, at any rate.

A small voice in the back of his head asked if perhaps Frank had gone to where he'd left Miss Warrington, to ensure that she hadn't escaped. He refused to even think the other, more ghastly suspicion—even in the privacy of his own mind.

That letter had been written in anger. There was no question. But Val refused to make accusations until he'd heard his cousin's explanation.

Only he couldn't help but worry that as he'd overlooked his brother's and even his father's more disagreeable traits, perhaps he'd also done so with Frank's temper. Did he wish to paper over his cousin's words simply because the alternative was to accept the truly upsetting nature of his boyhood friend's present character?

He was almost to the doors of the Albany when he saw a familiar figure walking toward him.

"I thought you'd be at the tailor's being measured for a wedding suit." A grin split Eversham's usually serious face. "I did warn you that Caro would find some way to eviscerate you for that invitation, didn't I? It didn't occur to me that she'd do so with a leg shackle, but that was a failure of imagination on my part."

"I'll remind you, Eversham," Val said with a scowl, "that's my betrothed you're speaking of. Keep a civil tongue in your head."

The detective's gray eyes went wide. "It's like that, is it? You have my abject apologies. I meant no insult."

"Oh, put away your letter of apology, man." Val rolled his eyes. "I'm not going to challenge you to a duel."

"I should think not." Eversham's inspector's expression was back in place, though his tone held just a hint of humor. "Dueling is illegal, and I would refuse the challenge."

Pinching the bridge of his nose, Val sighed. "Why are you at the Albany?" he asked. This was an odd location for him to stumble upon Eversham.

Eversham's face grew grave. "I called at your house only to be told you'd come here looking for your cousin. I suppose I was quicker on foot than your cab because of the traffic."

"You have news," Val said, feeling a sudden pang in the pit of his stomach. "Have you found her?"

But Eversham shook his head. "We've found one of the men who kidnapped Miss Warrington, however."

Val looked at him in surprise. "Where?"

"In the Thames," the detective said bluntly.

Val swore. "How do you know he was one of the abductors?"

"Our inside man in the neighborhood where we found the carriage was able to identify him."

"And this is someone you trust?" Val asked. But he knew Eversham wouldn't have come to him with the information if he was unsure. He was far too careful a detective to use unreliable details.

The other man nodded. "I was hoping your cousin would come to the morgue with me to confirm he's one of the men who took Miss Warrington."

What a time for Frank to go off without a word, Val fumed. "We can ask him once we get up to his rooms," he said, now more determined than ever to talk to him.

"So you believe him to be here?" Eversham asked as they walked into the building and climbed the stairs to the floor where Frank resided. "From what your butler said, he left your townhouse without a word to anyone. Which seems unusual for a man unable to leave his sickbed yesterday."

"He seemed well enough at breakfast," Val said. Though he suspected even if Frank had been feeling unwell, his cousin would very likely have tried to conceal it. He was stubborn that way. Especially if he had been planning to search for Miss Warrington and didn't wish to be kept from doing so.

He wanted more than anything to believe that was Frank's reason for leaving without word, and not some underhanded attempt at hiding the truth behind Miss Warrington's disappearance. "I don't believe he was feigning illness yesterday or wellness today, for what it's worth."

"That's good to hear," Eversham said mildly. "Let's hope we find him upstairs, then."

"What are you implying, Eversham?" Val asked as they neared his cousin's apartment.

"I also stopped by Half Moon Street." Eversham knocked on the entrance. "Mrs. Spencer told me about the letter you found from your cousin to Miss Warrington."

When no one answered, Val pounded on the door again, twice as loudly as Eversham had done.

"So, you've decided he'd make a good suspect now, is that it?" Val asked peevishly. He had no idea why he was being an ass to Eversham. It was Frank that Val was angry with. Angry for putting him in a position where he felt bound to defend him to Eversham. To Caro. Hell, he'd even felt as if he should apologize to Mrs. Spencer for Frank's letter to Miss Warrington. He'd never wanted to be so deeply embroiled in his cousin's affairs.

He'd certainly never wanted to be searching for him so he could demand whether he'd done some irreparable physical harm to his fiancée.

Adding to Val's annoyance, no one seemed inclined to answer their knocking.

Frowning, Eversham tried the knob.

The door swung inward.

Putting a finger to his lips, the detective crept stealthily into the room. Val followed, but the sight that greeted them brought them both up short.

The contents of every shelf had been scattered across the thick Aubusson carpets. Books were torn apart, paintings taken from the walls and ripped from their frames. The upholstered furniture was gutted and goose down floated eerily through the air in the wake of their entrance.

"The housekeeping staff at the Albany leaves much to be desired," Eversham said dryly before moving forward to the rest of the chambers.

Stepping into the dressing room, Val noted that whoever had made the mess hadn't spent as much time in the bedroom as in the sitting room.

"I see no sign of a valise." Eversham peered into the wardrobe. "And it looks as if some clothing is missing if one goes by the gaps in the wardrobe."

"That would have been from when I had my footman come yesterday," Val said. "It can't have been like this when he was here. He'd have alerted me to the fact."

"Good," Eversham said. "That tells us this must have been done last night or sometime today."

"That's something, I suppose," Val said. "What could they have been looking for?"

"That I cannot tell you." Eversham stooped to right a side table that had been thrown to the floor. As he did so, the drawer, which had been facing the floor, fell out with a clatter.

Eversham apologized but Val wasn't listening. He'd spotted a bundle of letters, tied with a ribbon, on the floor. It must have been wedged between the bottom of the drawer and the table frame.

"Something the thieves missed?" Eversham asked.

Val untied the ribbon holding the pages together, moving to the nearby window to examine them.

Dear Miss Warrington,

The vicar and his wife never took me into their confidence regarding your true parentage, and as you know, there was nothing further to be found in their belongings when they passed. The only knowledge I have been able to glean since we last corresponded is that their coachman retrieved you from an inn near Brighton Road. But as that was many years ago now, I doubt anyone there has any recollection of the matter. I beg you to let this rest. The Warringtons were good parents to you, and continuing this pursuit can only come to no good.

Miss Mary Killeen

"Letters," Val said shortly. "But they belong to Miss Warrington, not Frank."

He handed the bundle to Eversham, who read through them before handing them back.

"They're dated over a month ago," Eversham said. "Time enough for Miss Warrington to have visited Brighton."

Val cursed.

"I don't like this." Eversham frowned. "Removing a potential heir from the picture is a much better motive for a murder than it is for an abduction."

Val asked, "If Frank knew about this business in Brighton, why didn't he mention it, for God's sake?"

"We won't know until we speak to him," Eversham said. "What we do know is that one abductor is already dead. And your cousin is one of the only people who can identify the other."

For the first time, Val felt real fear for Frank. If he were innocent of Miss Warrington's abduction, and he was almost ready to believe that now, then his life was in danger. And now he appeared to be missing, too.

"It's possible he found this mess and went on the run before they could finish the job they started yesterday," Eversham said.

But Val wasn't fooled by his unusual optimism. "You don't believe that, do you?"

"I've been wrong before, Wrackham," the detective said.

Val just had to hope like hell—for Frank's sake—this was one of those rare times when Eversham had entirely missed the mark.

Chapter Thirteen

"What do you mean Mr. Thorn is gone?" Caro stared at Val where he stood in the front entry hall.

A discreet cough from behind alerted her that Newton was there waiting to take Val to meet with her father. "I'll need to speak with Lord Wrackham before he goes up to Papa, Newton."

"Very good, Miss Caroline," the older man said as he took Val's belongings.

Caro noted the fatigue in her fiancé's eyes as she tugged him into the nearest private chamber, a little-used parlor where her father sometimes met with fellow businessmen.

He'd changed clothes since that morning and was now attired in an expertly tailored suit of gray wool with a matching waistcoat and a snowy white shirt with a neatly tied cravat. It struck her once again just how handsome he was. The dark waves of his hair had been somewhat tamed but a rush of pleasure filled her as she recalled how her fingers had mussed it last evening. The rest of the world might know him like this—the polished aristocrat with an easy grace. But only she would be privy to his disheveled hair and passionate gazes now.

She felt a rush of affection for him in that moment. However the circumstances might have come about, she *was* glad to be marrying him.

"Come." She pulled him over to a large winged chair. "I think Papa has some brandy hidden away in here. You look as if you need it."

When Val didn't protest at her fussing, she knew just how upset he was by his cousin's disappearance. His face was pale, and his usual teasing had been replaced with grim silence. Even his earlier worry at Mr. Thorn's threatening letter was no match for his shattered expression now.

He was silent as she searched the cabinets, and when she pressed a glass of brandy into his hand, he took a healthy gulp before handing it back to her.

"I have no wish to be intoxicated when I speak with your father," he said with a crooked smile. She set the snifter on a nearby shelf, unsure how best to react to his attempt at normalcy.

Before she could speak, however, he took her hand and pulled her into his lap.

Caro squealed but let him pull her against him. Resting her cheek against his head, she said, "Tell me what happened."

Briefly, he explained what he and Eversham had found in the Albany. "While it's possible Frank disappeared of his own volition, either searching for Miss Warrington or in an effort to evade the men who searched his flat, Eversham suspects his life is in danger."

"You don't know that." Caro sat back to look at him. "There was no sign that your cousin was injured in his rooms, was there?"

At Val's shake of his head, she reached up to touch his face. "You mustn't let Eversham's assumption of the worst color your view of things. As a detective, he has seen far more darkness than you or I could ever imagine. He tends to adopt the more dire interpretation first, so if he's wrong, he can be pleasantly surprised."

"He said as much the same thing." Val nodded. "But it makes logical sense that if this relation of Miss Warrington's is willing to kidnap her—"

"We don't even know if that's who took her," Caro chided. "We must follow the evidence, rather than leaping to conclusions. Really, Val, this isn't like you in the least."

He dragged his thumb and forefinger over his eyes and rested his head against the back of the chair. "You're right, of course. I suppose the possibility of losing Frank has brought back all I felt when I lost Piers. Added to that, I am now the heir and so I feel a sense of responsibility for Frank."

Caro stroked a finger over one dark brow, then the other. She had so much affection for this infuriating, complicated man. She knew if she allowed herself to fall in love with him again, she'd be risking a worse heartache than the one she'd suffered four years ago. But they were to be inextricably linked now. Was it even now too late to protect her heart?

When she pulled her hand away, she kissed him softly

on the mouth. It was a kiss of comfort rather than passion, and after, she lay a hand over his chest, feeling the steady beat of his heart.

"I'm sorry about your brother," she said softly. "But you mustn't give up on Frank just yet. Nor will I give up on Effie."

"How can you be so optimistic?" he asked.

"Because for all of the terrible things that can go wrong," she said simply, "there are just as many wonderful things that can go right. Without hope, we may as well surrender to the dark."

"You're very wise." He smiled.

"That bit of wisdom is borrowed from my father," she said with a smile of her own. "I doubt he'd have managed to build a business empire without it."

"Speaking of your father..." Val sighed. "I suppose I'd better get up to his study."

"You needn't sound so unhappy about it," Caro said in mock dismay, climbing out of his lap.

Before he could apologize, she pulled him to his feet and smoothed the shoulders of his coat. "I know you didn't intend it that way," she assured him. "Neither of us is under the impression this is a love match."

It was a reminder for herself as much as it was for him. That she could fall in love with him again did not mean that she should.

At her words, she thought she saw his eyes darken, but the emotion was gone as quickly as it had come.

"But you deserve my respect," he said, gaze serious.

"Let us simply agree that the way this betrothal came about was unusual." Caro stepped back to survey her handiwork. However irritating he might be at times, she thought, she had first been drawn to his innate sense of kindness. He might have hurt her four years ago, but his slights had been unintentional. "Before you go up, I'd like to make a request."

She took his silence as permission to continue. "Mama is about to immerse herself, and by extension me, in plans for an elaborate, unnecessarily costly wedding. If at all possible, I would like to avoid that."

"Does not every young lady dream of an elaborate wedding?" Val raised a brow. "I should think you'd wish to oversee the cake, at the very least."

"This young lady," Caro said, with a moue of disapproval, "would prefer a small celebration with a few friends and family where she can avoid having her bridegroom paraded before her mama's friends like the largest fish in an angler's competition."

At his wide-eyed response, she sighed. "I do love Mama, but I also know her. She is thrilled at the notion of my marrying the heir to a dukedom and she won't be able to help herself if she's given free rein. It's not in her constitution to let such an occasion pass without letting the world know about this coup. Especially because she'll see it as a way of proving to those who look down their noses at Papa that his daughter is good enough for any of them."

"But that may benefit your father." Val frowned. "And to be clear, his daughter *is* good enough for any of them, but she's marrying *me*."

"Just the fact that we're marrying will be enough to quell Papa's fears." Caro smiled. "He doesn't care about proving anything to the *ton*. He only wants to know that his background hasn't kept me from making a good match."

"Then I will see to it." Val's eyes warmed. "Given that I haven't spoken to my parents about plans for the wedding yet, I think it best that we simply do as we wish and let them all follow along."

"Thank you," Caro said softly. "Besides, I would not wish a lavish celebration while Effie and your cousin are still missing. And, of course, the wedding must take place as soon as possible."

He winked at her. "That eager to bed me, are you?"

She laughed, her face heating. "You know very well, you rogue, that the haste is out of necessity to preserve what's left of my reputation."

"My father has a connection to the archbishop," Val assured her. "I should be able to obtain a special license by tomorrow if that suits."

Caro blinked. That was faster than even she'd imagined. "I suppose…yes."

"We needn't marry tomorrow, you know," he said, taking her hand and rubbing a soothing thumb over the back of it. "I'll only get the license then. We choose the date."

"No, of course not." She took a deep breath and reminded herself that she wanted this marriage. It would ensure that her rash behavior didn't reflect badly on her parents. And what's more, she wanted Val. She wasn't quite ready to open her heart to him again, but she wanted to be with him. Surely that was basis enough for a marriage.

Steeling her spine, she smiled brightly and opened the door into the hallway. "Mr. Newton," she called. "Lord Wrackham is ready to be taken up to Papa now."

Turning to Val, she nodded. "Good luck. I expect you'll be invited to stay for luncheon. Afterward we can go see Langham's bout."

He wanted to argue, she could tell, but Newton was there, and perhaps realizing argument was futile, he followed the butler up the main staircase.

"Am I dressed appropriately for a boxing match?" Caro asked from beside Val. He was driving them in his phaeton to Jim Hyde's club, where Langham's match was to take place.

"Never having brought a lady to a sporting event," Val responded as he steered them into the line of sporting carriages that were gathering outside of Hyde's, "I cannot really say. You do look lovely, however."

Her dark green silk gown with its contrasting blue jacket fit her to perfection. He wanted to put his mouth where a jaunty feather curled down from her hat to caress her cheek.

"And you're sure there will be an opportunity to speak with Langham before the bout begins?" Despite her eagerness to attend the event, it was evident from her wide eyes and glances at their fellow spectators that she was nervous. Val felt oddly protective at seeing the always confident Caro exhibiting signs of unease. He was coming to realize some of her bravado was merely a defense against those who would mock her for her boldness.

"I've been to hundreds of these fights," he assured her. "They almost never begin on time."

They'd come close enough to the venue now for Val to toss the reins to one of the dozens of street urchins who gathered on days such as this to earn a few coins. Soon enough, he was guiding Caro through the crowd and into the warehouse Jim Hyde had converted into a club.

He was eager to see the massive space where he'd covered countless matches in his role as sporting reporter for *The London Gazette* through Caro's eyes. He'd been interested in the "sweet science" of boxing since first learning about it at school, and when he'd had the opportunity, thanks to Kate, to follow its progress for his work, he'd jumped at the chance.

"Stay close to me," he said over the hum of voices as more and more people pressed into the rapidly filling space.

Beyond her head, he saw Jim Hyde in conversation with Langham. Both men towered over the room, with their large build and unusual height, and Val easily kept them in his sight as he and Caro made their way through the crush to where they stood near a pair of doors in the far wall.

When Val and Caro reached the two men, Hyde grinned down at Caro. "Miss Hardcastle, I haven't seen you since the Lake District. What a pleasure to welcome you to me club."

The big man executed a perfect bow over Caro's hand.

"Mr. Hyde." She smiled warmly. "I am looking forward to my first boxing match. I must compliment you on your magnificent club. It is really quite impressive. I had no notion it would be so fine on the inside."

Her reaction didn't surprise Val. He supposed most ladies unfamiliar with such venues thought all sporting events took place in grimy rooms that smelled of sweat, with rats darting around corners. The sweat was correct, but Hyde wouldn't countenance having rats about the place.

"It don't look like much from the outside," Hyde agreed without rancor, "but I made sure to do what I could to make the inside as fine as any boxing saloon in England."

"Miss Hardcastle." The Duke of Langham also bowed over Caro's hand. "I can't say I was expecting to see you here this afternoon. I hope you won't be too put off by the damage I intend to inflict upon my opponent."

Caro glanced around them, craning her neck. "Is he here? I don't wish to place a wager until I've had a chance to see both of you and make an assessment."

All three men laughed. "That would be me, Miss Hardcastle." Hyde grinned sheepishly. "I'm retired but every so often I find meself with a hankering to get back in the ring. So friends like 'is grace oblige me."

Val watched in amusement as Caro looked from one man to the other and back again. "Are you sure you wish to go through with this, your grace?" she asked Langham, glancing between the two men in alarm.

In truth, Langham and Hyde were well matched, despite the several stones by which Hyde outweighed the duke. Langham was younger and, despite his aristocratic ancestry, had done his share of brawling. Still, a novice like Caro wouldn't be able to see that.

Rubbing the back of his neck, Langham gave a theatrical sigh. "I have had second thoughts, Miss Hardcastle, but alas, I am already committed. And if I don't go through with it, the men who've bet on me will break my knees."

At Caro's gasp, Val hurried to assure her Langham was joking.

"I should have known better than to believe you," she chided the duke.

Hyde was called away just then, and Val decided they'd better speak to Langham while they had the chance.

He said with a casualness he didn't feel, "May Caro and I have a word with you in the dressing room?"

The duke's brow furrowed. But he didn't try to evade them. "Of course," he said, ushering them through the nearby door.

The room was sparsely furnished beyond a sofa and a few mismatched chairs. A dressing table held a variety of unguents and creams used for the treatment of bruises and the sorts of injuries caused by flying fists.

"Miss Hardcastle," the duke said, once Caro had been seated, "I would offer you a cup of tea, but I'm afraid the only beverages I have are whisky and gin. Neither of which I fear would meet with Wrackham's approval."

"We didn't come for a tea party." Val leaned against the wall nearest Caro, crossing his arms over his chest, his eyes flinty. Langham might have been his friend for years, but he didn't appreciate being lied to. His tone hardened. "We came because you didn't tell me the truth yesterday about the nature of your relationship with Miss Warrington."

The duke's jaw clenched. "I'm not sure what you mean, so perhaps you'd better state your business, Wrackham."

"You led me to believe that you are in a relationship with Nell Burgoyne," Val said. "I have since learned that not only have you spent time in the greenroom as part of Miss Warrington's coterie, but you were also seen leaving her townhouse in the early hours of the morning."

Langham's face progressed from disbelief to outright

scorn as Val spoke. "I don't know who's been telling you these things, but they've got their details wrong. The facts of what they told you are, yes, accurate, but not the reasons for my actions."

"Why don't you explain to us, your grace," Caro said firmly. "Because as it looks now, not only have you been unfaithful to Miss Burgoyne, but your behavior also makes you a suspect in Effie's disappearance."

The duke moved to where a bottle of whisky and a single glass stood. Pouring a few fingers, he took a large gulp before setting the glass down again.

Lowering himself into the chair beside Caro's, he addressed his words to her—ignoring Val. If it was his intention to annoy Val, he was succeeding. "Not that it's anyone's business, but Nell and I have not been together for several months now. Nell asked me to keep the matter quiet while she considers whom to bestow her favors upon next. So, there is no question of my being unfaithful. Not that the same sorts of rules apply between a man and his mistress as husbands and wives, mind you."

"Keep to the subject at hand, please, Langham." Val's voice held a warning note. He'd already risked Caro's reputation by bringing her here. He didn't need to worsen the situation by enlightening her on subjects she no doubt would claim it was high time she knew about.

"I'm hardly ignorant of the way such arrangements work, Val," Caro objected, shooting him an exasperated look. "Even if I weren't friends with Effie, Kate and I spoke at length with Julia yesterday. You needn't shield me like a hothouse flower."

"My apologies, Wrackham," the duke drawled before

Val could respond to Caro's scolding. "I'd assumed, since Miss Hardcastle seemed to think it appropriate to question me about my—"

Val cut him off. Between the duke and Caro, he was going to end up with back teeth ground down to nubs. "Move on to another topic."

"You've certainly brought the right man along to protect you, Miss Hardcastle." Langham winked. "Well done."

"Perhaps you can explain your actions, your grace?" Caro asked, not showing any response to Langham's outrageous flirting. The devil might be good with women, but he wasn't good with *his* woman. Val bit back a smile.

"I will tell you the truth, Miss Hardcastle," the duke said. "There is no romantic relationship between myself and Miss Warrington. As much as I admire her, she and I have only ever been friends."

"Then why gaze at her with longing at the theatre?" Caro asked. She sounded like Eversham questioning a witness.

"I don't know which occasion your spy was speaking of"—Langham crossed one long leg over the other—"but I can only guess that it was the night after that worm Tate accosted her in the greenroom. I wasn't there to hear what was said, but Nell told me Miss Warrington was quite shaken up. She asked me to come to the theatre the next night to make sure she did not have to suffer the man's verbal assault again."

"Nell asked you to do this even though you are no longer together?" Val asked, skeptical.

"I don't know how it is with you and your mistresses, Wrackham, but—" The duke broke off at Val's expression.

"That is to say, Nell and I are on good terms. I care about her and she is like a mother hen with the other actresses at the theatre. Even Miss Todd, who is as merciless as a tiger."

Val considered the veracity of what the duke was telling them. It would be foolish to lie when his story could be so easily checked with Nell. Furthermore, his explanation did make a degree of sense—and was more fitting behavior for the man Val had always considered a friend.

"And the early morning visit?" Caro pressed, clearly unwilling to let him brush by the other incident in Tate's accusation.

"Again, whoever your observer was, he misinterpreted the matter," Langham said breezily. "On that morning, Miss Warrington was not, in fact, even there."

"What do you mean?" Caro demanded. "Why were you there, then?"

"She'd asked me if I could assist her in finding some legal information." For the first time since he'd begun speaking, Langham looked uncomfortable. "I cannot help but feel as if I am breaking a confidence. Despite what you may think of me, I am not in the habit of betraying promises."

"Why you?" Val asked. His annoyance with the other man had lessened now that his behavior didn't seem nearly so suspicious. But he was curious about this legal business. "It's not as if you're a solicitor."

"Which is exactly what I told her." The duke shrugged. "I suppose the thought was that as a duke, I'd have dozens of solicitors at my disposal. And, if we are to be entirely honest, she was correct. I was able to connect her to a man who was able to answer her question within an afternoon.

"I simply dislike breaking my word not to disclose what I found." He scowled. "And in my defense, when you first came to me, Wrackham, you mentioned nothing about legalities. You said you suspected an obsessed admirer was responsible for her disappearance."

Caro's expression softened. "If it weren't of the utmost importance, your grace, we would not ask you to do so. Whatever she asked you to investigate might be the reason behind her abduction. You see, information has come to light that she was searching for her natural parents. And her disappearance might be related to that."

Langham cursed and paced to the other side of the room and back. He thrust a hand through his overlong hair as he stared into space for a moment. When he looked back at them, his gaze was determined. "I want you to find her. Because I do suspect this information might be what got her taken.

"From what I understand, Miss Warrington was raised by a rather strict vicar and his wife. At any rate, she learned— don't ask me how—the identity of her natural parents. I believe she suspected she might have been left a bequest. Her specific question for the solicitor was what would happen if the rightful heir to an estate appeared after the next in line had already taken control of the property. She never mentioned the names of her own family, but judging by the wealth and holdings of the estates she asked about, I suspect the inheritance in question would be sizeable."

"Large enough to kill over?" Caro asked the duke, her brows knitted.

"In my estimation, Miss Hardcastle," Langham said with a grim look, "yes."

Chapter Fourteen

Caro felt all the blood rush from her head as the room spun around her.

From far away, she heard both Val and the duke swear, and soon a glass was being pressed into her hand.

"Drink this," Val ordered, and for once she didn't feel the impulse to bristle at his commanding tone.

She did as he'd bade her, but as soon as she swallowed, a fit of coughing overcame her.

"That's foul," Caro rasped once she'd regained the ability to breathe. "Why do you drink it?"

"It has its benefits." The duke's voice was amused.

"And one usually sips it." Val's eyes smiled as he took the glass from her and handed it to Langham.

"You gulped it this afternoon," Caro accused Val. He'd seemed to enjoy it, too, she remembered.

"Because I'm accustomed to it," he explained. "You have to work up to a large swallow."

"You managed it better than most ladies of my acquaintance would have, Miss Hardcastle." There was a note of admiration in the duke's voice.

Then, recalling what had brought about her need for the whisky, Caro moaned in distress. "You don't really think Effie's dead, your grace, do you?"

She straightened, heartsick at the notion Effie might have been killed by someone who only saw her as a threat to their own inherited wealth. She'd come to love her friend over these past months, and she couldn't bear to think of someone silencing her dear voice forever.

"I apologize, Miss Hardcastle," the duke said, real regret in his tone. "I shouldn't have spoken so callously. Of course, we can't know what has become of her yet. Indeed, her disappearance may have nothing to do with the matter she asked me to investigate."

"But you don't really believe that," she said flatly.

When he hesitated, Val spoke up. "We'll have to find out who her parents might have been. It's possible the inheritance is inconsequential. Not every bequest is of an amount worth killing over."

"That is true," Caro said. But her usual optimism was eluding her at the moment, having been replaced by harsh reality. It was hardly unlike her to jump to—the sometimes wrong—conclusions, but this felt more like pragmatism than impulse. An effort to protect herself from the possibility that Effie might not be coming back. "We will have to hope that's the case."

Val stood from where he'd been crouched beside her chair and rested a hand on her shoulder. Caro was grateful for the touch. "I think it might be best for us to leave now."

"Oh!" Caro gasped and came to her feet. "We haven't delayed your match, have we, your grace?"

But the duke didn't seem alarmed. "Not at all. They can't start without me. And I daresay Hyde has the crowd convinced that I'm terrified to face him and have spent this time cowering. It will make my appearance now that much more thrilling."

Before they left, Caro took his hand. "Thank you for telling us what you know. I feel sure it will help us find her and Mr. Thorn."

"And Thorn?" Langham looked searchingly at Val.

"Gone since late morning," Val confirmed.

"I'm sorry," the duke said simply. "Let me know if there's any way I can be of help."

But all she wanted, Caro thought, was to find Effie and Mr. Thorn alive and unharmed. Even a duke of the realm couldn't make that happen.

After a night of fitful sleep—where he'd vacillated between lurid imaginings of Frank's body being fished from the river and brief, frustrating dreams of Caro—Val rose not long after dawn and dressed with care before setting out for Berkeley Square.

His father was an early riser and Val found him, having already breakfasted, going over correspondence with his private secretary in his study.

Upon seeing Val, however, the duke dismissed the young man. "I saw the announcement in the *Times*. You are going through with it, then?"

It was to be like that, was it?

"I compromised the lady's honor," Val said stiffly. "There is no question of not going through with it. Even if that was my wish, which it is not."

He'd hoped this conversation would be an easy one, but a lifetime's acquaintance with his father had warned him that his optimism was fruitless. His father could be amiable when he wished, but he did not care to be thwarted.

"I hope this wasn't some attempt on your part to put me in my place after I raised—very sensible—objections to your pursuit of the girl." The duke's tone was sharp. "I should have thought you were past the age for such petty rebellions."

"And I should have thought after your demand for me to marry—in this very chamber, no less—that you would be pleased at my swift acquiescence." Standing across the desk from his father, Val felt disappointment in the man for whom he'd once had the utmost respect. He'd known the duke was not perfect—as had been clear the previous night at the theatre—but perhaps naively, Val had assumed that once the announcement was made, his father would back down.

He could see now that he hadn't been explicit enough in his rebuke of the duke's attitude toward Caro and the Hardcastles in the theatre box. His own failure to object when his father and brother had so casually dismissed not only Caro and her parents, but also so many others over the years whom they deemed lesser beings, had no doubt led them to believe he agreed with their snobbish attitudes. It was time for him to make it clear to his father that no longer would he tolerate such talk.

"You cannot expect me to rejoice at the inferiority of the connection, surely?" the duke said. "The chit's mother might be the daughter of an earl, but the father's low birth negates any advantages. I would feel differently if the girl showed any refinement of manner, but it was clear from her boldness when she announced your betrothal for anyone within earshot to hear that she hasn't the poise to make a credible duchess."

"She," Val said sharply, "is a lady and has a name. Miss Caroline Hardcastle, soon to be Lady Wrackham. You may find her manner unrefined, but I find it refreshing. Indeed, I believe she has just the degree of backbone necessary to make her a formidable duchess. But more important, she pleases me and that is all that need concern you.

"What's more, I will expect you to treat Miss Hardcastle and her parents with the respect they are due as my bride and parents-in-law. There will be no cutting remarks or subtle insults, and if I so much as hear one suggestion from you that Caroline is somehow unworthy of being a part of this family, I will see to it that you have as little contact as possible with us, or any children we have in the future."

His words were harsh, Val knew, but if he wished to have any sort of relationship with his father going forward, this was the only way. He had little fear that the duke would cut him off entirely—the law ensured that he would be the next in line no matter what his father wanted, and financially, Val was stable enough to manage without funds from the estates until the time came for him to inherit. It was Val's hope that the duke would live for many years to come, and in good health, but if Val had to curtail his visits to his parents in that time, then he was prepared to do so for Caro's sake—and truthfully, his own.

The duke huffed, but any further argument was forestalled by the appearance of the duchess in the doorway.

"Valentine." She hurried forward to clasp him in an enveloping hug. "We saw the announcement in the papers this morning. I'm so pleased for you. Miss Hardcastle is a lovely young woman. I was afraid after the uproar of the evening that something might happen to upend things, but I'm so happy to see it did not."

Val held her close, grateful at least one of his parents was happy for his impending marriage. Caro's position in the family would be much easier—and much more comfortable—if she could count on the duchess as an ally. "Thank you, Mama. I am fond of Caroline and I hope that you will come to feel the same."

"I'm sure I will." The duchess pulled away, beaming. "Now, you must tell me what the plans are for the wedding. Will you wait for the reading of the banns?"

Val glanced at his father before answering her. "Special license. We see no reason to wait. Given how we are only just out of mourning, and the fact that Frank is missing, we thought it best to keep it a quiet affair."

The duke frowned. "What is this about Francis? Where is he?"

Seeing no sense in keeping them from the truth at this point, Val told them about Frank and Miss Warrington's betrothal, Miss Warrington's kidnapping, and Frank's subsequent disappearance. He had intended to ask his father for assistance that first day when he'd answered Frank's summons, but he'd chosen not to out of fear for how the duke would react to the news of Frank and Miss Warrington's betrothal. Now, however, with his cousin possibly in grave danger, he thought it best to disclose all.

To the duke's credit, he chose not to comment on Frank's betrothal to Miss Warrington. Instead, he focused on the investigation. "What does Eversham say? He seemed a capable enough man to me. I ought to contact the prime minister. I know the leadership at the Yard can be wrongheaded when investigating crimes they don't deem important, but Francis is the nephew of a duke. Surely they're aware of the influence I can bring to bear should they fail to find him."

"Eversham is well aware of Frank's family connections," Val assured him. "And he has the matter well in hand. Perhaps you would speak to Uncle Theo about the matter? I must confess, I don't know what to say to him. Especially given his disapproval of the relationship between Frank and Miss Warrington."

"I will call on him later this morning," the duke said grimly. "I had intended to see him later at the club regardless, but he needs to know his son is missing."

Hanging in the air was the reminder that the duke knew all too well what it was like to have a son in danger—and what consequences it could bring.

"What sort of lady is she, this Effie Warrington?" the duchess asked, putting a hand on Val's arm as the duke moved to stare out the window. "I know she is an actress, but is she a kind woman? Does she make Francis happy? He was always such a dear boy. I remember how inseparable the three of you were as children. I hope he has had some measure of happiness before—"

She broke off with a sniff, and Val pressed his handkerchief into her hand. "From what I understand, they have been very happy together. She is a dear friend of Caro and Kate's, so I do think she must be kind. I doubt either lady would have given her their attention if she were not."

The duchess beamed. "I like your Caro. She has a great deal of spirit, I think. And I must say, I am pleased to see you settle down."

"Thank you, Mama," Val told her. "I hope you will come to be good friends with her."

"I should like that," she said with a watery smile. "Very much."

"I'll walk down with you," the duke said when Val had bid her goodbye.

He braced himself for more objections about his marriage, but to his surprise, his father offered him a rare apology.

"I can be a narrow-minded arse sometimes," the duke said ruefully as they neared the entry hall. "And I was, perhaps, overly harsh in my remarks about Miss Hardcastle and her parents. I have no excuse for it, except to say that like many men of my generation, I forget sometimes that the old ways aren't always the best ways. And some of my attitudes are so deeply ingrained that it's difficult for me to see, until it's pointed out, that I'm acting like an opinionated old fool. Some of that is being a duke, mind you, but some of it is also a failure to recognize that the world has changed while I have not.

"I daresay," the duke continued, "it's a good thing for the peerage that you younger members are open-minded enough to marry outside the upper ten thousand."

Val knew better than to agree with his father's assessment

of himself. Instead, he said, "Thank you, sir. I know this isn't the marriage you had hoped for me, but you cannot expect me to be as pliable as my brother was. I am a different man with different ways and preferences. Caroline, for all that our marriage will have come about precipitately, suits me. She is a clever and kind woman, and I think if you will look past your objections to her background, you'll come to like her—maybe even grow fond of her."

In the time since Piers's death, their relationship had grown strained as Val bucked under the expectations of becoming the heir. Val truly hoped that he could have a more meaningful connection with his father going forward, but he meant his every word about eschewing the relationship if the duke didn't significantly alter his behavior toward Caro.

"I'm sure you're right," the duke said with a tight smile. Then his eyes grew troubled. "I hope that I've not made you feel as if I expect you to be a seamless replacement for your brother, Valentine. I know you are your own man and will go about taking up your duties in your own way. If I have insinuated that I found you wanting, I beg you will forgive me."

The duke swallowed, looking miserable. "I cannot afford to lose you as well."

Val turned and clasped his father by the shoulder. "You haven't lost me. Now, if you will exert yourself to be charming to my bride, and her family, I will be thoroughly appeased."

"I can do that," the duke said with only a small grimace.

It wasn't perfection, Val thought, but it was a start.

Chapter Fifteen

Caro was still abed the next morning, Ludwig curled in an almost perfect circle in her lap, a cup of steaming chocolate in her hand, when she heard her mother's shrill tones.

"What were you thinking?" her mother demanded, unceremoniously showing herself into Caro's bedchamber. "How could you have gone against my wishes like this?"

"Good morning to you, too, Mama." Caro took one last sip of her cocoa before handing the drink to her waiting maid.

Ludwig, who was not fond of Lady Lavinia even when she was at her most serene, dove beneath the counterpane. He remained as still as a stone near the foot of the bed, clearly unaware that the lump he'd formed in the smooth bedclothes made his location evident.

"Your papa just informed me that his lordship has requested the ceremony take place this very weekend,"

Mama fumed. "How am I to plan a wedding with so little notice? I had *thought* we might hold it at the chapel on the duke's estate so as to give the occasion the respect it deserves."

"Given that the family is only just out of mourning and that Val's cousin is missing, Mama, imposing upon them like that would be unnecessarily burdensome." Caro was careful to keep her voice calm so as not to further inflame her mother's nerves.

She loved Mama dearly, but she did have a tendency toward the dramatic when she was overset. And on this particular detail of her wedding plans, Caro was unwilling to compromise. She already knew that Val's father, at least, was displeased with his remaining son's choice of bride. But however pride and familial affection might urge her to follow Mama's lead—if only to prove to the duke and the rest of London society that she was unashamed of her father's origins—she refused to plan a large celebration while Effie and Mr. Thorn were missing and likely in danger.

"Oh," Mama said, deflated. "I hadn't realized Lord Wrackham's cousin was missing. How dreadful. Does it have something to do with your friend's disappearance?"

"We don't know yet," Caro explained. "But you can see why we don't wish to press the matter."

"I know they must be worried," Mama said, frowning, "but surely for a matter as important as the heir to the dukedom's wedding—"

Caro interrupted her. She knew how much it meant to Mama to prove—through Caro's marriage—that Papa was the equal of any puffed-up aristocrat who might snub him.

But the very fact that Caro was marrying into the Thorn family would have to be enough.

"Mama, neither Valentine nor I am willing to ask such a thing of the duke and duchess." Caro rose from her bed and slipped her arms into the dressing gown her maid had left out before making her discreet exit. "And we have agreed that we would like a small ceremony. I hope that you will respect our wishes."

Her mother's pretty face crumpled with disappointment. "But you are my only child, Caroline. I have been dreaming of your wedding since the day you were born!" Then, her expression hardening, she went on. "Not to mention that this is the perfect opportunity to show *them* that your papa is every bit as good as they are."

There was no need to ask Mama who "they" were. She'd been clear enough the night of their trip to the theatre that she resented the way her own family and the aristocracy looked down their nose at her husband.

"Surely the fact that I am marrying the heir to the Duke of Thornfield is enough," Caro reasoned. "It's not necessary to travel to their country estate for the nuptials to prove the point."

"I suppose not." Mama perched on the edge of the window seat with a sigh. "Of course, I have every sympathy for Valentine's parents. I cannot imagine how difficult it must have been for them to lose their son at such a young age. And it must be distressing that their nephew is missing. I simply want your wedding to be perfect—and not just because of what it will mean for your father. He only wants to see you happy. And he has a high opinion of your Lord Wrackham."

"They've only met a few times." Caro turned from where she'd been brushing her hair at her dressing table. "How can he have come to anything like a firm conclusion?"

Mama smiled at Caro, her eyes full of affection. "He's always been perceptive about people. It's what makes him a successful businessman. And I wonder you should ask such a question, given that it's a trait you've inherited from him."

Caro supposed that her mother was right. About Papa at least.

"I may be quick to judge," Caro said wryly, "but I'm not nearly so proficient as Papa at it."

Thinking of how wrong she'd been in her assessment of Val's character, she wondered that she could boast any powers of discernment at all.

"You're far better at it than you think," Mama said, her voice laced with pride. "Why do you think your readers are so drawn to your column with Kate? It's because you are both able to assess situations that are difficult for most mere mortals to even fathom. You make a determination on what happened and who might be responsible."

"But that's only reporting facts and interpreting them," Caro protested. "We don't solve cases like Eversham or the Yard does. We simply discuss the crimes and their implications for society and women in particular."

"Yes," Mama said patiently, "and part of that interpretation and discussion is making judgments. Not everyone always agrees with you, but if you weren't good at it, your readers would tell you. I've read everything you've written, and much as the subject matter disturbs me, I'm proud of what you and Kate have accomplished."

Caro had never considered the matter like that. She'd begun to question if her tendency to see situations in such stark contrasts was a weakness. It certainly hadn't helped her in her interactions with Val. But now she wondered if her difficulty had less to do with being wrong in her judgments and more to do with her tendency to distrust her instincts. The thought unraveled the knot that had been constricting her opinion of herself this past year. "Thank you, Mama. That means a great deal to me."

Caro gave her mother a quick hug.

"Does it mean enough for you to change your mind and allow me to plan a lavish wedding?" Mama's hopeful look was so blatantly false that Caro couldn't help but laugh.

"I'm afraid it doesn't." Caro had to credit her mother's persistence.

"'How sharper than a serpent's tooth it is to have a thankless child!'"

If Mama hadn't been born into the aristocracy, Caro thought, she might have made a very good actress. Aloud, she said, "I might be willing, if you are able to arrange it, to have the ceremony at St. George's, so as to increase the size of the guest list to include Papa's business associates. And whichever *ton* families you might wish to ask."

As most *ton* weddings took place at St. George's Church, Mama's eyes brightened. "I'm sure I would be able to arrange that. And we can have the wedding breakfast here. I know Mrs. Honeychurch and the rest of the staff will do their utmost to ensure we celebrate your nuptials properly. No matter how small a gathering you insist upon."

Grateful to have thwarted a titanic tantrum from her high-strung mother, Caro watched in amusement as Mama hurried in search of her maid.

Closing her bedchamber door, Caro set about dressing for the day. She had just set Ludwig down in his favorite window seat, having coaxed him out from beneath the covers, when a footman knocked on the door to let her know Miss Deaver had called.

She found Flora, neatly if simply attired in a pale gray silk with a straw hat and matching ribbons, in the blue drawing room. She was standing with her back to the fire.

"Flora, my dear." She hurried toward her friend. "It is good to see you. You're here on an errand for Kate, I suppose?"

It was too much to hope that the assistant had come with news. They were now nearing two days since Effie's abduction, and they still had only snatches of information that couldn't yet be pieced together into a coherent whole. And Mr. Thorn's disappearance had made the situation only more complicated.

Flora nodded. "I've come with Kate's notes on your draft for next week's column."

She reached for the leather case resting against a chair near the fireplace.

"Of course." Caro rubbed the spot between her eyebrows in frustration. "I can't believe I didn't remember them sooner." She had given the pages to Kate the afternoon they'd waited for Effie at Applegate's Tea Room. Had that really been only two days prior?

"You've had quite a few matters to distract you," Flora

pointed out. "And if it makes you feel less of a feather-brain, Kate has been just as preoccupied. We've all had a hard time concentrating this week."

Taking the papers from Flora, Caro was about to ask if she'd like to stay for a cup of tea when Newton knocked briskly. He announced Val and—to Caro's surprise—the Duke of Langham.

"Good morning, my dear." Val bowed over her hand, the touch of his lips against her bare skin sending a shiver through her.

Caro wondered if she'd ever become accustomed to the little jolt of awareness that ran through her whenever he entered a room. She was beginning to fear that trouble-some, impetuous part of her had already taken the leap into deeper feelings for him.

"And good morning to you, Miss Deaver," he said to Flora. But she was rather comically staring wide-eyed at Langham. Given the way the young lady followed his exploits in the papers, Caro supposed his presence was not unlike seeing a fictional character come to life. "May I present my friend, the Duke of Langham? Langham, this is the inestimable Miss Flora Deaver. She is Lady Katherine's right-hand woman at *The Gazette*."

Caro noted with some amusement that the duke seemed just as flummoxed by the sight of Flora.

Interesting.

The two remembered their manners, and Flora dropped into a deep curtsy while the duke bowed courteously over her hand.

"My apologies for persuading Wrackham to bring me along, Miss Hardcastle," the duke said once he'd regained his composure. "I remembered a detail about our mutual friend that I thought might be of interest."

"You may speak freely in front of Flora, your grace," Caro assured him. "She is assisting us with the search. Indeed, she's been doing essential research at the library at *The Gazette* in hopes of identifying the sender of a letter that we found in Effie's house."

Langham stared at the secretary for a long moment. Then, his blue eyes widened in recognition. "You're the same woman who was looking for records at Somerset House for Miss Warrington."

Flora looked uncomfortable at both the duke's scrutiny and his words.

Caro gasped. "Flora, you told us nothing of that!"

"I didn't believe it had anything to do with her disappearance. We all supposed one of her admirers from the theatre was responsible," Flora said a little defensively. "And she asked me not to tell anyone. I couldn't break her confidence."

"That's what I told them." Langham gazed sharply at Caro and Val. "But I can already see that you're inclined to take this person's word at face value, whereas I—a peer of the realm, and a friend—had to endure a very uncomfortable time being questioned by the two of you."

Flora audibly drew in a breath.

"Miss Deaver is a dear friend, your grace," Caro chided Langham after directing a pointed look at Val.

Taking the hint, Val cleared his throat. "Badly done, Langham. I believe you owe Miss Deaver an apology."

To his credit, though he still frowned, Langham took the correction in stride. "I can be a sharp-tongued bas— er, fellow, Miss Deaver." He bowed. "I hope you will accept my sincere apologies."

But the damage to Flora's hero worship of the duke had been done. "Of course, your grace," she said with a curtsy. The look she cast upon him, however, could have curdled milk.

"Now that that's settled," Caro said cheerily, trying to get them all back onto a friendly footing, "I am ringing for some refreshments, and you"—she nodded at Flora—"will tell us what you were looking for at Somerset House, and you"—she nodded at the duke—"will tell us whatever it is you remembered."

As she crossed to the bellpull, Langham murmured to Val, "Is she always this managing, Wrackham? I fear you may be in for a hard time of it."

"Some gentlemen are not afraid of an assertive lady," Flora said mildly. "I should have thought a duke who commands multiple estates and armies of staff would not balk at a woman who knows her own mind. But I suppose a title is only a word, after all."

When Caro turned back to her guests, she intercepted Flora and the duke trading scowls. Taking a seat beside Val, she said in a low voice, "I fear Flora may have just defenestrated your friend."

"There is no 'may' about it," Val said with admiration. "She did what Hyde could not." Caro surmised with surprise that despite Jim Hyde's expertise, he'd been unable to best Langham at their match the evening before.

"And what do you know of such things, Miss Deaver?" Langham asked with considerable hauteur, even going so far as to remove a quizzing glass from some inner pocket of his waistcoat. He glared at her through it. "You cannot be more than, what, one and twenty? I daresay you know no more than an alley cat about relations between men and women."

Flora raised her nose in the air with all the arrogance of a royal princess. "Cats are very intelligent. I won't have you malign them. And I am five and twenty, but since when does one's age have anything to do with one's understanding of interactions between the sexes? A girl of fifteen may possess an expert's knowledge of love and a man of fifty may be a quivering virgin. Of course, the aristocracy place—in my estimation—far too much emphasis on keeping ladies in the dark about such matters. But as you so helpfully pointed out, I am no one of importance and as such would not be shielded from that knowledge."

Caro had to press her hands against her sides to keep from applauding. She might have spoken out in praise of Flora's masterful setdown, but she feared giving the duke, whose glare at her friend was sharp enough to cut glass, time to respond would open the door to him being even ruder than before.

Fortunately, a footman arrived at that moment carrying a loaded tea tray.

"Would anyone like some tea?" she asked brightly.

Val had never seen Langham behave with such ill manners. Though he was known to be blunt, he was generally polite—especially with members of the fairer sex.

He could see that Caro was alarmed by their byplay. Since

he had been the one to bring Langham unannounced, he did what he could to pour oil on these troubled waters, as it were.

"Perhaps you can tell us what you remembered about Miss Warrington, Langham," he said to the other man. He was still glowering over his teacup at Miss Deaver, who appeared to be ignoring him. When Langham didn't respond, Val kicked him none too gently in the shin.

The duke threw an indignant look at Val, but he did cease looking daggers at Miss Deaver.

"You remembered something about Effie?" Caro's voice, in Val's opinion, held more patience than the man deserved.

"Yes," Langham said stiffly. "Or rather, the solicitor I sent her inquiry to."

"Well?" Miss Deaver prompted.

"I am collecting my thoughts," Langham said pettishly.

Caro sent Miss Deaver a chiding look. The young lady looked utterly unrepentant.

"Miss Warrington had wanted to know the legal ramifications of an heir appearing after they'd been presumed dead or lost." The duke then took his time selecting and biting into a cucumber sandwich. Once he finished chewing, he continued, "Phipps recalled that though she made no mention of a family name, Miss Warrington did express concern that if an heir had achieved a fame of sorts, a connection to her might put their reputation in jeopardy."

"I would hope that finding a long-lost relation who undertakes honest work would never come as an embarrassment," Caro said with a wave of her hand, "but we all know that plenty in the middle and upper classes would be scandalized to discover even a distant relation to an actress."

"But who would be in danger because of it?" Miss Deaver bit into a madeleine reflectively. "Surely an actress in the family couldn't irrefutably tarnish that many reasons for prominence."

"We'd be better off asking," Caro said thoughtfully, "who among the nobility have need of employment, and what sort of professional reputations would suffer from the emergence of a relation with a career on the stage. I would think we're most probably searching for younger sons."

"As a second son..." Val paused as he remembered his brother. He might be the heir now, but he hadn't always been. He doubted he'd ever forget that. "I can see your logic. And," he continued, "there are only a few acceptable professions I can think of. The military, the church, and politics."

"I can't think a military man would care one way or another about a connection to an actress," Langham said dismissively. "Too busy planning campaigns and pinning on medals. And they don't rely on family reputation so much as the other two do."

Val didn't disagree. "I'd rule out military men, too. Their careers aren't influenced by public opinion as much as those of clergymen and politicians. Though the latter would only matter for MPs, since the lords don't need to stand for election."

"Thank God," Langham muttered under his breath.

"And since the most recent Reform Act," Miss Deaver said, acid in her tone, "more younger sons of the aristocracy than ever are standing for Parliament, since so many funds are required for campaigning."

"I should think you'd be pleased at the expansion of the vote to more working men, Miss Deaver." The duke examined her with his quizzing glass once again.

"I'd be more pleased if the act had expanded the vote to women, too." There was no mistaking the young woman's resentment.

Thinking to forestall the argument between the two, Val spoke up. "So, we are agreed that the most likely candidates for Miss Warrington's hypocritical relations will either be MPs or clergymen?"

"With clergymen being the worst hypocrites of all," Langham agreed. "I should know—I've got enough of them in my family."

"They must be so proud." Miss Deaver smiled mockingly.

"Either of them would be plausible," Caro said. "Though my inclination is that it must be a politician. Especially the sorts who crusade for public morals. I firmly believe some I've seen would rather cut off an entire branch of the family tree before admitting to kinship with an actress. For all too many of the so-called 'righteous,' acting, for a woman, is only one step removed from prostitution. These men might enjoy attending the theatre, but I doubt any of them would welcome an actress to their dinner table, much less into their family."

"A valid point." Val nodded. "Though clergymen do like to present a certain appearance of virtue, what real consequence would there be for one if a relation to an actress was revealed? Defrocking is only for sins they've committed. And with the archbishop's support, I doubt they'd even lose a coveted posting. But a member of the House of Commons would have to contend with their voters. And a skillful opponent could weave scandal out of a newly discovered actress in the family, I have no doubt."

"Good," Langham said cheerfully. "Now we only have to ask every MP from a noble family if he's recently learned of a long-lost relation who happens to tread the boards. That should be easy enough."

"And I don't think we can entirely discount members of the House of Lords," Caro said, sounding almost apologetic. "That increases our pool of suspects, but we must remember that we are looking for someone who, firstly, inherited a large estate and, secondly, has a reputation to protect. That could be someone from either house of Parliament. Or even a cabinet member."

Val groaned. "Why does it feel as if every time we make progress, some new twist happens to take us back to where we began?"

Miss Deaver smiled slowly. "I might be able to clarify things."

From the leather case beside her chair, she retrieved a small notebook, flipped it open, then handed it to Caro.

"What's this, Flora?" she asked. From Val's vantage point, it looked like a list of some sort.

"I was able to examine what was left of the signet ring's impression from the sealing wax in Effie's hearth," Miss Deaver said. "I agreed with your assessment that the animal was a fox, and the rectangular bit, an arrow. I consulted with the herald at the College of Arms and we were able to compile a list of possibilities from every noble family in England."

"Flora," Caro whooped, "this is brilliant."

"Well done, Miss Deaver." Val had known her keen mind had earned Kate and Caro's respect, but he was beginning to think her skills might be put to better use deciphering codes for the Foreign Office.

"You should see this." Caro handed the notebook to him.

Curious, Val scanned the list.

"I want to see." Langham sounded like a small child trying to see around a crowd.

"I'm not sure you do," Miss Deaver said, even as Val passed the list to him. "Though perhaps you can explain why your family name is there?"

Chapter Sixteen

I daresay it's because there's a fox on my family crest,"
Langham responded with ill-disguised annoyance. "But
there's one reason why I don't belong there. I've never sent
any correspondence to Miss Warrington."

Caro could see that the duke was irritated, but Flora
could hardly have left him off her list of Effie's potential
relations. And how could she have known Val would bring
Langham to Caro's house?

Langham glared at Flora. "You've known this whole time
I was on your bloody"—Val coughed, and he amended his
epithet—"your infernal list."

"I did," Flora said unrepentantly. "But you can easily
eliminate yourself from suspicion."

Caro had come to the same conclusion. "Come to the
escritoire, your grace, and we can test the impression of
your signet ring against the original."

"Gladly," Langham said with another glare at Flora.

"Though since I don't give a hang about my reputation, I'd like to point out that I wouldn't be under suspicion by Miss Warrington's own estimation."

Caro thought the duke made a valid point, but none of them stopped him from comparing his ring impression with the wax seal.

Within minutes, the duke had pressed his signet into the melted puddle of wax Caro had heated.

Flora, she noted, was careful not to stand too close to the duke when she brought over the impression from Effie's for comparison.

"It is not a match." If Caro detected a hint of disappointment in her friend's voice, she could hardly blame her, given Langham's rude behavior. She'd thought him charming, if a bit fractious, at their meeting yesterday, but she suspected his manner today was closer to his usual demeanor.

"As I said." The duke sounded sullen. "There is a mark on the seal that is not present on mine."

"At least now you have been eliminated," Val said with an overabundance of good cheer.

"So, are we to question the heads of these families to determine which of them or their relations have some connection to Miss Warrington?" Langham demanded, looking at the list again. "I have some little acquaintance with Bute and Grafton—you will remember Grafton from school, Wrackham—though I don't know that they or their families are overly involved in Parliament. Waterbury is ninety if he's a day and rarely leaves his Yorkshire estate. His grandson is a rakehell, if I recall. Croyden and Fitzmaurice are entirely unknown to me."

"Which of them has an estate near Brighton?" Caro asked, recalling the letter Val had found in Mr. Thorn's rooms. "It cannot be a coincidence that Effie was handed off to the Warrington's near there."

"None of their family seats are in Sussex." Flora looked deflated. "I can see if any of them owns property there, but that will take more searching."

"It might be more expedient if we simply go to the coaching inn and ask about the estates nearby." Caro wished she weren't stranded in London until the wedding. Kate and Eversham could go, of course, but she selfishly wanted to be there.

"It would at that," Val said. There was a faraway look in his blue eyes.

Before she could press him on what he was thinking, Flora rose from her chair. "Lady Katherine will be wondering what's become of me." She smiled ruefully. "Thank you for the refreshments, Miss Har— I mean, Caro." Despite having been acquainted for more than a year, the other lady still had difficulty remembering Caro's admonition to address her informally.

To Val, who had risen with Langham, she said, "It was a pleasure to see you again, my lord."

She offered a deep curtsy to the duke. "Your grace, it has been…a memorable experience."

"Indeed," said Langham with a very correct bow. He watched her with open curiosity as she took up her leather case and left.

"I suppose I'd better be off as well." Val turned to Caro. "Langham, oblige me by preceding me downstairs, will you?"

"Certainly," the duke said. "Miss Hardcastle, it was a pleasure. Even the novelty of proving myself innocent of a crime."

Once Langham was gone, Val leaned in and took Caro's lips. When they were both breathless, he rested his forehead on hers. "I'm off to procure the special license."

He stepped back, and Caro took his hands. "Mama took the news of the expedited wedding plans better than I'd expected."

"That's a relief." Val wryly smiled. "How was that achieved?"

"I may have had to promise we'd marry at St. George's if at all possible," Caro said apologetically. She'd hoped to spare him an elaborate society wedding, but he of all people should understand the difficulties of dealing with determined parents. "So it's likely the guest list will expand somewhat."

But Val didn't appear bothered. "I'll speak with Mother. Perhaps she and your mama can join forces."

"Do you think that's wise?" Caro asked. The memory of his father's stiff response to the news of their engagement was still fresh in her mind. The duchess had seemed pleasant enough when they'd spoken, but she didn't know her very well. Perhaps she was simply better at hiding her displeasure than her husband. Caro would spare Mama the embarrassment if she could.

"Why wouldn't it be?" Val looked surprised.

"Well," Caro began stiffly, "your father wasn't pleased by the news of our betrothal, and though your mama appeared happy enough—"

Realization dawned in Val's blue eyes and he pulled her

to him in a quick hug. "I wasn't thinking when I spoke. I'm sorry he made you feel unwelcome."

She rested her head on his shoulder, inhaling the now familiar warm scent of lime and bergamot and relishing the feel of his arms around her.

"Come." Val drew her over to the settee to sit beside him. Taking her hand, he said, "I had a very frank discussion with my father this morning. My hope is you'll need not worry anymore about how he will treat either you or your parents."

Caro listened intently as Val told her about his discussion with the duke and how firmly he'd expressed his expectations for how Caro and her family were to be treated by the duke and duchess.

But when he shared his threat to keep himself or any children they might have from his parents, Caro gasped. "Val! How could you say such a thing? I don't wish to come between you and your family. It's bad enough that he doesn't think me good enough to marry you."

Val leaned forward and dipped his head, looking her in the eye. "*You* are my family now. Or you will be soon. As a duke, my father is used to having his own way in all things. He wouldn't have respected anything less than a full show of strength."

Tears welled in her eyes.

He kissed her softly.

"I only did what I should have done four years ago," he said once he'd pulled back. "I will never ever stand by as you endure disrespect at the hands of anyone, but particularly my family, ever again."

He'd apologized to her on the night of their betrothal, but Caro knew all too well that words didn't always match a person's deeds. The realization that he'd not only spoken truly, but also gone so far as to threaten his father with consequences if he showed Caro disrespect again, filled her with hope. It felt as if with every gesture, Val was adding kindling to the embers of their old love. "Thank you," she told him, her voice hoarse.

This time it was Caro who kissed Val, wrapping her arms around his neck to tell him how touched she was by his actions.

When they were both once again breathless, he set her away from him. "We most definitely need to plan this wedding for sooner rather than later."

"Agreed." Caro noted with amusement that she'd mussed his hair again.

Getting to his feet, Val gave her one last quick kiss. "I have to go before I maul you again. Besides, I want to speak with Eversham and see if he's learned anything new about the man in the river. I'll tell him what Flora discovered about the seal and our theories about Miss Warrington's relations."

"I suppose we should ask if he and Kate might be able to visit Brighton," Caro said, though she was unaccountably disappointed at the notion. But it was selfish of her to delay any chance at discovering some important clue simply because she wanted to be the one to follow the lead. "You can make the suggestion."

"I shall."

He was almost to the door when Caro gave in to the urge to follow him and ask, "Do you think we're making enough progress? I'm beginning to fear we may not find them. Certainly not before the wedding."

The knowledge that she and Val—who were as much of a cross-class match as Effie and Mr. Thorn—would wed while her friend and his cousin's lives hung in the balance made her deeply uncomfortable.

"Weren't you the one preaching the doctrine of hope to me?" Val reminded her. "I haven't given up on them yet. I know we'd both prefer to have them here with us, but the timing cannot be helped. And in the meantime, I'll make some discreet inquiries about any likely candidates from the House of Lords. Perhaps you, Kate, and Miss Deaver can explore some of the families in Miss Deaver's list? We'll find them."

Then, with one last kiss to her cheek, he was gone.

Chapter Seventeen

Caroline and Valentine were married three days later at St. George's Hanover Square—her mother had managed to secure the church with assistance from the duchess, who'd happily helped—with more friends and family in attendance than Caro had initially visualized.

But despite the ease with which she and Val had interacted in the days since their betrothal, neither of them had spoken of deeper feelings or hinted at the possibility of a return to the same tenderness they'd harbored when they'd first met. The kisses they'd shared proved the attraction was still there, but she was mindful now of how her own impetuosity had gotten her into trouble in the past. While Val had proven himself willing and able to stand up to his father on her behalf, it took time to rebuild trust. She had resolved to make the best of this marriage—even to enjoy the easy affection between them—but until she had full confidence in him, she would keep her heart to herself.

The wedding itself, however, did not fail to touch her.

As she'd intimated to her mother, she'd never dreamt of the day she'd wed, planning every last detail from the gown to the flowers and the breakfast afterward. But as she looked into Val's eyes when they exchanged their vows, she found herself wishing she had. This occasion deserved to have been planned down to the last flower petal, and she was sorry she'd not spent more time preparing for it. Then the bishop was pronouncing them man and wife, and Val was smiling down at her, his blue eyes filled with what appeared to be genuine happiness, and she had no more patience for regrets of any kind.

The breakfast afterward was to be held at the Hardcastle townhouse. Once in the carriage to Belgrave Square, Valentine surprised her by pulling her into his lap and kissing her thoroughly. His enthusiasm was contagious, and despite her determination to behave with decorum on this of all days, she found herself kissing him back with equal delight.

"Have I told you today how lovely you are, Lady Wrackham?" he asked after a long interlude. "I like whatever it is you've done with your hair." He lifted a finger to a ringlet that caressed her collarbone.

There had been no time to have a gown made up, but Caro had chosen to wear a Worth creation she'd been saving for a special occasion. The ivory silk went well with her dark hair and fair skin, and the scalloped bodice bared enough of her shoulders to feel daring while being entirely respectable. She'd felt beautiful as soon as she put it on, and Val's admiration when he spotted her on her father's arm had been gratifying.

"Not today." Her heart turned over in delight. She might have promised herself to keep from falling back into love with him for now, but in the face of his sweet words, it was impossible to remain entirely unmoved. "I will be sure to relay your compliment to my maid."

"But the compliment is meant for you, my lady," he said, his clear blue gaze intent. "The same style on another woman would leave me cold."

She should have ignored the small flattery, but Caro was uneasy with the exaggeration. "There's no need for hyperbole." When her heart fluttered again, she used his full name to put some needed distance between them. "I have no need for reassurances you won't have a wandering eye, Valentine."

He glanced up at her from where he'd been watching his finger stroke her shoulder. "Why would I have need to assure you of such a thing? Is there some question in your mind about my ability to remain faithful to my vows?"

All the playfulness in his manner was gone. He removed his hands from her bare skin and circled his arms loosely at her waist—as if merely ensuring she didn't tumble to the floor.

"We both know this isn't a love match," Caro reminded him. However happy her parents' marriage might be, she knew the same could not be said for others in genteel society. Val had shown himself willing to give her the protection of his name and to make a place for her in his aristocratic family, but she was mindful of the haste with which they'd come together. His friend Langham had been Nell Burgoyne's lover and Val was no innocent—why was it unthinkable to imagine he might behave like other men of his class? "We may have been rubbing along well enough together of late, but I don't have to tell you that we've barely had a civil word for one another these past years. I merely wished to assure you that there will be no need for false compliments or promises you may not wish to keep."

Val lifted her away from him to sit on the opposite seat, and Caro felt the absence of his warmth like a physical loss. "We're nearing Belgrave Square," he said, looking out the window of the carriage.

"You agree with me, do you not?" Caro asked, somewhat surprised by his response. After all, he hadn't professed his undying love to her any more than she had to him. She was merely trying to assure him that she would not expect more from him than he was willing, or able, to give her. And if a tiny voice said that this would keep her heart from breaking in the event that he ever did stray, well, that was neither here nor there.

"We should begin as we mean to go on," she continued. "We'll be much more comfortable this way."

She said "we," but Caro knew it was her own peace of mind she was trying to protect with her assurances.

"I'm not sure which sentiment I find more insulting." His vehemence surprised her. "That you seem to take it for granted than I am incapable of fidelity, or that you did not include yourself in this proclamation. As if it is a given that you will have no trouble keeping your vows."

Caro had supposed herself to be the only one in danger of losing herself to old emotions, but should she take his outburst as a sign that Val might harbor more tender feelings for her than she'd imagined? It was tempting to think so, but what if she'd read the situation incorrectly and he was merely reacting out of wounded pride? "I wasn't trying to insult you," she said carefully, not quite sure how to smooth over his pique. "I merely wished to let you know that—"

"That you will be happy to look the other way while I take untold numbers of lovers over the course of our marriage," he interrupted. The bitterness in his voice was a stark reminder of the Val she'd seen before their betrothal. Since their first meeting at Effie's house, he'd relaxed around her more and more, returning to the easygoing man she'd once known. His attitude now, however, was like a door closing in her face. "I believe I took your meaning, my lady. There is nothing wrong with my understanding."

She'd hurt him, Caro realized. She was sure of it. In her attempt to guard her own feelings, she'd selfishly hurt his. But before she could formulate an apology, the carriage rolled to a stop.

Not wanting to send him into their wedding breakfast in his current mood, she did what she could to make amends. Before the coachman could open the door, Caro put a hand on Val's arm, hoping he wouldn't rip away from her. "I'm sorry if I hurt you with my rash words, Val. There's no time to explain now, but I can assure you I had no intention of—"

"As you say, we've arrived, Lady Wrackham," he interrupted, though she was relieved to see his posture had relaxed slightly. His refusal to meet her eyes, however, only heightened her anxiety.

"Now," he said, glancing between the carriage window and her, "we mustn't go into our wedding breakfast looking as if we've been arguing."

Considering how her parents would react to such a sight, she nodded her agreement.

"I know hiding your emotions isn't what you're accustomed to"—his smile didn't quite reach his eyes—"but you'll need to at least make a show of happiness when we go in."

You'd be surprised at how good I am at concealing what I feel. But there was no more time.

"Of course I can," she said aloud.

Then, fearing she may have just done irreparable damage to their marriage before it was even an hour old, Caro allowed him to hand her down from the carriage and prepared herself to fool the people she loved most into thinking she was happy.

Val should have known better than to let himself relax. During the ceremony he'd even felt happy, for God's sake. That hadn't happened in well over a year.

He wasn't sure what he had expected from Caro. Nothing in her brave little speech had been wrong. Theirs hadn't begun as a love match. But the affection between them had given him hope they could build a relationship that would stand the test of time.

Of course, he hadn't expected Caro to boldly tell him she didn't give a hang if he broke his vows. Especially not minutes after they'd exchanged them. He'd meant every word of what he'd declared back in St. George's. He would remain faithful to her for the rest of their lives.

He knew he'd reacted badly. But he'd been so insulted—

and unaccountably hurt—by what she said that hiding his reaction had been impossible. Which, truthfully, wasn't like him. Only, he'd been behaving out of character ever since that first meeting at Half Moon Street. Something about Caro prevented him from hiding his emotions behind his usual veneer of civility. Where she was concerned, he was a bundle of uncontrolled chaos.

But given her apology, perhaps her permission to stray was a preemptive protection in the event that he did intend to break their vows? He'd shown her his willingness to defend her from his family, but he hadn't given any indication that this marriage was more than one of convenience.

All these thoughts ran through his mind as, after the formal meal, Val smiled, shook hands, and accepted congratulations from far more guests than he'd thought could possibly have received invitations in the short time between the betrothal announcement and the wedding. He'd underestimated the determination of Lady Lavinia and his mother to make their wedding the event of the season.

"Only married a few scant hours," Langham drawled beside him, "and already grinning like a besotted fool."

If only he knew, Val thought wryly. "I believe one is allowed to smile at one's wedding, Langham," he said. "Indeed, if I did not, I fear my bride would regret her decision to accept my offer most heartily."

"Since your bride has been looking your way," Langham said with a nod in Caro's direction, "as if she believes you will begin rending your clothes and moaning like Hamlet's ghost any moment, I think she may already have done so."

Val jerked his head to where Caro was standing with

Kate and was startled to see that she was indeed watching him with a worried expression. Regretting his harsh words in the carriage, he smiled and hoped she would read in it the apology he intended. The tightness in her shoulders relaxed and she gave him a shy smile in return.

"I've never seen a quarrel made up via a series of glances," Langham said, his voice tinged with awe, "but damned if you haven't just managed it. I suppose it's how some cultures do all their communicating, though I'm not sure I could pull it off myself."

"Is there a reason you're here?" Val retrieved a glass of champagne from a passing footman.

"You invited me," Langham reminded him with a scowl. "And I was gracious enough to accept, though you chose not to ask me to stand up with you. I really think you will come to regret choosing a policeman over a duke when you look back on this day."

"I'm a detective inspector." Eversham had come to stand on Val's other side. "You wouldn't like it if I called you a baronet, would you?"

Langham's eyes widened. "Is that the equivalent?"

Eversham nodded.

The duke didn't seem particularly upset by his faux pas, however. "I had no idea you lot had such an affection for rank. Though I suppose I can respect it. I wouldn't allow a baronet to wax my boots."

"I should be grateful you deem viscounts worthy of friendship." Val raised his glass to the duke. "Though it does make me wonder what you must have thought when I was a mere lord."

"A duke's son is still of greater worth than a baronet,"

Langham said blithely, with no apparent shame at his snobbery. "Why even bother with the title? It's so negligible as to be worthless."

"Except, of course," Eversham said mildly, "for no title at all. Should all us commoners simply walk off the nearest cliff en masse?"

"Of course not." Langham waved his hand generously. "You aren't a commoner. You're a detective inspector. Entirely different matter."

Eversham gave Langham a pained look, but he didn't respond to the duke's words. To Val he said, "Have you told her yet?"

"Told whom what?" Langham interrupted.

"There hasn't been time," Val said, ignoring the duke. He had planned to share the news in the carriage ride from the church to Belgrave Square, but that hadn't been possible, as it turned out.

"I dislike it when people speak in riddles." Langham's tone was impatient. Then, seeing another footman passing with a tray of champagne, he claimed a glass for himself. "Explain yourselves."

"Since you weren't included in this conversation," Val said, not caring if he was being rude, "there's no need."

"I was conversing with you first," the duke reminded Val dryly. "Between the two of us, I'm accustomed to being the one with rag manners. I never expected it of the oh-so-well-behaved Lord Wrackham."

Val almost corrected the other man's assessment of Val's behavior these days, but this was neither the time nor place. "You're still the more ill-mannered of the two of us," he said instead.

"He's right, though," Eversham said with what sounded like reluctance. "I interrupted. The fault lies with me."

The duke raised a brow. "I told you."

Val exhaled in exasperation. He might as well tell Langham. The man was a duke and didn't quite understand that he wasn't entitled to everything he asked for. Teaching him the error of his ways would take more time than days in the year. "Eversham was asking if I'd informed Caro of where we are going on our wedding journey, and I replied that I have not."

"Why haven't you?" Langham asked.

"Yes," Caro said, approaching the men, with Kate at her side. "Why haven't you?"

Val surveyed her. They'd sat next to one another during the formal meal but afterward, as the guests circulated the Hardcastle drawing rooms, halls, and various other public areas that had been opened for the gathering, they'd kept apart. As if by mutual consent, giving each other time to lick their proverbial wounds. Their earlier silent exchange had reassured him, but he knew they'd need to talk further at some point about their quarrel.

She was just as lovely as when he'd laid eyes on her that morning at the church. He'd always thought her a remarkably pretty woman, but knowing it was their wedding day had given her an extra glow of ethereal beauty. Of course, when he'd tried to tell her so, she'd told him not to flatter her. Did she doubt his sincerity? Come to think of it, her rebuff seemed all of a piece with her permission for him to be unfaithful. He understood real forgiveness took time, but he intended for this marriage to be a happy one. He'd have to redouble his efforts to earn her trust. Otherwise, he foresaw years of them treating each other like polite strangers, and he had no wish for that kind of superficial relationship.

In answer to her question, he said, in a teasing tone, "It's meant to be a surprise."

"But you know you'd much rather tell me now, wouldn't you?" she asked him playfully, though her gaze was shadowed.

Thinking to distract her from their earlier rift, he decided it would be best to simply go ahead and tell her. "I thought we'd travel to Brighton," he said, hoping she'd interpret his gesture in the spirit in which it had been intended.

With Eversham having been pulled into another investigation at the Yard and Kate unable to leave the paper, they hadn't been available to travel to Sussex as Val and Caro had hoped. So knowing that his bride had desperately wanted to make the journey, Val had arranged for them to do just that. Given that the seaside was a popular destination for such trips, no one would question the choice.

As he'd hoped, Caro's eyes widened with pleasure—to his surprise, tears. "Oh dear," she said, attempting to regain her composure.

"Here." Val handed her his handkerchief, then ushered her into an antechamber away from curious eyes.

Once they were safely in the room, which looked to be more of a storage closet, Val spoke. "Are you unhappy about Brighton, or…?" He let the question hang in the air, letting her fill in the rest.

Caro gave him a watery smile. "Quite the opposite. It's only that I've been thinking of Effie and Mr. Thorn and though I know they would understand—"

"You felt disloyal for celebrating while they might be in danger, or worse?" Val gave up the fight and pulled her to him.

"You've felt it, too?" she asked, her head pressed against his chest.

She was doubtlessly crushing his neckcloth or wrinkling his lapel, but Val couldn't find it in himself to care. "I was glad to have Eversham stand up with me, but it should have been Frank."

"It should have been your brother," she said softly.

The hand he'd been using to stroke over her back stilled. "I'm not sure about that." He should probably have said the words while looking her in the eye, but he was still too brittle from their earlier argument to risk seeing skepticism there. "I haven't forgotten it was his cruel words that played a part in our broken betrothal. Even if he were still alive, I wouldn't have had him play such a key role in our wedding, Caro. That would be an enormous show of disrespect for you."

He might have been too afraid to look at her, but she had the courage he lacked. Pulling back, she met his gaze with her dark brown one. "Thank you, Val. You have no idea how much it means to me that you'd put me first in such a way. But he was your brother. I was hurt by what he said, but please don't stifle your memories of him for my sake."

"You are far more generous than either he or I deserve." Val smiled. "I'm a lucky man."

Now, however, she looked away. "About what I said before. It truly was not my intention to hurt you."

"Let us agree that it's been a day of many emotions for

both of us and leave it at that, shall we?" He didn't want to argue. And perhaps it would be better if for now, they set aside the hard questions of how they would navigate the treacherous waters of marriage and simply enjoy the inaugural voyage.

With a little sigh, she nodded. "When do we leave for Brighton?" she asked, her voice breathless.

"We'll spend tonight in my townhouse and take the train to the coast in the morning."

The blush that spread over her cheeks reminded him that they hadn't exactly discussed the expectations for the wedding night.

"I am, of course," he said with more calm than he felt, "willing to give you time to adjust to our being married, if you wish to delay the actual consummation. Though to borrow a phrase you used earlier, I think we should 'begin as we mean to go on.'"

"And you mean to go on by bedding me?" To her credit, she didn't back down from the question and met his gaze with a bold one of her own. She wasn't missish, his new bride.

"Frequently," Val responded. In truth, if he had his choice in the matter, he'd have thrown her over his shoulder and carried her off to bed as soon as the ceremony was finished. But there were conventions to uphold. And there would be time enough tonight to show her how much he wanted her. His body tightened as he imagined her wedding coiffure mussed and her lips plump from his kisses. As if she'd guessed the direction of his thoughts, Caro's blush deepened.

"Begetting an heir is, of course, one of the main reasons

I'm required to marry," Val continued, his voice a little rough now. "Though I've no plans to get you so frequently with child that you spend the next twenty years wishing me to go to the devil. You will find me quite willing to do what I can to prevent conception after we've got an heir and a spare in the nursery."

"We should perhaps have discussed this before the wedding," Caro said wryly. "Not that I didn't already know the expectations. Or that the notion of frequent childbirth would have changed anything about our need to marry. It just occurred to me that so many conversations like this one—of true import—don't happen until the proverbial horse has gotten out."

"Then let us agree to make an effort to have these conversations while the horse is still in the barn," Val said with amusement. Leave it to Caro to put such a delicate matter in such a matter-of-fact way.

"Agreed. And to answer your question"—she turned red again—"I don't wish to wait."

She leaned into him and he brought his forehead to hers. "Let us begin as we mean to go on," she said.

Tenderness blended with relief as he took her lips.

He couldn't wait for their first adventure as man and wife.

Chapter Eighteen

When the carriage rolled to a stop before Val's town-house, Caro was struck with a rare feeling of nervousness. She'd been here only a few days ago, but she hadn't viewed it with any kind of proprietary air, though they'd been betrothed at the time.

It occurred to her that she was about to enter her new home, the first in which she would preside as mistress.

Grateful for Val's strong arm beneath her hand as he guided her up the steps, she looked up to see his butler—now her butler, too—Foyle, standing with solemn dignity at the open door.

Bowing deeply, the handsome man of middle years smiled far more cheerily than on her previous visit. "Lord Wrackham, Lady Wrackham, may I offer my congratulations on your wedding." It was clear from the way he beamed at Val that he held his master in some affection.

To Caro he said, "Welcome to your new home, my lady. I hope you will be happy here."

At the man's heartfelt words, Caro felt a pang of gratitude. He had no need to be so kind. Indeed, knowing that servants could enforce the rules of social hierarchy as strictly as, or even worse than, their employers, she'd feared the response of Val's servants. They had every right to expect a noble mistress and might scorn her.

It was a relief that Foyle, at least, welcomed her.

Once they entered the house, an even more heartening sight greeted her. Every servant in Val's employ, from groom to kitchen maid, stood in parallel lines leading up to the main staircase.

The housekeeper, Mrs. Oakes, dipped into a curtsy. "Congratulations, my lord, my lady. On behalf of the staff of Wrackham House, it's my pleasure to welcome you to your new home."

It took every ounce of self-control Caro possessed to maintain her calm while she surveyed the array of people before them. She no doubt clung more tightly than necessary to Val's arm as one by one, Mrs. Oakes introduced each of the twenty-five servants. Knowing how much she had valued being treated as an individual when she was at school, Caro made sure to repeat each name as it was given to her and ask each person a question that would make them feel valued. It may not be the way of the aristocracy—once, she had overheard the daughter of a marquess say staff were barely people—but Caro was determined to treat them as she would wish to be treated.

At the end of the line, there was only the cook, Mrs. Stevenson, and the two kitchen maids flanking her.

"My lady," the ruddy-faced woman said breathlessly, "I cannot tell ye how honored we are t'have ye here. I've read every one of yer books, and the recipe for trifle in volume three of *Hardcastle's Guide to English Cookery* is one of the master's favorites."

Caro stared stunned at the beaming woman. Was ever there a more welcome compliment than to have one's own cook praise your recipes?

Val's eyes widened—apparently he hadn't known the recipe was one of Caro's. "She's telling the truth." He laughed. "That's one of my favorite puddings."

She'd stepped out of the carriage afraid she would muck matters up with her lack of aristocratic origins, but instead, she had been presented with a houseful clearly intent on welcoming their beloved master's new bride. To finish matters off like a gorgeous ripe strawberry atop a perfectly glazed sponge, here was the cook telling her that her new husband favored a recipe she'd developed years before they'd even met.

"Mrs. Stevenson, I cannot tell you how delighted I am to hear you've found my books useful," she said, trying to ignore the effervescent lightness in her chest. "That his lordship counts my trifle among his favorite desserts, however, is simply beyond anything I'd imagined."

"Oh, he's quite fond of several recipes from all three volumes," the cook assured her, "but he's got a sweet tooth, does the master, and never turns down a pudding."

This was the first Caro had heard of Val favoring any sort of food, she thought, giving him a sidelong look. Clearly, there were many things they still had to learn about one another.

"I hope you won't mind if I venture into the kitchen from time to time to try out new recipes, Mrs. Stevenson," Caro said to the still-smiling cook. Given how the rest of the servants were watching them in amazement, she suspected that the mobcapped woman was not generally known for her merry disposition. "I haven't written any new cook-books in some time, but perhaps a home of my own will inspire me to develop some new ideas for publication."

"I would be delighted, my lady." Mrs. Stevenson curt-sied. Then, emphasizing the sentiment, she said, "It will be a *pleasure*, my lady. A right pleasure."

Mrs. Oakes stepped forward then and informed them that Caro's maid was waiting upstairs. "And your cat has settled into your rooms, my lady, but if you wish him to stay in the kitchen, we can have him moved."

Val turned to Caroline with surprise and, if she didn't mistake his expression, some alarm. "I thought Ludwig was staying with Miss Deaver until our return from Brighton."

"So did I." Caro frowned. "How did he arrive here, Mrs. Oakes?"

"Miss Deaver brought him this afternoon," the house-keeper said. "She said that she was called away on family business and would be unable to care for him as you'd agreed."

Caro had never heard Flora speak of her family before. In truth, she'd assumed the girl to be an orphan, though she realized now that had been a foolish thought. But the fact that she'd come in person to deliver Ludwig eased her mind. Given that both Effie and Mr. Thorn were missing, she had no wish to lose track of Flora as well. Besides, she had doubtlessly given more information to Kate, who was, after all, her employer.

"Thank you for letting me know, Mrs. Oakes," she told the housekeeper. "Ludwig can remain in my chamber for the time being. I'll have to arrange something else for him for the duration of our journey."

"I wonder what took Flora away," Caro said as she and Val made their way up the main staircase. "It's not like her to break a commitment."

"I have no idea." Val rested his hand on Caro's back as they climbed. "But what a delight that we have extra time with Ludwig to look forward to."

There was something about his tone that made Caro doubt Val's sincerity. It would seem that she wasn't the only one who had changes to become accustomed to.

Clearly, Val thought as he watched Caro pull away from him and hurry ahead to greet her infernal cat, he would need to find some way of diverting his feline nemesis for at least long enough to consummate the marriage. That Miss Deaver had been called away on this of all days was a misfortune of catastrophic proportions.

Oh God. He was so far gone he was punning. *Cat*as-trophic proportions, indeed.

Not quite as amusing was their argument earlier, he thought as he followed at a more sedate pace, giving Caro time to greet the hell-born Ludwig.

Caro might not be ready to trust him fully yet, but he was intent on showing her that she had nothing to fear from him. His outsized response to her seeming indifference at him taking a mistress might have prodded him into realizing that he was well on his way to being half in love with her again already, but he wasn't ready to tell her so. Both of them, it would seem, were reluctant to risk their hearts so soon after reaching their uneasy truce.

But if they were to make a success of this marriage—however hastily contracted—they would need to surrender some control to one another. Otherwise, they would be stuck at arm's length for the rest of their lives.

That she'd agreed that they should sleep together had come as a relief. The thought of waiting—which he'd been prepared to do so if she'd asked it of him—had made him want to weep. Since their encounter after the fracas at the theatre—hell, since their aborted betrothal four years ago—he'd been desperate for her. He'd never been so consumed with need for a woman. How soft would her skin feel against his tongue? What sounds would she make when he touched her? If he were to be honest with himself, he'd spent years wondering what they'd be like together.

Whatever reservations he had about how successfully they would manage to make a life together, about their compatibility in bed he had no doubts.

When he reached her new bedchamber, which he'd had the good sense to have refurbished before taking over the house after Cynthia had left for her parents' home, he crossed his arms and leaned against the doorframe, watching her with a mixture of desire and affection.

For all that he genuinely believed the cat would stab him to death in his sleep if it could but hold a knife, it was hard not to smile when Caro cooed over the little monster.

Said monster was currently fast asleep on the bed. Caro had climbed up to snuggle against the lucky cat. Though from Val's vantage point, he had a stellar view of her first-class bottom, so he was not entirely displeased.

"My poor boy." She smoothed a hand over the cat's angular head. "You've been here all alone, haven't you?"

From what Val could tell, the cat wasn't in need of soothing, but he knew better than to come between a woman and her cat.

A sturdy redhead, who Val assumed was Caro's maid, came out of the dressing room then. "He's fine, milady." She shook her head ruefully. "Spent some time sniffing every last corner of your rooms, then came in here and jumped up on the bed and fell fast asleep."

"He can be very sensitive," Caro told Val. The cat's brown ears twitched at the sound of her voice. "But since he's traveled with me, I suppose he's more adaptable than other cats to new environments."

"That's good, I suppose." But if Ludwig had responded positively to the sound of his mistress's voice, his response to Val's was quite the opposite. Lifting his head, the cat looked directly at him and pointedly hissed.

"He most definitely hates me." He narrowed his eyes at the cat, who proceeded to lick his paw, as if to show he was no longer interested in Val in the least. But Val knew better. Their one meeting prior to this, at Val's house in the Lake District years ago, had been just as fractious.

"Ludwig, that's not nice," Caro chided the cat. "He doesn't hate you," she said to Val. "He barely even knows you."

While it was true that Caro had obtained her feline

companion after the dissolution of their first betrothal, Val had little doubt that even had he and Ludwig years to become better acquainted, they would still only very barely tolerate one another.

Val gave the cat a narrow-eyed glare. "Still, he definitely wants me dead."

Rising from the bed, Caro came toward him and slipped her arms around his neck. Her maid had discreetly disappeared into the dressing room. "I hope you aren't jealous of a cat, Valentine. Because that would seem very foolish indeed."

"Of course I'm not," he lied. "It's not as if he's seen you naked and slept with you for years."

She giggled. "I don't think it's quite the same."

"I should hope not." He pulled her against him, kissing her hard. "Now, I'll leave you to rest for the afternoon and settle in a little. We'll have supper in my room, I think. I don't wish to encroach on his majesty's territory."

"He'll come around," Caro assured him, leaning her head against his chest.

"He'll have to." Val shrugged. "I'm not going anywhere."

They stood together like that for a few moments. Despite Caro's seeming ease at touching him, he hadn't missed her fine tremor when his arms came around her. She had faced so many obstacles that would leave lesser women in tears, but this unexpected intimacy was what gave her pause.

He was humbled that despite her fear and mistrust, she was willing to take this leap of faith with him. He vowed then and there to do his damndest to appreciate that precious gift.

"I don't suppose you'd care to nap…together?" Caro

asked softly, keeping her head down, showing a shyness he'd never seen from her before. He was more charmed than he'd admit by this new side of his normally bold wife.

And he couldn't help but wonder. Did she mean "nap" or *nap*?

He supposed he was about to find out.

"I'd be delighted."

Chapter Nineteen

A drowsy feeling of well-being surrounded Caro like a cocoon.

The pillow beneath her cheek was deliciously warm and smelled enticingly of bergamot and lime. The scent made her insides tingle and her hands clench.

Val, her mind whispered.

Her eyes flew open in alarm, and she struggled to sit up.

Then, almost as quickly, she remembered the events of the day and collapsed onto his chest.

"Easy," his deep voice rumbled beneath her ear. "I thought you were going to sleep for days."

She yawned. "Preparing for a wedding is hard work."

"Harder than working in a hot kitchen testing recipes?" he asked wryly. "Or writing a celebrated newspaper column?"

She laughed. "Since you've also written books and for the paper, I think you should know the answer to that."

"But I haven't planned a wedding," he countered, stroking a hand down her back.

They'd both removed their shoes and stockings. Val had taken off his coat, and Caro had changed into a dressing gown because lying down would have been impossible in her corset, petticoat, and skirt. As a result, they were as close to undressed as they'd ever been in one another's company.

She stared at the canopy above her head. "It wasn't so much more difficult as more rushed. Fortunately, I had servants to help with packing my belongings, and Mama and Kate did a great deal as well. So perhaps it wasn't so much the planning that fatigued me as anxiety."

He looked down at her with a smile. "I was nervous as well."

His admission startled her. "You were? I didn't realize men suffered from wedding-related nerves." It had never occurred to her that men would feel any sort of negative emotions about their nuptials. "What is there to be nervous about? You can maintain your life just as it was before the ceremony if you wish. You needn't give up any ownership of your property. You continue to live in your own house, sleep in your own bed. Nothing really needs to change for you."

She considered mentioning that if he had a mistress, he could keep her as well, but considering their earlier argument, she thought it best to keep that thought to herself. And if she were honest, despite her earlier assurances, she was fairly certain she'd claw out the other woman's eyes if she ever learned her existence was anything more than hypothetical.

"Men have every advantage in marriage," she finished. "Women have none."

"You really dislike my sex, don't you?" he asked with an uncomfortable laugh.

"Your sex," she emphasized. "Not you. If I didn't like you, I would never have agreed to marry you. Or rather, I would have been much less willing. If my father had been threatened with ruin, I very likely would have married even someone as loathsome as Lord Tate—though thankfully he is already wed, so that would not have been a possibility."

"I don't like to think of you married to anyone else," Val said roughly, pulling her onto his chest again. "You're mine now."

His possessiveness sent a thrill of pleasure through her. As much as Caro valued her independence, on some level, she'd always longed to feel as if she belonged to someone. And, conversely, to have someone belong to her. For better or worse, as their vows said, they were each other's now. The thought was comforting but also a little terrifying.

Turning the subject back to a less alarming topic, she asked, "But you said you were nervous. Why?"

"Well," he said, stroking a hand down her arm, "contrary to what you think, I cannot maintain my life just as it's always been. Nor would I wish to. If you were hoping for the sort of husband who will merely say hello in the breakfast room and only occasionally come to your bed, you are to be sorely disappointed."

"No, of course not," Caro responded, unable to stop the little flip in her stomach at the mention of bed. "I don't wish us to have that sort of marriage either."

He looked as if he'd say more, but then he shook his head a little, as if thinking better of it. "Just rest assured that I'm not entirely undaunted by our new situation."

"I didn't say that," she protested, "but—"

"But, yes, agreed. I won't need to make as many adjustments as you will," he finished. "That's evident just in the fact that you've had to move your belongings into my home instead of the other way round."

"I somehow do not think you would be comfortable living under the same roof with my mother." Caro laughed.

She suspected his shudder was not entirely feigned.

"But," she argued, stroking a finger down his chest, "there are certain advantages for married ladies."

She looked up at him through her lashes, watching the way the evening light limned the contours of his nearly too-handsome features. It was almost fantastical to think she was here in a bed at long last with the man who'd first awakened her to the possibilities of passion all those years ago. They'd never tasted it, of course, but her heart whispered, *Better late than never.*

She raised her hand to trace the curve of his lip with her finger.

His eyes grew heavy with what she instinctively knew was desire. And when she stroked his lip again, he opened his mouth to gently bite her finger.

She'd barely gasped at the contact when he shifted. She went from reclining on his chest to lying on her back with all his muscled hardness braced over her.

"Perhaps you'd better tell me about these advantages." His voice was husky. He leaned down and kissed her with exquisite slowness.

When he moved away, she took his face in her hands and pulled him back down to her. Just as it had been that night in the carriage, the connection between them was hot as the flame in a gas lamp. She'd never felt anything as delicious as the touch of his tongue. The heat of his body, everywhere he touched, every caress, set off a series of reactions that reverberated from the surface of her skin to deep inside where need was building.

Still kissing her, Val used one hand to keep himself from crushing her with his weight and slipped the other past where her dressing gown gaped open. When his hand cupped the fullness of her breast, Caroline gasped against his mouth.

In between kisses, he said, "If there's anything I do, any touch you dislike, you have only to tell me and I will stop."

She could not imagine him doing anything that she wouldn't enjoy, but she knew that not all men would even bother with such concerns, let alone say them once they were married and had no need for consent according to the law.

Oddly, his words made the gravity of their actions seem even more immediate. "Yes," she said softly. "I will tell you."

He gave her one last kiss before he pulled away from her, stood by the side of the bed, and began removing his clothes.

"What are you doing?" Caro shrieked, feeling disappointingly like a shrinking virgin but unable to stifle her surprise. She hastily covered her eyes before he got to his trousers.

"Darling," he said wryly, "I can keep my trousers on if you wish, but I can assure you it's much more comfortable if they're off."

"I know that," she said, peeking through her fingers. "I just thought—"

She felt the bed dip with his weight as he climbed back on. Fortunately, they'd turned the bedclothes down earlier, so her modesty was saved when he used them to cover himself.

"There," he said with a solemnity that sounded suspiciously as if he was trying not to laugh, "your maidenly blushes are saved."

"I've never blushed a day in my life," Caroline lied. "I've had your tongue in my mouth on multiple occasions. I've seen the Elgin Marbles many times. In fact, I—"

He cut her off with a kiss and pulled her against him beneath the covers. "You're blushing right now," he murmured against her lips. "In fact, let's see how far down it goes."

He helped her out of her dressing gown before tossing it onto the floor.

Adopting a serious expression, he inspected her skin from her neck down to the tops of her breasts. "Oh yes, it's definitely spreading. I'd better experiment and see if stimulus changes things."

The touch of his tongue, and then his mouth on her breast, arrested her laughter. The contact sent a jolt of sensation down to that place at her center where she was suddenly restless with the need to be touched.

As if he'd heard her thoughts, Val stroked a hand down over her abdomen, settling it there for a moment. His mouth tugged on her nipple and her hips shifted restlessly. With his free hand, he caressed her other breast, and only when she moaned did he relent and move the hand at her pubis to dip down over the spot that ached. He slicked a finger into the moisture there and Caro's hips lifted again.

He teased and stroked her until her body was vibrating with need, and when he pressed into her with first one finger, then another, she gasped at the flash of pleasure it sent through her. "More," she demanded, though she wasn't sure what more she wanted. Only that she needed it.

When he began kissing his way down her body, she almost wept. "What are you doing?"

She felt the warm puff of his breath against her skin. "I'm trying to give you what you asked for, dear wife. Trust me."

But it was difficult to do so when her body was aching with unfulfilled passion.

He slid his arms beneath her legs and braced her knees over his shoulders. Then she recalled an illustration she'd seen once in a book the girls had passed around at school. Her eyes widened. "Oh! Is that something that people do outside of books?"

She gasped at the sensation of his soft huff of laughter against her mons.

"It's something the people in this bed can do if you like it," he said, kissing her on the inner thigh.

His hot breath on her most intimate parts felt odd, yet utterly intoxicating, and when she felt his tongue on the sensitive bud at the heart of her, she wasn't too shy to thread her hands into his hair and clasp him to her.

Over and over again he stroked his tongue there and

soon used his fingers to press into that empty space that longed to be filled. Alternating between his tongue and his fingers, he brought her to the edge of bliss more than once, then finally, gloriously, he kept going until, like a shooting star, she splintered into a million tiny pieces and slowly fell back to earth.

Chapter Twenty

While Caro came back down to earth, Val tried to get himself under control. He'd never felt this kind of overwhelming desire. Perhaps it was from the duration of his longing for her, or simply the fact that she was—at long last—his wife. Whatever the reason, he needed her now.

"What if we didn't wait until tonight?" he asked, sliding skin on skin up her body until his thighs were cradled between hers. If she wanted to wait, he would simply have to douse his entire body in a cold bath. It would be unpleasant, but he could endure it for her sake.

Her eyes were still drowsy with the aftermath of her pleasure, but at his words, they widened. "I thought we'd already decided not to wait." She glanced down to where his hardness nudged against her center. "In fact," she said on a groan, "I think it would be best if we didn't." She bent her knees, which lifted her softness to stroke against him.

Bracing on one arm, Val used his other to take himself in hand. "There may be pain," he said tersely. "But I'll try my best to make it as brief as possible."

"I know you will." She leaned up to kiss him. "I trust you."

He knew it wasn't an easy admission for his proud wife to make, but Val was too overwhelmed with emotion to say so. He let his kiss tell her what his words could not, and with one sure thrust, he pressed into her. He felt her gasp against his shoulder where she gripped him tightly, and he regretted causing her pain. Then pulling back, he felt her body close around him, as if to keep him within her. Closing his eyes against the pleasure, he kept going until he was almost to the edge, then thrust back in again, this time seating himself fully inside her body.

"All right?" he gritted out, every muscle in his body tight in an effort to keep from pounding into her.

"Yes," she said in a strained voice. "It's uncomfortable but not painful exactly."

"Too uncomfortable to continue?" he asked carefully. He would stop if she needed him to.

She thrust up her hips experimentally. "Oh, no, please continue," she said a little breathlessly.

That was all the encouragement he needed to begin a series of steady strokes that soon had her moving against him in a rhythm as old as time. It wasn't his first sexual experience, of course, but it was his first time making love to Caro, and with every touch, every stroke, his body knew this was different. He'd known all those years ago it would be good between them, but what he hadn't realized was just how holding, touching, loving her like this, would fill his heart.

He could feel her breathing becoming erratic as her hips began to thrust up with more force. With one hand he reached down to caress the bud of her pleasure and was rewarded by a soft cry as Caro flew over the edge and lost herself in the aether.

With a curse, Val let himself go, pushing into her again and again and again, until he felt the telltale tingle at the base of his spine that signaled his impending climax. With one last thrust, he gave a sharp cry and hurtled into nothingness, pouring himself into her.

When he came back to himself, he was ashamed to realize he'd collapsed on top of her.

"I'm sorry," he said, scrambling to move over.

But Caro, who'd been holding him close, clung tighter. "Don't go yet," she said softly. "I like it. The weight of you lying on me."

Puzzled, he let himself relax again. "Far be it for me to contradict a lady."

"It's pleasing to me." She laughed. "It's…it's primitive maybe. Which probably makes me every sort of hypocrite, considering how much I rail against women's roles."

"Not necessarily." He cushioned his head against her breast. "This is simply what you like. Instinctively maybe. There can't be anything wrong with instinct, can there?" He realized as he spoke that perhaps his words could apply to himself as well as Caro. Ever since they'd met again, he'd dismissed his chaotic emotions as base impulses, but really, hadn't he just been acting on instinct? Where Caro was concerned, at least, it seemed he was most often led by his heart. And that wasn't anything to feel shame over. No more than the way she liked the weight of his body on hers.

His whole life he'd been taught to suppress his own impulses. Whether holding his temper or being polite to people he found insufferable, or even obeying his father in choosing a bride not based on his own preferences but what society demanded of him.

But he was learning his feelings for Caro were true. And if that was true, then surely he could trust his instincts elsewhere. The revelation left him a little awed.

"Maybe," Caro agreed, unaware of his thoughts. "So long as it doesn't infringe upon someone else's freedom, I suppose it's allowable."

He felt her hand stroke over his back and downward, his eyes growing heavy.

"We had our wedding night in the evening." She giggled.

Val glanced up at her. "You don't mind, do you?"

"Not at all," she said with a smile in her voice. "I don't know why I'd always imagined relations would be in the dead of night, long after everyone in the world was fast asleep. I suppose it can be done during the daylight as well? Fascinating!"

He smiled sleepily at her amazement. Wait until he showed her relations could be had in any room of the house—or out of doors, even!

"What are you laughing at?" she asked suspiciously. "Are you laughing at me? I was a perfect innocent, wasn't I? It's quite lowering, really."

He pushed up so he could see her better. "I'm definitely not laughing at you. You were perfect." He punctuated his words with a kiss. "I couldn't have asked for a sweeter wedding day. Thank you."

She blushed, and Val felt himself rising to the occasion again. His body, however, could wait, he thought as he shifted to lie at her side. They had all the time in the world, and she would be sore.

Moving to press her head onto his shoulder. "Thank you." She kissed his chin. "I know this wasn't what either of us was looking for, but I will try to be a good wife to you."

His heart swelled with affection at her words, though he had to resist correcting her. In truth, this was exactly what he'd been looking for. If he hadn't already been half in love with her, that artless confession would have done it. Then she yawned, utterly adorable, and he feared he'd fallen even further.

"Come," he said, pulling the bedclothes up over them, "let's get a bit of rest before supper."

But even before he'd finished his words, she had closed her eyes and curled up against him.

Suddenly exhausted himself, Val wrapped an arm around her and slept.

The next morning, after several reminders from Caro that her maid should send word immediately if Ludwig needed her for any reason, the newlyweds set out to the train station and boarded a private car for their trip to Brighton.

"You know he'll be fine." Val patted her hand as they sat together near the window. "My household hasn't lost a cat yet."

"You must think me a ninny," she said ruefully. Showing Val just how much she doted on Ludwig left her feeling vulnerable. Then again, the cat's friendship had been a balm to her ever since she'd found him, a scrawny kitten, scrounging in the mews behind her parents' Belgrave Square mansion not long after she'd ended their first engagement.

"I don't think you a ninny at all," he assured her. "There are any number of peers of the realm who treat their hunting dogs better than their own children. At least you aren't pampering Ludwig in the hopes he'll help you kill other defenseless animals."

"I doubt he could bestir himself to do any sort of work." Caro laughed. "He's very much a gentleman of leisure."

That Val held such views wasn't a surprise, given that his brother had died while taking a risky jump on a hunt. Fox hunting, and indeed, any number of sports favored by the aristocracy, had always struck her as particularly barbaric. In yet another way, she saw Val was out of step with his peers.

He was a good man. And the more she came to know him—not just the face he showed the rest of the world—the more she was realizing he *was* worthy of her trust. They'd lingered in bed that morning for as long as possible before the train departure time had forced them to rise and dress for the journey.

Caroline had known Val would be an attentive lover. He approached everything with a certain degree of single-minded focus, and it stood to reason that in this he would be no different. But she'd found herself undone by the tenderness with which he'd brought her to completion again and again after that first admittedly rushed coupling. She'd almost felt as if he'd been saving all his passion for her over the years they'd been apart.

She acknowledged now that the attempts she'd made to put distance between them—feeble though they had been—had failed miserably when faced with the intimacy of the marriage bed. She'd had no idea just how difficult it would be to keep herself emotionally removed from him when he was making love to her. Hiding herself from him was impossible while they were as close as two people could be. In those moments, their disparate upbringings and past conflicts had seemed unimportant.

Loving him would be so easy. She just had to let herself fall.

But soon enough she had been reminded that the intimacy was an illusion. From the deference of the servants to the Wrackham crest on the door of their carriage, there were countless reminders that in marrying her, Val had lifted her out of the middle class, into which she'd been born, and into the aristocracy.

Only, she was no longer caught up in her hurt and betrayal over how Val and his family had treated her. He'd done so much to prove to her that he was no longer the same man who had stood by while his brother insulted her. His ultimatum to his father and constant, calm reassurances of his loyalty to her had gone a long way to earning her trust again.

All these thoughts assailed her as she sat beside him in the sumptuously furnished private train carriage.

"Penny for your thoughts?" said the man in question.

"You can nap if you like. We've got a bit longer before our arrival."

"You needn't look so smug." Caro mock scowled at him. "Especially considering you're the reason for my fatigue."

"I didn't want to say anything." Val shrugged modestly. "I don't like to boast."

She surveyed him with a raised brow. "Ah, yes. Your prodigious skills in the bedroom are second only to your legendary modesty."

"I'm so pleased you noticed." He reached down to take her hand—palm to palm, fingers entwined—in his. "I do believe I surpassed myself last night."

"I dare not pay you another compliment"—Caro's smile belied her mournful tone—"lest we are crushed under the weight of your conceit."

She felt strangely proud at his shout of laughter.

They sat in companionable silence before the need to be busy prompted her to open the small bag she'd kept beside her for the journey. She extracted a small notebook and pencil.

"We can use this time to prepare for the visit to the Hen and Hound." She smoothed the blank page before her.

"Unlike your cat, you, my dear, are always working," Val said with affection. "I don't suppose you have the rest of the letters between Miss Warrington and Mary Killeen?"

Wordlessly, she plucked the bundle of letters from the bag and handed them to him.

"Excellent." He opened and set about arranging them—chronologically, she saw, looking over.

He scanned the first one. "I hadn't had a chance to

read these since Eversham and I found them. It appears that Miss Killeen was a servant in the Reverend and Mrs. Warrington's household. But she seems reluctant to speak of the matter." He shuffled through the papers. "It took five letters for her to divulge that Miss Warrington was retrieved from the Hen and Hound."

Caro nodded and began writing the details in her notebook. "Perhaps the need for secrecy was impressed upon her by Effie's adopted parents. I suppose discretion is one of the conditions of arrangements like this. If Mary Killeen knew the identity of the family who gave Effie away, she may have been too afraid to disclose such information by letter."

"They should be able to tell us at the inn which are the larger properties in the surrounding area. Hopefully one of the families thereabouts will correspond with one of the names on Miss Deaver's list," Val said.

"I still don't quite understand." Caro tapped her chin with the pencil. "Why would it be so important for her birth family to stop Effie from learning about her origins? It's not as if she'd be entitled to any entailed properties if she's legitimate—and if she's legitimate, why send her away at all? If her birth is illegitimate—a strong possibility, given the need to hide her—then she has no claim on any unentailed estate or moneys unless there was a specific bequest to her."

A sudden fear ran through her at the thought of how far they still were from understanding what had happened to Effie and why. "We must find her, Val. I'm beginning to wonder if we ever will."

"It's been a relatively short time since she'd gone

missing." Val wrapped an arm around her. "And if Eversham learns something while we're in Brighton, Kate has promised to send word."

Despite their efforts, neither Kate nor Eversham had discovered any likely candidates for Effie's relative among the list of families Flora had compiled for them. Which meant that this trip to Brighton was their best chance at learning who Effie's birth parents had been.

"You're right. I just want to know where they are." Caro leaned her head against his shoulder. "She seemed so happy when last I saw her. She was so excited for the opening of her new play. And only a few days later she was gone."

"We will find them," Val assured her. "Don't give up your optimism just yet."

"I haven't. But I fear that if this trip doesn't produce results, they may be lost to us forever."

Chapter Twenty-One

They checked into their room at the hotel, which, to Caro's delight, overlooked the sea. It was still early enough in the day that Val was able to hire a carriage to take them to the village of Laycock.

The Hen and Hound was a bustling country inn with hiring stables next door, dashing any hopes that their arrival would go unnoticed.

Thankfully their attire marked them as quality, and Caro and Val were shown to a private parlor almost immediately. When Val requested a word with the owner, the serving maid looked curious but left at once to relay the request.

"I hadn't expected such a thriving business." Caro took a sip of the tea she'd requested, while Val sampled the local beer. "I'd imagined an out-of-the-way place where one might expect havey-cavey exchanges of babies to occur. Not a busy establishment where hundreds of travelers must pass by a day."

"Reality so rarely turns out to be as exciting as one's imagination." Val stretched his long legs out before him and took a drink of his own beverage. "But it stands to reason that if one were hoping to escape notice, the better alternative would be someplace like this. It's difficult to take note of something out of the ordinary when everything is constantly changing."

"That makes sense," Caro said, nodding. She only hoped that this trip would move them closer to learning what had happened to Effie and Mr. Thorn. Despite knowing that Kate and Eversham were still working on the case back in London, she couldn't help but feel a bit guilty at leaving them for a wedding trip. Even if by mutual agreement, she and Val had made it an investigative one. Finding a solid lead would go a long way toward assuaging her conscience. "Only someone watching closely would know whether the person who arrived with an infant was the same who left with one."

A brisk knock heralded the opening of the parlor door and the arrival of the inn's owner.

"You asked to speak with me, Lord and Lady Wrackham?" asked a pretty Black woman wearing a serviceable blue gown covered with a pristine white apron. "I'm Mrs. Trelawney and this is my inn."

Caro and Val nodded their greetings and invited her to sit down with them, but she declined. "If I sit, I won't want to get up again, and I've too much to do with luncheon coming up. How can I help?"

Quickly, Caro explained what they'd learned from Mary Killeen's letter about infant Effie being given to the Warringtons there some twenty years ago. "But I fear you would have been far too young then to have known the family."

Mrs. Trelawney laughed. "I don't know whether to be insulted or to thank you, milady. I was here twenty years ago, but my husband and I had only just taken over the inn. He was a navy man and brought me back with him from Trinidad. When he died, I became the owner."

"That must have been a large undertaking," Val said, his voice sympathetic. "How long had you been married by then?"

"Over a decade," Mrs. Trelawney said sadly. "But I knew enough about the business by then to know what to do. And the crowd you see now is far more than we had twenty years ago. Which is why I do recall the day the Reverend and Mrs. Warrington took in an infant."

"You do?" Caro asked, sitting up straighter. She'd barely hoped such a memory was possible.

"Indeed, milady," said the innkeeper. "I remember because there was a dustup between the woman who brought the child and the lord who owns the largest property hereabouts. My husband and two of our men had to physically remove him from the premises."

"That must have been difficult," Val remarked. "It isn't easy to go against a peer even when he's in the wrong. Your husband must have been sure of himself."

"Lord Croyden was so deep in his cups that I don't think he remembered afterward what had happened." Mrs. Trelawney laughed.

Croyden was one of the names from the list Flora had compiled—Caro's eyes flew to Val's. His gaze told her that his interest was just as piqued as hers by Mrs. Trelawney's words. At last, they'd found a lead.

"And if my husband hadn't done so, the earl might have harmed the child," the woman continued. "He claimed the babe was his and that the woman who'd given her to the Warringtons had stolen her."

"Stolen her how?" Caro asked.

"I don't know what he meant, milady. He wasn't married at the time, as far as we knew. My husband and I thought that the poor thing must be the product of an affair."

"Was the woman who brought the child that day her mother?"

"She seemed too old." Mrs. Trelawney frowned. "I got the impression that she was a relation of the child's mother. But where she is or whether she's even still alive, I do not know."

The innkeeper shook her head. "I haven't thought about that day for almost twenty years. What makes you come here asking questions all these years later?" Then her eyes lit up. "Never say you were that babe, milady!"

Before Caro could correct her, Mrs. Trelawney said enthusiastically, "There's a rumor—though, of course, I have no way to know if it's true—that his lordship left a sizeable bequest to any natural children of his. Perhaps you can make a claim."

Caro and Val exchanged a look, though Caro tried not to show any reaction to that bit of information.

"No," she said. "We believe a dear friend of ours might be that child, however. Unfortunately, she's gone missing. We found a note among her things where she was looking into her parentage after being taken in by the Warringtons all those years ago, and we thought perhaps coming here might lead us to finding her."

"The poor lady," Mrs. Trelawney said softly. "I had hoped she went on to live a happy life."

"Does Lord Croyden still live in this area?" Val's voice was deceptively casual; then turning to Caro, he added, "If so, perhaps we can pay a call on him, my dear."

Their hostess shook her head. "I'm afraid the old earl died around the same time as my poor husband. The new earl is there, of course, but I doubt he'd know anything about the matter. He's a cold one, he is. And he won't thank you for bringing up his predecessor. He's always on about how the former earl didn't act like a man of his station should. Too quick to mix with the lower classes and didn't hold himself aloof enough from those beneath him. If you ask me, he's just jealous because he's not as well-liked as the other man was."

He sounded just the sort who would wish to keep any kinship between himself and an actress from becoming public, Caro thought.

"If that's the case, then I understand why you would think he wouldn't be of much help," Val was saying to Mrs. Trelawney. "I daresay he wishes to erase the fact that his father ever held the title at all."

"Oh, the old earl was his uncle," Mrs. Trelawney corrected. "When the new Lord Croyden inherited the title, he came to the estate and cleared out everyone who worked there. Some had been employed by the earldom for generations. It isn't even the family's primary residence, but his lordship was convinced everyone was loyal to the old earl. It was a cruel thing he did, make no mistake. I was able to give as many of them a job here and at the carriage yard as I could. When people depend on you for their livelihood, it's not right to turn them out for no reason other than pure meanness."

She shook her head in disgust. "I suspect the only reason he stays at Croyden House at all is because he'd got workmen making improvements to the family's primary residence in Kent. Rumor has it that he's all but torn down Croyden Keep and is having it rebuilt with all sorts of improvements. That must have cost him a few farthings. I wonder he hasn't tried to sell Croyden House to pay for it, but I suppose he doesn't want to admit he needs the blunt."

"Now, I really must go," the innkeeper said. "I hope I was able to help you?"

"You were." Caro said as she and Val rose. "Very much so. We can't thank you enough."

"I don't like to think of that poor young woman missing," Mrs. Trelawney said with a troubled look. "I hope you're able to find her safe."

The newlyweds walked back out to the main entrance of the inn where vehicles were lining up to deposit travelers at the door. As they stepped outside, one such carriage, highly polished and exquisitely laid out, was rolling away toward the road. Caro couldn't be sure from this distance, but she thought there was a fox on the insignia on its left side.

"Pardon me," she said to an ostler standing nearby. "Do you know to whom that carriage belongs? I'm sure I know the owner but I can't think of his name."

"That's Lord Croyden's carriage, milady." The man

frowned. "He's off to London for the season. But if you don't mind my saying so, I shouldn't think a nice lady like yourself would have much use for him."

This final connection felt like opening a window that had been long sealed shut.

Val soon had them back in the carriage, and they were on their way.

Inside, Val turned to Caro. "We've found him. Croyden must be the relative Miss Warrington was searching for. The man who wrote to her. He's not a second son, but he's well-known for his haranguing speeches in the Lords."

Unable to contain her agitation, she grabbed his hand, clinging to it tightly. "Thank you for arranging this trip. I will never forget it."

Her apologetic tone must have alerted him to her intent.

"We're returning to London today, aren't we?" Val gave an exaggerated sigh.

"Do not pretend that you aren't just as eager as I am to question Lord Croyden, for I will not believe you."

"Fine." Val fiddled with the dangling ribbon of her hat. "I'm just as eager to speak with Croyden as you are." His eyes narrowed. "I especially wish to know what he's done with my cousin. For I have little doubt he's the one who hired whoever demolished his rooms and made him disappear."

"I believe this is the chance we've been waiting for." Caro rested her head against his shoulder, feeling the full weight of relief from their discovery combine with her exhaustion from last night's lack of sleep. Suddenly, she was unable to keep her eyes open.

"I think so, too," she heard Val say into her hair. Then she fell fast asleep.

After returning the hired carriage and informing the hotel that they would not, after all, be staying in Brighton for the next few days, Caro and Val booked tickets back to London on the next train and were at Wrackham House by teatime.

"I'll send a note round to Kate letting her know what we learned, and then we can leave for Croyden's," Caro said once she'd changed and refreshed herself. They'd stopped for a brief luncheon before boarding, and from the way she was pacing, she was ready to venture back out and beard the earl in his den.

Val, however, suspected that like Tate, Lord Croyden would not wish to discuss such a delicate matter as a family scandal before a lady. He disliked asking her to keep away from such an important interview, especially given how much he knew she'd been looking forward to questioning Croyden herself. In truth, he was damned tired of protecting the fragile feelings of misogynists at the expense of Caro's.

"Before you argue," he began, pulling her to sit beside him on the settee, "let me explain my reasoning."

Her belongings had been unpacked and arranged throughout the sitting room adjacent to her bedchamber, and it looked as if she'd always lived here. The realization made him unaccountably happy. If he thought it odd that his wife had a large dollhouse furnished with tiny figures reenacting famous murder scenes, well, who was he to judge? He himself had a room dedicated to boxing, complete with a bag filled with sand affixed to the ceiling, on which he practiced pummeling when the mood struck.

She stroked Ludwig, who had leapt into her lap the moment she sat down. "This sounds like something I will dislike immensely."

Val watched the cat with no little degree of jealousy. "It's not as bad as that," he reassured her. "I just think you should let Eversham and me pay a call on Croyden first."

"But I want to question him myself." Caro straightened in her annoyance, and in turn, Ludwig jumped down before leaping up onto the table that held the dollhouse. Then, she deflated. "For the same reason I suppose I had to let you question Lord Tate?"

"I'm sorry, my dear." Val got up and crouched before her chair. "You know if I didn't think the fellow would cut up rough, I wouldn't suggest it. But the sooner we can question him, the sooner we can learn if he's had anything to do with Miss Warrington's and Frank's disappearances."

"You're right," Caro said, absently smoothing a hand over his hair. "But you must promise to tell us as soon as possible if you learn something important."

"I promise." Val kissed her palm before rising to his feet. "Now, I'll go track down Eversham to accompany me. What will you do while I'm gone?"

"I'll pay a call on Kate, I suppose," she said. "Perhaps she'll have learned something new in our"—she looked at the watch pinned to her bosom—"six hours' absence from town."

"Thank you, best wife." He kissed her cheek, grateful

she hadn't been too hurt by his suggestion. "I'll come by Kate's house afterward with Eversham in tow to report back on what we learn from Croyden."

"I'm not sure how I feel about having a husband squire me about town," Caro said, in a return to their earlier playfulness. "It's quite a change from my usual independence."

"I have no wish to curb your freedoms, Lady Wrackham," he said with all sincerity. "Only to share some of your adventures." Her independence was one of the things he liked best about her. She wasn't afraid to fight for what she believed in. Or for her friends and family. If it ever came to it—though he'd do his damndest to ensure that she never felt the need—he knew she'd slay metaphorical dragons for him, too.

How could he not love her?

Not ready to share what he'd just accepted about his feelings for her, he slipped from her room and was soon catching a hansom cab, which he instructed to take him to Scotland Yard.

He found Eversham in his oak-paneled office behind a large desk covered in paperwork.

"You look as if you could use an excuse to run away." Val noted the scowl on his friend's face as he signed one sheet and moved it to another stack.

Eversham's eyes lit with relief. "If you've come with one at the ready, I will pay you any sum you name. No one becomes a detective inspector in order to fill out requisitions for uniforms."

"You needn't pay me anything," Val assured him. "If anything, you'll be doing me a favor."

Eversham leaned back in his chair. "Wait a moment.

Aren't you supposed to be on your wedding trip in Brighton right now?"

Val explained his and Caro's reasons for returning to London.

Eversham whistled. "Croyden does sound as if he had motive to keep the connection between himself and Miss Warrington from becoming public. He likely feared either her profession or position as her uncle's illegitimate child would bring scandal on his reputation for righteousness."

"And if what Mrs. Trelawney said about his renovations on the estate in Kent is true," Val said, "it doesn't sound as if he'd wish to give up any funds that might have been intended for Miss Warrington in his uncle's will. It sounds as if he's spared no expense in updating Croyden Keep."

Rising from behind his desk, Eversham retrieved his hat and coat from the hook behind the door. "Let's go find out."

When they arrived at the towering Croyden townhouse in St. James's Square, Val let out a low whistle. It was the sort of old-fashioned London manor that many peers had abandoned for the more updated houses in fashionable Mayfair or Belgravia, where such modern conveniences as running water and gas lighting might be had. Val's grandfather had abandoned the former family townhouse in St. James's Square decades ago in favor of the present one located in Berkeley Square. But clearly the Croyden family had been unwilling or unable to do so.

Another indication that the earl had been unwilling to give up any money intended for Miss Warrington in his uncle's will?

"You'd better let me do most of the questioning at first,"

Val said to Eversham as they made their way up the steps. "Give your name as Mr. Eversham."

"Who is leading this investigation?" Eversham raised a brow. "I think I know well enough how to put a suspect at ease."

Val had barely time enough to apologize hastily before the door opened.

"Lord Wrackham and Mr. Andrew Eversham for Lord Croyden," Val told the ancient servant who greeted them. Taking their cards—to Val's surprise, Eversham had cards for his personal use, with no mention of his role with Scotland Yard—the butler ushered them into the house. "I'll see if his lordship is available."

The interior itself was scrupulously clean, every surface polished within an inch of its life. The entryway looked to be Jacobean in style and boasted a domed fresco on the ceiling and a gleaming marble floor.

"He doesn't seem to be hurting for cash," said Eversham in a low voice after the butler had left them in a small parlor. "The gold leaf in the ceiling alone must be worth a mint. Though I suppose if he's renovating the other house up to this same standard, that would cost quite a bit. Miss Warrington's inheritance could likely buy quite a lot of marble floors."

Val tended to agree, though he noticed that some of the empty insets looked as if they'd once held statuary. Could Croyden have been selling off objets d'art in order to obtain money for his renovations?

When Eversham gave a strangled cough, Val turned to see what had plagued him. The detective pointed toward the intricately carved fireplace.

"I can't imagine a man so wedded to proselytizing being too comfortable with that," Eversham said wryly. "If the other house is similar, it's no wonder he's all but torn it down and built it back up again."

"What do you me—" Val looked closer. "Oh."

What had at first looked to be a pastoral scene of shepherds and maids was actually rampant satyrs frolicking with naked nymphs.

"Oh, indeed," Eversham agreed. "I can't imagine this is the only room with such adornments. No one whose tastes run to this sort of thing ever thinks, 'Yes, this is just the right amount of depravity—we can stop now.'"

Val would have agreed but the ancient butler had returned. "His lordship will see you."

The old man then turned and left the room.

Exchanging a look, Val and Eversham followed the old man upstairs.

When they arrived at what looked to be Croyden's study, the butler ushered them inside, then beat a hasty retreat.

The earl was seated not behind his desk but at a table, on which stacks of documents were piled. It faced one of the massive floor-to-ceiling bookshelves that lined the walls. He had an almost ethereally pale complexion, as smooth as the polished marble floor in the hall. His hair, a sandy light brown, was receding. "I hope you have a good reason for calling. I'm quite busy as you can see and can only spare a moment, Lord Wrackham, Mr. Eversham."

As welcomes went, Croyden's was sorely lacking.

"I've come to ask you some questions about your late uncle, Croyden." Val didn't bother waiting for the other man to invite him to sit before dropping into an armchair.

The fireplace nearby was more decorous than the one downstairs, Val noted.

Eversham, following Val's lead, took the chair opposite.

"What about my uncle?" the earl said curtly, not bothering to look up from his papers. "He was a drunkard and a rake. And he's long dead, so I don't know what you could possibly wish to ask."

"I'm more interested in his daughter," Val said, matching the earl's tone. "Do you know anything about her?"

Croyden finally looked up. "That slut? It should surprise no one that my uncle's only child grew up to strut on the stage. Her maternal grandmother went to the trouble to place her with a very respectable family, but blood will out."

"But doesn't that same blood run in your veins?" Eversham asked thoughtfully. "I should think you'd be a bit more understanding, given the circumstances."

"My father was the only morally upright member of that family. And I was lucky enough to follow in his footsteps. But Miss Effie Warrington takes after her lowborn mother and my rakehell uncle. For all that he was of noble birth, he never much cared for mixing with people of his own class. A disappointment to his family, make no mistake about that. We would never condescend to such low company; I can assure you."

If the rest of Croyden's family shared his winning personality, Val thought, then he could hardly blame the man's uncle for eschewing them for more pleasant companions.

"Can you tell us if your uncle left Miss Warrington any sort of inheritance in his will?" he asked the earl, watching carefully to see how he reacted.

Croyden's dark eyes narrowed. "Yes, as it happens. She came to me some weeks ago to ask about it. Of course, I sent her to my solicitor who handles all those matters for me."

"Why wasn't she contacted at the time of your uncle's death?" Eversham asked, his tone much as Val would imagine it if he were questioning a Billingsgate gangster.

"That had nothing to do with me," Croyden said dismissively. "I had no hand in the way the estate was dispersed. That was up to the solicitors and the trustees."

"What else did you discuss with Miss Warrington?" Val asked. He didn't like to admit it, but Croyden was likely correct about contacting the heirs being the duty of the solicitors. Even if he wasn't responsible for her disappearance, then perhaps whatever else he'd told her might give them a clue to her disappearance.

"I gave her the name of her mother." The earl had abandoned all pretense of paying attention to the papers before him now, glaring at them in agitation. "She was a local girl in the village who died giving birth to her. Then I sent her on her way."

"What of Miss Warrington's maternal grandparents?" Val asked.

"Long dead. They were heartbroken, apparently, by their daughter's fall from grace and passed not long after her."

"So, you're her only living family," Eversham said. "I should think a man like you, who seems to pride himself on correct behavior, would have been more welcoming."

Croyden snorted with derision. "I am not her family. She is the illegitimate child of my late uncle. We have no connection. What's more, by treading the boards, she's made herself unfit for any sort of aristocratic company. Unless, of course, it's some noble protector who pays for her favors."

Val stretched his legs out before him, masking his disgust at the other man's snobbish sentiments but giving no indication that he planned on leaving. "Are you aware that Miss Warrington was abducted from her own carriage last week?"

He watched the man's expression very closely to gauge his reaction. But if anything, the earl's face grew more offended. "Why should I know anything about it? If the silly bitch got on the wrong side of one of her protectors, it's nothing to do with me."

Val glanced at Eversham to see what he thought of the man's story but interpreting the detective's expression was impossible.

Getting to his feet, Val stepped over to the table where Croyden had spread out his documents. It was difficult to tell without a closer examination, but he thought they looked like legal papers. "Thank you for your assistance. I will ask that if you see Miss Warrington again, you get in touch with me. You may not give a hang what happens to her, but she has friends who don't wish her to be harmed."

"I didn't say I wished harm on her," the other man said pettishly. "I simply don't wish her to associate with my family."

"Yes, that makes all the difference," Eversham agreed with mock seriousness.

Val and Eversham didn't speak until they'd retrieved their hats and coats from the decrepit butler and stepped outside.

"I hope that entire house is filled with filthy carvings." Val cursed. "What a miserable bastard."

"He's not the worst I've met," Eversham said, "but he's certainly near the top of the list. I can't imagine Miss Warrington would have chosen to see him again willingly if he was as charming to her as he was to us."

"Nor I." Val stepped out into the street. "And despite his protestations, I can't say I believed him overly much. He might have sent her to his solicitor, but did you see how he paused before when I asked about her abduction? He definitely knows something."

Eversham scowled. "Agreed. I think we need to find this solicitor of his."

"I promised Caro we'd meet her at your house to tell her and Kate what we learned," Val said, hoping his tone was casual enough not to raise Eversham's brows too much. He was a newlywed, after all. He was entitled to indulge his wife as much as he wished.

To his surprise, however, the other man didn't comment. Only agreed and turned to wave down a hansom cab.

"Aren't you going to mention something about my being wound round Caro's little finger?" Val demanded, unable to move beyond his suspicion that the detective was mocking him somehow. Eversham had greatly enjoyed seeing his discomfort after he'd issued that fateful theatre invitation to Caro's parents, after all.

"My dear fellow." Eversham clapped him on the shoulder as they waited for the cab to roll to a stop before them. "I know all too well what hell there would be to pay if either one of us was to go off on our own without reporting back to our wives. You might be new to this marriage business, but I am not. I have no wish to spend my night sleeping in the best guest bedchamber."

"You make a good point," Val admitted, though he doubted Caro would ever refuse him her bed for such a small mistake. Would she?

He wouldn't take the chance. After giving the cabbie their intended destination, he added, "An extra pound if you get us there in half the time."

Chapter Twenty-Two

Caro used her walk to Kate's house to expend some of her nervous energy.

It really was too unfair that she'd been unable to call upon Lord Croyden with the men, but she had to admit that Val's reasoning was sound. A man like that would never let down his guard with a woman present.

When she was shown into Kate's drawing room, she saw her friend had other guests.

"Caro, what on earth are you doing back so soon?" Her friend rose to greet her. "You and Val are well, I hope?"

Accepting her hug, Caro rushed to reassure her. "We're fine. We simply"—she looked at the assembled company, not wishing to reveal too much before strangers—"decided we'd rather be in London than Brighton."

Kate gave her a knowing look. "You're just in time, then, to meet the newest members of our salon."

Caro turned to her friend in surprise. So far as she knew,

there had been no plans for a salon meeting today. Unless something had happened while she was away?

Taking a seat in her favorite overstuffed chair, she gratefully accepted a cup of tea from Kate and glanced at the two other women seated at the tea table.

"This is Miss Lucy Penhallow." Kate gestured to a pretty young woman with large blue eyes and butter-yellow curls. "She is a cousin of Andrews's if you'll believe it. I can't wait to introduce them."

"I've been quite eager to meet him ever since I learned of the connection." Miss Penhallow grinned. "The rest of our family are deadly dull. Of course, I've read your column since it started running in *The Gazette*. I was telling Lady Katherine that I was unable to come sooner because I was waiting to escape my dragon of a chaperone. She's finally gone to visit her mother in Scotland for a week, so here I am."

Caro blinked at the stream of words, which had been delivered almost in one breath. She could very well see that a chaperone would have her work cut out with this girl. "I'm so pleased you were able to come at last, Miss Penhallow." She gave her a warm smile. It was difficult to imagine any blood connection between this young woman and the taciturn Andrew Eversham, but she supposed all sorts happened in families.

"And this is Lady Tate," Kate said of her other guest. "I believe you visited her home last week, Caroline?"

Caro, who had choked on her tea at Kate's introduction, took a moment to regain her composure. "Lady Tate," she said, after clearing her throat, "what a delight to meet you. I indeed enjoyed some delicious pastries at your home."

"I was so cross to learn that *the* Miss Caroline Hardcastle had called while I was out." Lady Tate, a handsome brunette with a wide smile and a petite build, spoke with more emotion than was usually encouraged in ladies of her station. "I've read all of your columns, Miss Hardcastle. As I was telling Lady Katherine, I'd never worked up the courage to write or come to one of your salons, but when I received her invitation to tea, I knew I could not refuse."

At Caro's questioning look, Kate said, "I remembered your comment about Lady Tate being an admirer of ours, and when I received Lucy's request to pay a call this afternoon, I sent a note round to Lady Tate as well."

It was a plausible enough explanation, but Caro knew her friend must have had another reason to wish to speak with Lady Tate. She'd simply have to be patient until Kate could disclose her thinking once the callers left.

The four chatted amiably about crime and their own lives before the subject of Caro's wedding came up.

"Lord Wrackham and I left for Brighton just this morning," she said with a laugh, "but I found I was too worried about my dear cat, Ludwig. My friend who usually looks after him when I'm out of town was unable to do so this time, and I simply couldn't rest knowing he was alone."

"But isn't he alone now?" Miss Penhallow asked, with more logic than Caro was comfortable needing an explanation for at the moment.

"Oh, he's with my maid. She'd gone with us to Brighton, so now that we're both back, he's quite happy again."

"Brighton is lovely at this time of year," Lady Tate said with feeling. "I don't get to the coast nearly as much as I'd like these days."

Caroline's pulse picked up. "But you were just there visiting your sister, were you not?" After all, Tate's alibi for the day of Effie's disappearance had been that he and his wife were visiting her sister in Brighton.

The dark-haired woman looked confused. "I'm not sure where you heard that, but I have no relations in Brighton. I haven't been in nearly three years."

Caro touched her forehead. "I beg your pardon. I must have confused something your husband told Lord Wrackham the other day with an anecdote from one of the wedding guests. Really, I'm not sure if I'm coming or going."

The moment of awkwardness passed, and soon enough, Kate was bidding her guests goodbye.

"They're gone now," Kate said when they heard the front door shut. "Tell me why you're back so soon."

Caro explained how she and Val had learned at the Hen and Hound that Effie's natural father was the uncle of the present Lord Croyden. "The crest on the seal from Effie's house matches the Croyden coat of arms, which means he's been in correspondence with her."

"And would have every reason to wish she'd disappear. Especially if he feared she would publicize the connection."

Unable to sit still, Caro paced before the fireplace. "But if Croyden is responsible for Effie's disappearance, then why would Lord Tate lie about where he was the day she was abducted?"

"Oh, I'd forgotten." Kate gasped. "He said he and his wife were in Brighton on the day she vanished. Of course."

"What if it's not Croyden at all?" Caro asked in a rush. "What if it's always been Tate, but we were simply too ready to believe his lie about being away on the day Effie was taken?"

"The man lied to you and his household. He even went so far as to purchase sweets, claiming they were from Brighton." Kate gave her a sympathetic pat on the arm. "You can hardly be expected to have seen through it."

But Caro was already thinking back over what Val had related to her about his conversation with Tate that day. "I think I may know where he could be hiding her."

"Where?" Kate demanded, leaning forward eagerly.

"Tate told Val he'd already purchased a house for when Effie became his mistress," Caro explained, "but she'd refused him. What if he's hidden her away there?"

"It's a possibility." Kate sat back. "A definite possibility. But how can we find it?"

"Who else would know the details of such a transaction?" Caro asked, relieved that Kate hadn't dismissed her out of hand. "His man of business."

"And our new friend Lady Tate would be more than happy to recommend her husband's man of business to us." Kate's eyes lit with excitement.

Caro moved to the desk by the window, writing quickly. "What are you doing?"

"I'm leaving a note for Val and Eversham," Caro said over her shoulder.

Kate snorted. "Barely married a day and already you're playing by your husband's rules."

Caro preferred to think of her action a precaution in the event that she and Kate ran into trouble, but she didn't argue with Kate's assessment. She folded the note and faced her friend. "I'll give this to your butler on the way out."

"Did you bring your little pistol, or do we need to stop at your house on the way?" Kate asked as they hurried to the entryway.

"Of course I brought it." Caro was beginning to wonder if her friend knew her at all.

Stopping in the middle of the staircase, Kate turned, her eyes wide. "On a visit to me? I was joking!"

"But I had to get here, Kate," Caro reminded her. "Who knows what danger I might encounter on the streets of London?"

Kate's mouth snapped shut.

"You make a good point."

Eversham and Val arrived at the former's home fully expecting to find their wives waiting, albeit impatiently, for news of their interview with Lord Croyden.

Instead, they found only a cryptic note from Caro:

> *Tate didn't go to Brighton. Going to find his mistress's house. Suspect that may be where he's keeping Effie. Love, C and K*

"Damn it." Despite the brevity of the missive, Val knew precisely what Caro had meant. "Tate lied to us about being in Brighton on the day Effie was abducted. I don't know how they found out, but if that's true, then who knows what else he may have lied about."

"But how would they know where this house is?" Eversham asked. "It's not as if he advertised it."

"If I were going to set up a mistress," Val said thoughtfully, "and needed a house for that purpose, I'd entrust said purchase to my man of business."

"Do you know who Tate uses?"

"As a matter of fact, I do." Val grinned. "The aristocracy is bloody insular, and we all use the same people. In this case, Tate and my father share a solicitor. I saw him when I was signing papers at the firm when I took over control of the Wrackham properties after my brother's death."

"Well, then, what are we waiting for?" Eversham headed for the door.

Only moments after they'd arrived, the two men were leaving again.

The house, whose address they'd learned from Lord Tate's man of business after Caro had employed a few false tears to distract him while Kate extracted the address from the file on the solicitor's desk, was situated on a quiet street in Marylebone. It was by no means a fashionable neighborhood, but neither was it somewhere Lord Tate's comings and goings would be overly suspect. In fact, the solicitor had said Tate specifically asked for a property where he might go about his business without interference from the other residents of the area. From the looks of the other houses nearby, which were well-kept and of modest size, the prosperous merchants and professionals who lived here would see him as just another neighbor.

"What do you think?" Caro asked. She and Kate stood just out of view of the front door of 24 Portland Place. "How shall we get inside?"

"I still think we should wait for Eversham and Val," Kate said with a worried glance at her friend. "Or better yet, we should just go get them now that we've found the house."

"But what if it were you in there?" Caro demanded. "If it were me, I'd want my friends to do whatever they could to set me free as quickly as possible."

"You know that I would, too." Kate frowned. "I simply think it wouldn't hurt to be cautious."

"That's why I left the note. If we should meet with trouble, Val and Eversham will be able to trace us here."

"Caro," her friend said, affection blending with exasperation, "you know there are a hundred reasons why they might not get here in time to help us."

Caro sighed. Kate was right. And what's more, Caro knew that it had been her own precipitate behavior that had landed her in trouble on more than one occasion. Her instincts might be telling her she needed to find a way inside the house, but the cautious thing to do would be to come back later with Val and Eversham.

"All right," she told Kate. "We'll go home and wait for—"

She broke off when Kate suddenly gripped her by the arm and pulled her to where an abandoned cart rested against a nearby curb.

"What is it?" Caro demanded.

Wordlessly, Kate pointed at a man jogging down the steps of the house in question. Caro turned to Kate, puzzled. She'd never seen the brown-haired man before.

"Who is he?"

"Lord Croyden," Kate whispered. "I recognize him from his picture in the paper. We've run enough stories on him over the years."

"It can't be a coincidence that he's coming out of the house Tate bought for Effie." Caro's mind raced with possibilities. "Could they be working together?"

"They could be," Kate said softly. "One wants her, and the other wants her out of the way. It seems to me with a little negotiation, they can achieve both ends."

As they watched, Croyden hurried past them and rounded the corner to a side street.

"We have to get inside," Caro said in a low voice. "What if he was there to give orders for Effie to be killed because Val and Eversham came asking questions about her? Unlike Tate, *he* needs her gone."

She'd been ready to curb her impulses and wait, but now that there was a strong possibility that Effie was in immediate danger, she couldn't leave her there.

"All right, let's go."

Caro threw her arms around her friend—in fear and solidarity. "What's our plan? Should we pose as church visitors?"

"Our clothing is too posh for that. Why not introduce ourselves as new neighbors?"

"It needs to be something that will get us inside the house." Caro tapped a finger on her chin. What was a good reason to let a stranger in your home?

"I've got it!" Caro said with excitement. "Before we moved to our—well, Mama and Papa's, now—current house, we lived in Bloomsbury. One day an older woman came to the door saying she'd grown up there and wondered if she might wander through for a bit for old times' sake. Mama was reluctant, but Papa is a soft touch and gave the lady a tour. She was quite sentimental, and even Mama was moved before the end of the woman's visit."

Kate looked deep in thought. "It would give us a reason to get a foot in the door at the very least. And we can talk our way past the servants if we need to."

"I don't think we'll have to," Caro said. "I can be very convincing."

Three minutes later they were knocking on the entrance of twenty-four. It was opened by an older woman, perhaps a housekeeper, who didn't look the least bit friendly.

"Good afternoon, ma'am," Caro began, handkerchief already in her hand. "I hate to bother you, but my sister and I were wondering if we might be able to have a tour of the house? This was our childhood home and…and—" She broke off and dissolved into weeping.

Through her lashes, she could see that the woman didn't appear to be moved by the display.

"There, there, sister." Kate patted her on the back. "You see, we grew up in this house and we've only recently lost our dear mother. And Hortense thought that it would do her good to see the site of so many of our happy girlhood—"

The grim-faced woman cut her off. "Master won't like it."

If she had anything to add, she chose to keep it to herself.

"But if your master is here," Kate said firmly, "perhaps we can speak to him. I'm sure he wouldn't wish to disappoint two ladies."

Caro froze. She'd met Tate. If he was there, then as

soon as he saw her, he would know they were definitely not there to see their former home. But it was too late to warn her friend now.

"Ain't here."

Caro continued her sniveling, even as she felt only relief at learning Tate was absent. Still, they had to find some way to persuade this woman to let them in. "But Mama!" she wailed, impressed at her own volume.

The noise roused a reaction from the housekeeper. She shouted up the stairs behind them, making Caro wish she could cover her ears against the din.

"Mick!" she yelled. When there was no answer, she repeated herself. "Hey, Mick!"

Finally, her summons brought a male servant. He scowled at the taciturn woman. "What's this, then?"

"Want a tour of the house," she said, clearly no more talkative with her compatriots.

"Oh, please, sir." Kate gave a winning smile to the man. "You see, we were raised in this house, and we wondered if we might have a look around. We've only just lost our dear mother, and it would do my poor sister good to be here where we shared so many happy memories with her."

Caro was pleased to see that Kate's pleading tone, coupled with a strategic bite to her lower lip, was working on the man. His expression, while still not welcoming, had softened ever so slightly.

"Orright, then." His flat stare reminded Caro that they were dealing with people who might very well be hardened criminals. "But there's some parts of the house where ye can't go. No funny business or you'll be sorry."

The threat should have seemed like something out of

a penny dreadful, but his words sounded deadly serious to Caro's ears. Fear ran through her.

She mopped her eyes with the handkerchief, hoping he didn't see through their ruse. "Thank you, sir. I cannot thank you enough."

"Lost me mam a couple year ago," the man said. "Course she weren't nothing but a liar and a whore, but ain't the point, izzit?"

And just like that Caro dismissed her guilt like so many dandelion seeds in the wind.

"Gert'll take ye round." He nodded to the woman who'd stood scowling as they'd chatted.

"And who is your master, Mick?" asked Caro. "So I'll know who to send our thank-you note to. You really can't know how much this means to us."

"Truly." Kate slipped her arm through Caro's.

"Why don't ye just get on wi' yer tour, then," he said sharply, "'fore I change me mind."

"Of course." Caro waited for Gert to lead them upstairs.

When she just continued to stand there, Kate prompted, "Gert? Can we go upstairs now?"

As if waking from a trance, Gert nodded and started up the staircase.

The house itself was well-kept, the scent of lemon strong as they made their way up the steps.

They'd only reached the first landing when the front door slammed open, and a voice carried up to them.

"Who were those women at the door?" demanded Lord Tate. "I could see them from the carriage but I didn't recognize them."

"Just some leaky birds grew up in the house wanting

to take a look fer old times' sake," Mick told him with a marked lack of deference. "Nothing to lose yer top over."

Caro and Kate pressed forward into Gert, all but pushing her down in their haste to make it upstairs before Tate saw them. Unfortunately, Gert apparently rushed for no one, and it wasn't long before footsteps hurried up behind them.

"Here now, ladies." Tate's tone was querulous. "You'll have to leave. This house isn't open for tours."

But they ignored him, keeping on until they reached the first landing, where he managed to step in front of them. When he saw Caro, his eyes widened in shock. "You!"

"Oh, hello, Lord Tate; how do you do?" Caro hoped she appeared to be genuinely surprised. "What a coincidence. Is this your house? My friend Kate grew up here and wanted to see her childhood home again. Her mother just recently died, you see, and—"

"Sister," said Gert, choosing that moment to volunteer information. "Said she was yer sister."

Tate's expression turned ugly. "Mick, get up here!"

Before Kate and Caro could act, the two men had gripped them and hustled them up the stairs.

"You don't want to do this, Lord Tate," Kate said firmly. "Both Caroline and I will be missed."

Caro noted that she didn't include that her husband was with Scotland Yard or that Caro was the daughter-in-law of a duke. Though those facts might inspire Tate to let them go, they could also encourage him to do something violent to ensure they were never found.

"Shut up." Tate pushed them into a room along the hallway. "Shut up. Let me think."

He slammed the door behind them, and Caro heard the sound of a key turning in the lock.

The chamber was dark except for a sliver of light coming from the edges of the window coverings. Hurrying to open them, Caro bumped her shin against a footstool and cursed. Finally, she was able to open the curtains in a cloud of dust that set her coughing.

Obviously, whoever had kept the rest of the house clean wasn't allowed in here.

"Caro! Caro, come here!" Kate said from the other side of the room, where an ancient bedstead had been pushed against the far wall. The faded canopy hangings appeared to be the same fabric as the draperies at the windows and looked to be just as dusty. Kate was seated on the edge of the mattress.

Next to her was a body.

When she reached the bed, Caro was fully expecting to see Effie. Her shock was such that she, too, had to collapse onto the mattress.

"Oh my God. It's Mr. Thorn."

Chapter Twenty-Three

It was clear from his pallor that Francis Thorn was very ill. His hair, which had been clean and neat when Caro had last seen him, was now greasy and lank. From the unwashed stench of him, he'd been in this state for several days.

"Mr. Thorn?" Caro patted him on the cheek, only to find him feverish. "It's Caroline Hardcastle. Do you remember me?" She didn't bother telling him about the wedding. She didn't want to confuse him.

His eyes opened abruptly, and he gave a shout, striking out, narrowly missing her face. It took both Caro and Kate to hold him down. "We are friends, Mr. Thorn," Caro assured him. "You met me at Effie's house after she was abducted. And you've known Kate—Lady Katherine—for years. Do you remember us?"

Finally, he seemed to understand her words and fell

back to the pillow. "Miss Hardcastle," he said in a weak voice. "Val's Caro. And Kate. Why are you here?"

Relieved that he was conscious, Caro sat on the edge of the bed. "We've come to rescue you. Both you and Effie."

The man gave a low moan. "Effie. I tried to get her out of this place, but they soon recaptured me and separated us."

Caro wanted to ask how long ago that had been, but it was evident he was too weak to withstand such a barrage of questions. Instead, she asked, "Who did this to you? Are you injured?"

He nodded and shifted on the bed to lift his shirt, revealing what appeared to be a knife wound in his side. "Bastard stabbed me," he bit out.

"Who?" Kate asked, from Caro's other side. "Who stabbed you?"

"One of Croyden's men." He scowled. "They took me when I wouldn't tell them where Effie's letters from Mary Killeen were. When they started watching Effie's house, I took them to my rooms for safekeeping. They were her only proof connecting her to the old earl. Croyden's man said he wanted all traces of Effie's connections to him erased. Didn't know it was him until then, though. Swear it."

"The scoundrel," Caro said in a low voice. "He and Tate are definitely working together, then?"

Thorn nodded. "Didn't know about Tate."

He was obviously tiring, his words slurring and a sheen of sweat coating his face. Caro feared that they'd not be able to get him to safety before he succumbed to the infection in his wound. "That's enough for now," she told him. "You rest and we'll do what we can to get out of here."

"And Effie." He clasped her by the arm, his grip surprisingly strong as he nearly sat all the way up. "Don't forget to find my Effie."

"We will," Caro assured him in a soothing tone. "We won't forget Effie."

Her words must have eased his mind because he slumped back down onto the pillow and he closed his eyes again.

Caro and Kate moved away from the bed so that they could confer without disturbing him.

"He needs medical attention." Kate frowned. "It doesn't seem as if they've done anything to see to his wound at all."

"Mick and Gert don't appear to be the most conscientious of jail keepers," Caro agreed.

"My question is," Kate began, "where is Effie? Is she even being held here?"

"We have to search the house. I can't imagine a more convenient location for them to be holding her than here, but we won't know until we've looked." Caro scanned the room for anything they might use to clean Mr. Thorn's wound. "If I were them, I'd try to keep the prisoners separated, if only to keep them from working together to escape."

There was a cold pitcher of water near the fireplace, but that was all. An injury like Frank's would need hot water, and something to disinfect it.

"What's the plan?" Kate asked. "Frank doesn't have much time. And we don't know how long Val and Andrew's interview with Croyden will take before they see your note. Fortunately, Val should be able to convince Tate's man of business to give him the address on his own, since he won't have a letter of introduction from Lady Tate as we did."

Caro went to see if the window might offer a means of escape but found that iron bars had been installed to prevent them from being opened. "I'm not sure what kind of man chooses to have the windows in his mistress's house fitted with bars, but my guess is not a good one."

"One who chooses to kidnap a woman when she rejects him, so no, not a good man," Kate returned dryly.

It had been just before dusk when they arrived, and already the sky outside was darkening. They had to find a way out, but how?

Pacing, Caro felt the weight of her pistol hit against her thigh. She'd long ago made sure all her gowns were made with pockets, and today she was especially glad of it. "I've got my pistol," she told Kate in a low voice. "We've got to get out of this room and find Effie."

Kate stepped closer so no one listening in the hall could hear them. "How?"

"I could try to shoot the lock off the door," Caro offered.

"It's on the outside," Kate countered. "Otherwise, that might have worked."

Biting back a curse, Caro bit her lip and thought. What would cause their captors to unlock the door?

"We could scream," Kate suggested. "They might be curious enough to come running."

"I can't imagine Effie and Mr. Thorn haven't already tried that." Caro sighed. "We need to frighten Gert and Mick into opening the door. They obviously don't care about the health of Mr. Thorn."

"They might care very much about the health of a viscount's wife, who will one day be the wife of a duke," Kate said. "I wasn't sure how Tate would respond as it's unlikely he'll ever hang for his crimes, but as for Gert and Mick...I'd imagine they'd do just about anything to ensure you stay alive."

Caro added, "My father's name might help. Everyone in London knows Hardcastle Fine Foods. Money might be enough to persuade Mick and Gert where the milk of human kindness will not."

"I like it." Kate nodded.

They took a few moments to solidify their plan before setting it into motion.

First, Caro arranged herself on the floor in front of the fireplace, the iron poker lying beside her as if it had been used to strike her. Hidden from view was her pistol, which she held in her pocket. One of the pillows from the bed also half covered her as if Mr. Thorn had tossed it to the floor in his haste to attack. He was clearly far too weak to have done anything like that, but the plan only needed their captors to act on their first reaction and come inside.

"Ready?" Kate asked.

"Ready."

"Okay, go."

Caro sat up and let out a bloodcurdling scream. "Mr. Thorn, no! What are you doing?" She screamed again and Kate dropped a book they'd found in a near-empty bookcase onto the floor.

"Take that, you brute!" Kate cried, then picked up the book and dropped it again. "Caroline? Caroline? Speak to me!"

She waited exactly ten seconds before she began pounding on the door. "Mick! Gert! Please come quickly! Mr. Thorn has attacked Lady Wrackham! She's bleeding! Oh, you must come! What will the viscount, or his father the duke, do if she dies? She's the heiress to Hardcastle Fine Foods, for heaven's sake!"

When there was no response from downstairs, Kate pummeled on the door again, calling out to their captors once more. This time, they were rewarded by the sound of footsteps on the staircase.

"Orright, orright," they heard Mick muttering. "Keep yer hat on."

"Oh, please, Mick," Kate cried. "You must help her!"

"Lady, ye best be telling the truth or ye'll feel the back o' me hand."

They heard the sound of a key being inserted into the lock followed by the snick of it being turned.

Kate, who had picked up one of the other fireplace tools, stood with her arm down, the iron shovel hidden in her skirts. The door opened inward, and she stepped behind it as Mick entered to see Caro lying on the floor.

"Where's t'other bird?" He glanced around before stepping closer to Caro. Kate took the opportunity to fell him with the iron shovel.

He dropped to the floor with much less grace than Caro had used when arranging herself.

"Really, Mick." Caro shook her head at his clumsiness. "I'd expected more fight from a man like you."

"Just another in a long line of men who underestimate ladies," Kate said, shaking out her arm.

Caro got herself up from the floor and brushed off her

gown. "We have to search for Effie now while we have a chance."

"Agreed." Kate bent down to remove the key from Mick's hand and slipped it into her own dress pocket. Then, moving to the table beside the bed, where poor Mr. Thorn lay looking no better, she picked up a candleholder and lit the taper with a match from the box nearby.

While she did that, Caro walked quickly to the curtains, and one at a time she removed the thick cords being used to hold them back from where they hung on hooks on either side of the window. "We can't afford for Mick to wake up and hurt Mr. Thorn again, or come after us," she explained at Kate's questioning look. Crouching on the floor, she bound first the prone man's hands, and then his feet. Silently, she sent a prayer of thanks to the groom who'd taught her to tie a sturdy knot in case she ever had to secure a horse with rope instead of a bridle.

Rising to her feet, she noticed that Kate still held the small shovel in her hand. "You'd better exchange that for the poker. I suspect it will be easier to swing in a pinch."

Kate did just that and the two peered out into the hallway beyond.

It seemed deserted. They stepped out and went in search of Effie.

A glance down the hall showed them that there were three additional rooms, and the stairs led up to another floor above.

Their room had been on the east side of the house facing the street. Quietly, they tried the door to a room facing the back garden. Kate held the candle high so they could see inside, but the room was empty of both furniture and people.

The other two rooms on the floor were the same.

Silently, Caro pointed above them and Kate nodded. They made their way as quietly as they could to the level above.

The layout there was identical to the one below. Four rooms off a narrow hallway.

Going in the order they'd followed before, they first tried the room above the one in which they and Mr. Thorn had been imprisoned. This room also had bedroom furniture, but it was empty of anyone.

Unable to hold back the desperation filling her, Caro gritted her teeth. Where was Effie? Had they removed her from the house after locking Caro and Kate away? If that was the case, they might never see her again.

Kate laid a hand on her upper arm and gave it a squeeze. "We'll find her," she mouthed.

Nodding, Caro kept going toward the room facing the back garden. When they reached the door, however, she heard a faint cry. Her pulse quickening, she tried to turn the knob, but it was locked.

Afraid to make any noise lest she alert Gert and Tate that they'd escaped, Caro gestured silently for Kate to use the key from Mick. Silently, Kate turned it in the lock and they pushed gently on the door.

"Who is it? Who's there?" a voice called from inside the room. "I won't let you touch me, Tate. I thought I'd made that plain enough. Now, leave me alone!"

When she saw that Caro and Kate had entered instead of Lord Tate, Effie—her hair disheveled and her clothing wrinkled—gasped. Her red-rimmed eyes widened and she began to cry.

"Thank God you've come," she wept as Caro rushed to her side and hugged her close. "I was so frightened. They've got Francis. We must find him."

Once Val mentioned his father to the man who served as solicitor for both the duke and Lord Tate, it was a matter of minutes before he and Eversham were back out in the street hailing a hansom cab for Portland Place.

"Having a duke for a father must be a useful card to have up your sleeve." Eversham glanced at Val once they were in the carriage.

"You could have your grandfather to use on such occasions if you'd get that stick out of your backside and reconcile with your father's family," Val said with a sideways glance of his own. Eversham's father, a country vicar, was the son of a baronet but had been cut off by his family when he'd chosen to marry below his station. Though his parents had long ago reconciled with the family, Eversham was unwilling to make nice with the people who had rejected not only his parents, but by extension him.

"Not for the wide world." Eversham shook his head. "There are too many expectations. I'm content with my parents and Kate. And when I have need of assistance from the upper crust, I have you." This last he said with a broad wink.

"I'm just happy my father's name was enough to get us the address of Tate's property." Val tapped his hand against his thigh in agitation, unable to forget the reason for their errand.

From the set of Eversham's clenched jaw, he hadn't forgotten either.

"They aren't foolhardy," Val said aloud. "Do they take risks I wish they wouldn't? Yes. But they are clever and I know Caro can talk her way out of any scrape."

"You sound as if you're trying to convince yourself, my friend," said Eversham wryly. "I know because a similar litany is running through my head, only it has to do with Kate's resourcefulness."

"If I hadn't been so quick to believe Tate's claim that he'd been in Brighton that day, we might have caught him sooner," Val said darkly. "I thought myself such a good judge of character."

"I've been with the Yard for years." Eversham clapped him on the shoulder. "While I do have a sense of when I'm being lied to, it's not foolproof. No one is right one hundred percent of the time. That's why we gather evidence to prove cases rather than simply jumping to conclusions based on gut instinct."

"Well, I should have gotten some damned evidence, then." Val thought back to how he'd left Caro to question the maid. If he'd insisted on Tate allowing her to be present when he'd questioned the man, might she have seen through him? The possibility filled him with regret at his decision to accede to Tate's wishes that day.

It wasn't the only instance he wished he'd behaved differently.

Why hadn't he told her he loved her that afternoon as soon as he'd realized it? That he'd very likely never stopped loving her. Foolishly he'd thought there would be time later. Now he might not ever get the chance.

By God, if—no, *when*—he found her, he'd tell her so.

"They're fine, Val," Eversham assured him. "We don't even know for sure that they've found Tate's love nest."

"We don't know that, no. But as we've both agreed, they're too clever for their own good."

Eversham cursed.

They were silent for the rest of the drive, each man locked in his own grim thoughts.

When the cab stopped a few doors down from 24 Portland Place, it was in the gloaming, that time when the last light of the day cast an otherworldly blue sheen on the world.

The lamplighter was still making his way down the street and hadn't reached this end yet.

Paying the cabbie, they disembarked and looked down toward the house where they suspected Tate was holding Effie.

"How will we play this?" Val asked as they walked slowly toward their destination. "Should we try to approach from the rear?"

"Let's try to determine how the house is laid out first," Eversham said. "We don't want any surprises."

But as they got closer, they could hear Tate and Lord Croyden arguing on the front stoop of number twenty-four. Master criminals, Val thought, these two were not.

"You imbecile," Croyden sneered at Tate. "Are you insane? You didn't tell me that the chit's paramour is the nephew of a duke, and now you've kidnapped a viscountess?! Do you wish to hang?"

"They don't hang lords," Tate snapped. "And what else could I do? Those bloody women were already inside the damned house! I acted in haste. I'd like to see what you'd do in the circumstances. You're so afraid to get your hands dirty, but then you moan when things don't go precisely the way you want."

"I let you be the one to take the girl, you ingrate. I could have killed her and been done with it, if not for you," Croyden hissed. "And my men managed to spirit Thorn away without one killing the other. You couldn't even choose your henchmen properly. And keep your voice down. The entire neighborhood can hear you."

"The houses on either side are empty," Tate said. "It's one of the reasons I chose this place from among those shown to me by my solicitor."

"Well, in one instance you made a wise decision." Croyden sounded begrudging.

"And how was I to know Mick would take exception to Davy's insult of his mother and murder him? At least that's one less thug to pay off once all of this is over."

Still one house down, Val and Eversham exchanged looks. "So Croyden was lying, after all," Val hissed.

"He seemed devious to me at the time." Eversham shrugged. "We need to get in there and rescue our wives."

"I say we take them by surprise." Val wanted to pound his fist into the face of the man who'd just confessed to kidnapping his wife. And he didn't feel the least bit ashamed of the impulse. He loved his wife and would always protect her—there was nothing wrong with that. "We can overpower them. I'll take Tate; you take Croyden."

Nodding, Eversham said, "On three. One, two, three."

Both men rushed the remaining steps leading to number twenty-four.

Still arguing, Tate and Croyden didn't realize they were

under siege until it was too late. Given how much they'd wanted to get their hands on the men who'd kidnapped Caro and Kate, it took a lamentably short time for Val and Eversham to subdue the two lords.

"How dare you!" Croyden shouted as Eversham wrenched his hands behind his back, tying them with a length of cord. "Who do you think you are?"

"I'm a detective inspector with Scotland Yard. And you and your cohort just confessed to kidnapping Miss Effie Warrington, Mr. Francis Thorn, and Lady Wrackham." Eversham tossed another length of cord to Val.

Not even struggling to resist, Tate held his bleeding nose between his fingers. "It's broken, you brute."

"Good," Val said coldly, twisting the man's free arm behind his back. "Now, tell me where my wife and Lady Katherine are."

"Upstairs," said Tate, though it sounded more like "ubdairs" because of his nose. "I dob hab de key."

"What do you mean you don't have the key?" Val snapped.

"He's had a couple staying here taking care of Miss Warrington and her swain," Lord Croyden said with disgust. "Though who knows where they are."

Val's eyes widened in shock. Frank was there? He fought to keep himself from sagging against the nearest wall in relief. Frank was alive. Now, if he could only find Caro safe…

Eversham had led Croyden inside to stand against the entrance wall. Val pulled Tate's hand down from his nose, tied it with his other wrist already behind his back, then led him over to the wall opposite Croyden.

"Can you handle these two for a moment while I—"

"Val? Is that you?"

He broke off at the sound of Caro's voice.

"Caro?" He made sure Eversham had Tate, then took the stairs two at a time until he met Caro on the landing where she threw herself into his arms.

"I knew you'd come!"

"Of course I did," he said into her hair. "Tate and Croyden said you were locked in a room upstairs."

"We escaped before you arrived," Kate said from behind Caro. "And we found Effie."

"And Mr. Thorn." Caro pulled away from him. "He's upstairs but he's burning with fever. He needs a doctor. He was stabbed by one of the men who abducted him."

Standing aside to let Kate continue down to where Eversham was waiting, Val asked Caro, "Where is he? Where's Frank?"

He'd already lost Piers; he'd be damned if he'd lose the cousin he loved like a brother.

"I'll show you," Caro said, leading him up the stairs.

The room where Frank had been kept prisoner was redolent with the smell of infection and unwashed skin.

On the floor before the fireplace lay a man in workman's clothes, his hands and feet bound. Val turned to Caro. "Who is this?"

"Oh, that's Mick." She waved a hand dismissively. "He was the one who helped Lord Tate lock us up in here. Kate had to cosh him with a fireplace implement so I wouldn't have to shoot him. Then I tied him up so he couldn't come after us. There was a woman named Gert as well, but I'm not sure where she's gone. Perhaps out the back."

Val gaped. Not only had she and Kate defended

themselves ably against these ruffians, but they'd found Miss Warrington and Frank. Very likely they would have managed to dispatch Tate and Croyden if given more time. He gazed at her in wonder.

"Come see your cousin." She pulled him toward the other side of the room.

A young woman, whom he presumed to be Effie Warrington, was kneeling beside the bed. A single candle was lit on the bedside table.

Val stepped forward, Caro's hand gripped tightly in his, and saw his cousin looking very ill indeed.

"We need to get him out of here," Miss Warrington said in a low voice, holding Frank's hand up to her cheek. "Francis, I'm so sorry they hurt you. You should have let them take me."

"Couldn't let them take m' best girl," Frank said weakly.

Eversham, who'd just entered the room behind them, said, "I'll go find the watchman and have him bring some men from the Yard. While I'm out there, I'll send the coachman for a physician for your cousin."

Val nodded, grateful for his friend's offer and for Caro there beside him as a sudden wave of emotion washed over him.

"Thank you," he said to the detective. "Truly."

With a brisk nod, Eversham gripped him by the shoulder and then headed back downstairs.

"If we can find the kitchen," Caro said, leading him out of the room with a gesture at Frank and Miss Warrington's close embrace, "I'll boil some water so that we can make Mr. Thorn more comfortable. Perhaps there's even a cake of soap or some clean cloths about somewhere."

She didn't sound particularly hopeful.

As they headed downstairs, they could hear their prisoners sniping at one another.

"None of this would have happened if that damned actress had simply agreed to leave my family alone," said Croyden in an aggrieved tone.

"The funny thing is, my lord," Caro told him as they neared the bottom of the steps, "Effie had no intention of using her connection to help her career. She merely wished to know her family. She's engaged to marry Francis Thorn, who just so happens to be the nephew of the Duke of Thornfield. Your thugs might have tried to kill him, but they haven't succeeded. Effie has no need of you. She'll have far more illustrious relations soon enough.

"I find I rather like it when I can use the Thornfield name to put a villain in his place." She grinned at Val, who smiled back.

"Marry Thorn?" Tate blurted out. Though with his injured nose, it sounded like "Marry Dorn?" "She can't marry Thorn!"

"Oh, I believe she can," Kate said with a satisfied smile. "In fact, she's free to do whatever she wishes."

"Because despite all that you've tried," Caro finished, "you have no power over her. You are nothing but a rotten cur."

"Are you going to let her speak to me with such disrespect?" Tate demanded of Val.

"The thing is, Tate," Val said evenly, "respect is something that has to be earned. And I can't think of a single thing you've done to make yourself worthy of the regard you mistakenly think is your due. I agree with her. You *are* a rotten cur."

When Caro slipped her arm through his, Val felt like the luckiest man in England.

"I love you," he said aloud before he could stop himself.

Caro turned to stare at him. "You do?"

"I do." He felt as if his heart would beat out of his chest. "Have done for about four years now."

"Ever since we...our first betrothal?"

"Ever since," he confirmed.

Before he could even catch his breath, Caro had launched herself at him and thrown her arms around his neck. "I love you, too."

"You do?" he asked, after he'd kissed her thoroughly.

"I do," she said. "Ever since."

"I'm going to be sick," Lord Croyden said from where he sat on the floor.

"Me too," Tate echoed, though again, it was more like "me doo."

In unison, Val, Kate, and Caro turned to the men and said, "Shut. Up."

Chapter Twenty-Four

Two weeks later

The applause crescendoed through the Lyceum Theatre as the cast of *Hamlet*, including the former Miss Effie Warrington, now Mrs. Francis Thorn, took their final bows.

"He's looking better, don't you think?" Val asked Caro, with a nod to his cousin, who was beaming with pride at his new wife's performance. "I think marriage must agree with him."

"It certainly seems to agree with Effie." Caro slipped her hand into Val's arm. "I've never seen her perform better. It's a pity she's decided to give it all up. Though, I suppose, even if she didn't wish to settle down with Mr. Thorn, the unwanted attention from men like Tate would make it less palatable to her now. Why must men ruin everything? I think we've got two of the last good ones, Kate."

"I'm relieved to hear you say so," Val said wryly as he slipped her wrap over her shoulders in preparation for them to leave. "Otherwise, Eversham and I would have to throw ourselves from the top of the clock tower in Westminster."

"Speak for yourself, man." Eversham shuddered. "Have you seen what a body looks like after a fall like that?"

As they reached the antechamber just outside the box, the duchess turned to Caro and Val. "We will see you at dinner next week, won't we? I'm having Cook prepare your favorite trifle, Valentine."

"We'll be there, Duchess," Caro said before Val could reply. She didn't divulge that the recipe was one of hers. After Val's warning, the duke had been on his best behavior with Caro. She'd even come to hold him and the duchess, who was lovely, in some affection. But she wasn't sure her father-in-law was quite ready to grapple with the realization that many of the recipes he happily consumed for years had been crafted by his son's wife.

"Excellent." The duchess beamed. "We'll see you then."

They made their goodbyes, since Val, Caro, and the Evershams intended to speak with Effie in the greenroom.

"Where has Francis gotten off to?" the duke asked his wife as they turned to go.

"No doubt he's gone to find his wife," Caro heard the duchess say in a stage whisper as they stepped into the corridor. "We're quite lucky with Caroline, you know. What if Valentine had decided to wed an actress?"

While Val and Eversham stood talking nearby, Caro and Kate took a moment to themselves.

"There, you see, Caro." Kate grinned. "You're practically royalty in their eyes compared to poor Effie."

"They're trying," Caro said, defending Val's parents. "The duke has become an avid reader of our column. He likes to question me about some of our bolder assertions, but I can tell he enjoys our chats. And I believe the duchess is just pleased to see Val happy. Mama is the one who's out of sorts. She's still resentful that I refused to pressure the duke and duchess to hold the wedding at their country estate."

"Parents," Kate said with a rueful smile. "Always wishing we'd have done things exactly the way they'd have."

"At least they haven't begun pressuring us for an heir yet," Caro said. She knew, of course, that she and Val were obligated to provide for the next in line to the Thornfield dukedom, but the possibility of the duke and duchess intruding vocally in what was, to her, a private matter gave her nightmares.

"Imagine the conversation," Caro continued with a grimace. "'Another cup of tea, dear? Has my virile son's seed not sprouted in your womb yet?'"

Kate burst out laughing. "What's awful is that I can imagine the duchess saying those exact words. And now I will never forget the mental image of it."

"What are the two of you up to?" Val asked, coming up to take Caro's arm. "No good, I'm sure."

"How dare you, sir." Caro scowled up at him, though her smile lit her eyes. "We are merely discussing how best to be the good biddable wives you both desire."

Pulling her against him, he stole a kiss. "Whatever gave you the impression I want a biddable wife?"

"Isn't that what every man wants?" she asked a little breathlessly, looking up into his laughing eyes. It was hard to believe that in the course of only a few weeks, he'd gone from the man she most loved to loathe, to the husband she needed more than oxygen.

"Not this man," he said softly, but before he could kiss her again, Eversham cleared his throat loudly.

"You're not alone here, you know."

Val gave a gusty sigh and they turned to face the other couple. "Apologies. We're still newlyweds, you know."

"Oh, we know." Kate rolled her eyes. "The crowd seems to have dissipated a bit. Shall we try our luck with the greenroom now?"

When they reached the parlor where the cast gathered after the production, they found that a bevy of admirers still surrounded Effie. But once she saw Caro and Kate, she pushed past the crowd to speak to them.

Frank stood off to the side watching her, his expression inscrutable.

"It appears she's been missed," Val said to his cousin as he and Eversham came to a stop beside him. He gave a low whistle at the dozens of bouquets on the table behind her. "She's very much been missed, I think."

"Effie is one of the most talented actresses of her time," Frank said simply. "It's no wonder that she has legions of admirers. I daresay she always will."

Turning to Eversham, he asked, "Is there any word on Tate and Croyden?"

"Nothing new." Eversham shrugged. "They are both due to stand trial soon. They won't hang, of course, because they're peers, but if convicted, they should face a stiff penalty. They can request trial in the House of Lords, but since their victims were highly connected to one of their own, it's unlikely they will escape punishment as they wish."

"Thank God," Frank said with ill-disguised relief.

Mick, who had murdered the man who helped him and Tate kidnap Effie, had already been put to death. Though Val hadn't felt sorry for the fellow, given his misdeeds, it did disgust him to see the way in which justice seemed to operate on two tiers: the harsher one reserved for those without the rank or connections to protect them.

"She's safe now." Val clapped his cousin on the back.

"You're right," Frank said, relaxing a little. "I just can't face losing her again. You don't understand, Val."

Val squeezed his shoulder. "I do understand." He looked pointedly at where Caro was engaged in an animated conversation with Kate and Effie. "I understand all too well."

Recognition dawned in Frank's eyes. "I suppose you do at that."

On the other side of the room, Effie was beaming. "I know you've said it's not necessary, Caro, Kate, but I cannot thank you enough."

After discussing the play, Kate and Caro had asked Effie how her husband was faring, prompting her expression of gratitude.

"If you hadn't arrived when you did, and if we hadn't gotten him to a physician, I don't know what would have happened," Effie said with the intensity of a woman who'd almost lost the love of her life. "I'd never have found a way to escape and get a doctor for Frank on my own."

"We're just happy he's recovering and you were able to marry at last," Caro assured her. After the near loss of his only son, Mr. Thorn's father had surprisingly relented on his stance against his son's relationship with Effie. But relent he had, and before Mr. Thorn had even left his sickbed, they'd been wed. "And you both seem to be thriving in the married state, I must say."

"And so do you, Caro." Effie grinned.

"What will you do after the play is concluded?" Kate asked, turning the subject.

Effie's cheeks colored. "I was hoping to speak to you both about that," she said with a small smile. "You see, I was wondering if perhaps you could use some assistance with the salons, on those days when you are unable to lead the meetings? I enjoy them so much and I do have some experience speaking before crowds."

Caro blinked. While it was true that sometimes she was often pressed to find time to lead the salons, they were also the highlight of her week. Still, she liked the idea of taking on another leader for the groups.

"I think that's a marvelous notion, Effie." Caro smiled. "You would be perfect for the role."

"I love the idea," Kate said decisively. "But you've only just married; surely you won't have time for such an endeavor."

"Oh, we are in love, but we don't wish to live in one another's pockets." Effie laughed. "He will have his club, after all. He can manage without me for a few hours a week. I won't give up my independence simply because we're married now."

"I think we know a little bit about that," Caro said.

Epilogue

Later that evening, Caro lay back against her husband's chest, the movement causing a ripple of water to cascade over the edge of the bathtub.

"Are you sure your valet doesn't become upset when we make a mess like this?" Caro gave a worried look to the pile of extra toweling stacked neatly on a nearby bench.

"Of course he doesn't." Val pressed a kiss into her bare shoulder. "He lives to mop up watery puddles."

"He does?" Caro asked skeptically, turning to look at him, though it was difficult in her present position.

"No," her husband admitted, situating her in a more comfortable position—one that didn't threaten to emasculate him. "But you mustn't be afraid of him. He likes you. It's Ludwig he has issues with."

Caro's cat had made the regrettable decision to sharpen his claws on Val's best boots, and ever since, Ludwig and the valet had been at odds. Though she wasn't sure Ludwig knew or cared about the fastidious servant's ire.

As if he'd known he was the subject of discussion, the cat chose that moment to saunter in. Then he disappeared below view of the sides of the tub.

"He's drinking the water again, isn't he?" Val asked, though the sound of rapid slurping made the question moot.

"Do you mind him very much?" Caro leaned her head back on his shoulder, rubbing her foot along his calf.

After using the access to her neck to scrape his teeth lightly across the place where it met her shoulder, he pulled back a little at her question. "Of course I don't mind him. He's yours. Besides, we've come to an understanding. It's all been settled between us now."

"Oh, you have, have you?" Caro had come to learn so many facets of his personality, but this playful side was one she especially loved. "And what is it that you've agreed to?"

"Ludwig has agreed that so long as I do not keep him from his daily allowance of cuddles," Val said, stroking a hand over her breast, "then he won't keep me from mine."

"That's mag"—Caro gasped when he pinched her nipple—"nanimous of him."

"He's nothing if not a gentleman," Val agreed, sliding his hand down her chest and over her stomach to touch her center.

And for a long time, there was no talking.

Once they'd left the cooling bathwater, dried themselves, and climbed into his bed, Val drew her against him. "The truth of it is, Caroline, that I would endure any number of cats, dogs, and hedgehogs if it meant I got to spend the rest of my life with you. So, one persnickety feline barely signifies."

Caro placed her hands on either side of his face. "I love you. So much. And what's more, I trust you. I never thought I'd be able to feel so again. We wasted so much time in those years we spent apart."

"But if you hadn't broken things off, we might not have found our way to this perfect moment," Val said, his eyes smiling down at her.

She thought about his words for the barest second.

Maybe he was right. One different step along the way and they could have missed out on all this. She'd never been one to believe in the vagaries of fate, but she did believe in love.

"It is a perfect moment, isn't it?" she asked, kissing him softly.

And if they were lucky, there would be a million other perfect moments left to come.

Acknowledgments

Bringing a book from inception to publication is never easy, but this one, written and revised during a global pandemic, has been especially difficult. Thanks, as always, to my agent, Holly Root, who makes badassery look easy, and the whole Root Literary team. Thanks to my amazing editors at Forever, Amy Pierpont and Sam Brody, who somehow managed, amidst the aforementioned pandemic, to help me transform Caro and Val's story from its very messy first iteration into final, splendid form. Thanks for contending with my pandemic brain, y'all! Thanks also to the production team at Forever, including my copyeditor Kristin Nappier and production editor Luria Rittenberg— you guys are saints. And a huge huzzah for the entire Forever Marketing & Publicity Team, especially director Jodi Rosoff and assistant director Estelle Hallick—y'all are a delight and I'm so thankful for your hard work!

And, of course, thanks to my wonderful readers. Every review that called *A Lady's Guide to Mischief and Mayhem* "fun" gave me life while I was working on this book! I hope you enjoy this adventure with Caro and Val.

Any mistakes are, of course, my own.

The inimitable Miss Flora Deaver may just have met her match in the brash, arrogant—and infuriatingly *irresistible*—Duke of Langham.
Don't miss their swoonworthy romance!

Available Fall 2022

READING GROUP GUIDE FOR

An Heiress's Guide to Deception and Desire

A Letter from the Author

Dear Reader,

Have you ever encountered a piece of media—a movie, book, or photograph—that made you feel truly seen and understood for the first time? Maybe it spoke to some inner part of you that you'd always thought would be ridiculed if you told it to the world. Or maybe it helped you understand something about yourself that had always puzzled you.

This is what happened to me when I first listened to the podcast *My Favorite Murder*. When hosts Karen Kilgariff and Georgia Hardstark told how they'd launch into a disturbing tale of a serial killer's exploits at a party, only to watch their fellow partygoers slowly back away, I shouted with laughter but also shook my head ruefully because been there, done that. And like Karen and Georgia, my interest in true crime has not been about glorifying the monsters who commit murder, but about trying to understand what happened, why, and how to make sure it never happens to me!

When it came time to plan my next historical romance series—because in addition to the complicated mystery, I need my books to have a happy ever after—I wanted to find some way to pay homage to Karen and Georgia and their empathetic podcast. So, *A Lady's Guide to Mischief and Mayhem*, Victorian England's version of a true-crime podcast, was born. The first book introduced readers to the unconventional Miss Caro Hardcastle; her rock star of a cat, Ludwig; and the man she can't stop bickering with, Lord Valentine Thorn.

Caro and Val's book, *An Heiress's Guide to Deception and Desire*, takes the reader into the world of the Victorian theatre. I was a drama minor in college, and one of the highlights of my studies was a trip to London where I saw countless West End productions. I've always loved glimpses into that world in other historical romances, and while I've included visits to the theatre in other books of mine, this is my first where the characters go behind the stage and into the world of the players and their production.

As my author tagline suggests, the inspirations for all my books are the witty banter of Jane Austen and the intricately crafted whodunnits of Agatha Christie. I had so much fun writing *An Heiress's Guide to Deception and Desire*. I sincerely hope you have just as much fun reading it!

Ever yours,
Manda

Discussion Questions

1. Birth order for the aristocracy of nineteenth-century England meant more than the elder being bossy or the baby being spoiled. In Val's case, as the younger son he was able to behave as he pleased until his brother died without having produced an heir. Val inherits both his brother's courtesy title of Viscount Wrackham and his position as next in line to the Thornfield dukedom. One difficulty Val experiences is his father's expectations for him to marry and produce an heir as soon as possible. What other kind of difficulties might a surprise title cause for younger sons who never expected to shoulder that kind of responsibility?

2. The nineteenth century saw lavish estates like those of Val's father, the Duke of Thornfield, lose income as tenant farmers left the country in droves to take jobs in factories like those of Caro's father in the city. This created an opportunity for

families such as Caro's to arrange marriages for their daughters with the sort of titled men who might have previously looked down their noses at Caro's lack of pedigree. For what reasons might Lady Hardcastle wish for Caro to marry into an aristocratic family when her daughter is assured to be wealthy no matter whom she weds?

3. With the rise of the middle class, Victorian London society saw a much stricter enforcement of rules of conduct for young ladies—much more so than the previous generation, the Regency. Why might the newly elevated matrons of the middle class feel the need to be more exacting with regard to policing their daughters' behavior? How might the return of Caro's parents from abroad have influenced her desire to marry and set up a household of her own? Why might it have been frowned upon for her to do this on her own as Effie did?

4. Victorian publishing did a booming business in both conduct manuals and books like *Mrs. Beeton's Book of Household Management*. Considering the boom in middle-class households, why might this have been the case? Why would Caro's decision to write cookbooks have been considered vulgar by some in the middle and upper classes?

5. The theatre of this era was known for its audiences to be raucous, and it was more of an opportunity

for the occupants of the private boxes to see and be seen. How is this different from the way our own theatre audiences behave?

6. Actresses and opera singers were commonly considered by the middle and upper classes to be of loose morals during this time, yet the greenrooms of West End theatres were teeming with men seeking to turn these performers into mistresses. What role might misogyny have played in this dynamic? How might Caro and Kate's welcoming of Effie into their literary salon have been considered a rejection of this attitude?

7. Because of the social rules of this era, men were allowed to conduct lives outside the home that were wholly hidden from their wives, mothers, and daughters. Nowhere was this more evident than in the gentlemen's club, where ladies were not only forbidden from becoming members but also from entering at all. How might literary salons like the one started by Caro and Kate have offered a similar safe haven for women of this time?

8. While there were printed versions of the code of correct behavior for ladies, gentlemen had largely unwritten rules for behaving honorably. Why, aside from his attraction and affection for her, might Val have felt bound to offer marriage to Caro after their appearance in the theatre lobby? How

might such marriages made to preserve a lady's reputation have led to unhappy marriages? What do you think about the notion of "compromised virtue" in general? What role might the rules of inheritance have played in its prevalence?

9. Quick trips to the seaside, such as the one Caro and Val take for their wedding journey, were far more difficult before the advent of rail travel. How might the choice of where railroad stations were built have affected the economies of villages along the roads that were once the main routes from London to other cities and towns? How might the ease of travel have made it more difficult for the authorities to solve crimes?

10. If you were to create a code of conduct for behavior in the present day, what rules would you list? How would your rules differ from the ones ladies like Caro were expected to follow?

Further Reading

Beeton, Isabella. *Mrs. Beeton's Household Management*. Ware, UK: Wordsworth Reference, 2006.

Doughan, David, and Peter Gordon. *Women, Clubs and Associations in Britain*. London: Routledge, 2006.

Flanders, Judith. *Inside the Victorian Home: A Portrait of Domestic Life in Victorian England*. New York: W.W. Norton, 2006.

Foulkes, Richard. *Shakespeare and the Victorian Stage*. Cambridge: Cambridge University Press, 2008.

Furger, Andres. *Driving: The Horse, the Man and the Carriage from 1700 up to the Present Day*. Hildesheim: Olms, 2009.

Langland, Elizabeth. *Nobody's Angels: Middle-Class Women and Domestic Ideology in Victorian Culture*. Ithaca: Cornell University Press, 1995.

Poovey, Mary. *Uneven Developments: The Ideological Work of Gender in Mid-Victorian England*. Chicago: University of Chicago Press, 1998.

Ruskin, John. "Sesame and Lilies." In *The Works of John Ruskin*. Cambridge: Cambridge University Press, 2010.

Summerscale, Kate. *The Suspicions of Mr. Whicher.* New York: Bloomsbury, 2009.

Summerscale, Kate. *The Wicked Boy: An Infamous Murder in Victorian London.* New York: Penguin Press, 2017.

About the Author

Manda Collins grew up on a combination of Nancy Drew books and Jane Austen novels, and her own brand of historical romantic suspense is the result. A former academic librarian, she holds master's degrees in English and in library and information studies. Her novel *Duke with Benefits* was named a *Kirkus* Best Romance of 2017. She lives on the Gulf Coast with a squirrel-fighting cat and more books than are strictly necessary.